Taking Chances

BOOK YOUR PLACE ON OUR WEBSITE AND MAKE THE ARABESQUE ROMANCE CONNECTION!

We've created a customized website just for our very special Arabesque readers, where you can get the inside scoop on everything that's going on with Arabesque romance novels.

When you come online, you'll have the exciting opportunity to:

- View covers of upcoming books

- Learn about our future publishing schedule (listed by publication month and author)

- Find out when your favorite authors will be visiting a city near you

- Search for and order backlist books

- Check out author bios and background information

- Send e-mail to your favorite authors

- Join us in weekly chats with authors, readers and other guests

- Get writing guidelines

- AND MUCH MORE!

Visit our website at
http://www.arabesquebooks.com

Taking Chances

Angela Weaver

ARABESQUE

BET☆ BOOKS

BET Publications, LLC
http://www.bet.com
http://www.arabesquebooks.com

ARABESQUE BOOKS are published by

BET Publications, LLC
c/o BET BOOKS
One BET Plaza
1900 W Place NE
Washington, DC 20018-1211

All Kensington Titles, Imprints, and Distributed Lines are available at special quantity discounts for bulk purchases for sales promotions, premiums, fund-raising, and educational or institutional use. Special book excerpts or customized printings can also be created to fit specific needs. For details, write or phone the office of the Kensington special sales manager: Kensington Publishing Corp., 850 Third Avenue, New York, NY 10022, attn: Special Sales Department, Phone: 1-800-221-2647.

First Trade Paperback Printing: January 2006

10 9 8 7 6 5 4 3 2 1

Printed in the United States of America

For Greg–
Thank you.

When love beckons to you, follow him.
    —*The Prophet*

Chapter 1

Bolivia

Regan Blackfox ran her manicured fingertips over the cool semitranslucent silk of her black kimono. The thousand-dollar negligee served no other purpose than to please her target. To tantalize the man in front of her.

The U.S. government doesn't negotiate with drug lords, even those who kidnap our ambassadors.

That statement brought Regan halfway around the world, thrown into frantic last-minute mission preparation and dropped off in a high-class bordello.

Regan peered from underneath thick false lashes as Javier Merona disrobed and entered into the marble whirlpool Jacuzzi. He was shorter than her five feet ten inches. Dyed jet-black hair, and a thick neck supported the man's small head. From the short stature and extended belly, she ascertained that the ex-general didn't heavily indulge in the narcotics he sold throughout the world.

"You will join me, won't you, *cara*?" he queried after undressing and settling into the steamy water. His fluid Portuguese belied peasant origins. And his delicately worded question was in fact a thinly veiled order. She'd memorized his file. Merona hadn't finished high school because he'd been expelled for stabbing another student. Fitting with this personality profile, the drug czar had never forgotten the insult. As soon as he'd established his base of power, the man had personally driven back to his little village with five mercenaries and executed the school's principal.

Regan raised her head, then smiled sweetly while stepping into the bathing chamber. In the guise of a high-class courtesan, she'd spent the past two hours being modest and deferential. She'd admired Merona's home, fed him oysters in a half shell, peeled grapes, and sipped wine from his priceless golden Spanish goblets. And with every touch of his thick fingers against her skin, she'd inwardly cringed, but outwardly welcomed his attention.

The people who had trained her for this moment not only knew Javier Merona intimately but had also taught her well. The profile she'd been instructed to memorize listed the scent of cologne he wore, what brand of underwear lined his drawers by the dozens, his sexual proclivities, his taste in food, even what side of the bed the narcotics kingpin slept on. As the clock struck six, Regan pushed back her growing excitement.

Now it would all end.

"I'm sorry," she began without a trace of regret in her tone, "but I have another appointment, *Senhor* Merona." That said, the National Security Agency counterintelligence agent reached her right hand underneath her robe, drew her gun, and aimed. The small-faced Andean drug cartel leader was just how she wanted him to be, naked and vulnerable, but far from helpless.

Careful to keep her expression neutral, Regan continued. "We can do this the easy way or we can do this hard way, Merona, it's up to you. But either way, Ambassador Richards leaves here tonight," Regan warned.

"Puta! I will kill—" He reached for a pistol lying beside a full bottle of champagne and two empty glasses.

She'd twice pulled the trigger of the silencer-equipped

nine-millimeter before his arm could clear the soap bubbles. Pushing back the bile in her throat, Regan turned
away from the man sinking down into the churning water.
Like a nation at war against drugs, Regan had eliminated
a threat to her life and the national security of the United
States. Plus, she'd done it in self-defense, thus getting
around the U.S. government's policy against assassination.
Yet beneath the bravado, a moment of clear thinking sur-
faced and an image of her older brother raced across her
mind. Guilt slammed into her chest at what he would think
if he'd ever discovered that his sister had killed a man.
Caleb, the emergency room doctor, dedicated his life to
saving others, and she'd just taken one and would take
more before the night ended.

Regan tore off the robe and left it on the marble floor.
Moving silently out of the bathroom, she reached into the
overnight case she'd brought with her, pulled back the false
side, and took out her black jumpsuit and supplies. It took
her less than three minutes to change and tie her hair back.
Once again, she reached into the bag and placed the communications headset in her ear. She tapped the headset's
transmitter, then spoke into the microphone. "Merona's out
of the picture. I'm heading for the control room."

Five breaths passed before the receiver in her ear crackled. "Team Three is in position and waiting. Helicopters
are set to pull you out at 2000 hours. Snipers are ready for
you to say go."

After slipping on two nylon thigh holsters and loading her weapons, she strapped a small bag of explosives
to her chest. Regan scanned the room, and her lips
curled down in distaste. The cocaine billionaire had
spared no expense building his lavish estate and procur-
ing the sixty-four-thousand-acre retreat north of Santa
Ana on the Beni River, and about three hundred miles
south of the Brazilian border. In a country roughly three
times the size of Montana but with mountains and vol-
canoes, Merona's ranch had been under intense scrutiny

by the CIA even prior to the construction crew breaking ground for the foundation.

Regan edged close to the windows and peeked outside, immediately spotting the sentries moving around the electrified fencing. Looking over the jungle and toward the horizon, she noted that the military's weather forecaster had been right on the mark. The overcast sky would hide the bright harvest moon and allow the Delta Force ground team to move undetected up to the perimeter and grant the Pave Low helicopters a safe approach.

Once she'd taken up her position by the only door leading out of the suite, Regan looked at her watch before putting her hand on the door handle. Four years of NSA training, six weeks of building a false identity as a high class courtesan, five days of rehearsal in a full-scale replica of the three-story mansion came down to thirty minutes.

If she failed to reach the control room in time, only a team of Delta operatives would not only be walking onto a field of land mines and motion sensors, but the U.S. ambassador to Bolivia, who happened to also be the uncle of the newly elected president of the United States, would die. She forced herself to breathe in and out to reign in the adrenaline prickling her skin. When her hands steadied, Regan adjusted her grip on the gun barrel.

What had she learned during her modified Delta training? she asked herself. The answer came in the form of a mental shout. *Failure is not an option.*

Using the back of the door as a shield, Regan pulled out an identical fully loaded weapon, which sat in her thigh holster, ticked off the safety, and counted to thirty. She said a quick prayer and pushed down on the door handle. She took a step back and stood with her back against the wall. Either one of two things would happen: curiosity would kill the cat and the guards would enter, or she'd have to go out into the hallway and significantly increase the risk of being noticed by the security cameras.

Regan gave them until the count of sixty to enter the

room. Her heart stopped and then restarted at the count of fifty when two sets of booted feet entered the room.

Moving from behind the door, Regan dove toward the floor. The cartel gunmen's surprise gave her a second of tactical advantage, and that was more than she needed. Before her shoulders hit the carpet, Regan rolled and came up firing, taking out two heavily armed members of Merona's personal guards.

After pulling the men deeper into the bedroom, she peeked out into the hallway and waited. Thanks to having poured over the endless architectural schematics and coaching, she knew the inside of the mansion better than the layout of the house where she grew up. As expected, she caught a glimpse of a rotational security camera. It was ten yards from the bedroom to the end of the hall, and she had to cross that space before the camera cycled back.

Ace spoke in the mike in her ear, a soft whisper that had she not expected would have made her turn her head to see if he was standing behind her. "Nichols, have you taken out the cameras yet?"

"No," Regan answered. She stuck her head out again, then without waiting ran as fast as she could down the hallway. She skittered to a halt directly underneath the camera, then reached up and pulled out the cords. Not waiting a breath, Regan took off around the corner and made her way up the back stairs and toward the security control room. Not a second too soon, either. Because as soon as she crept around the last corner, the door opened and a man was carrying semiautomatic weapons and a bag of trash. It had taken her longer to make it into the control room than expected because of the extra unmapped surveillance cameras. Regan made a mental note to tell her boss that the CIA blueprints had not been as accurate as they'd boasted.

Putting her hand on the metal handle, little by little she pressed it downward. The entrance to the control room wasn't even locked. After neutralizing the lone guard and the room's operators, she closed and locked the door behind her.

"I've secured the control room." Regan turned her head, looking from one corner of the TV panels and computer systems to the other.

Stepping in between the slumped bodies of control room operators, she touched her fingers to the keyboard. "Rerouting backup alarm system and shutting down motion detectors." Reaching into the pack strapped to her chest, she pulled out a relay device and attached it to the main panel.

Returning her attention to the computer, Regan entered a memorized script and watched as Global Positioning coordinates flew across the screen. She had just evened the odds. Now Delta Team Three would be able to approach the compound without setting off the land mines. "Upload started."

Her receiver crackled. "It's coming across now."

Again reaching into her pack, Regan set the timer and placed an explosive device behind a wall of equipment. Then after double-checking to assure herself that no one would detect it, she looked back at the monitor. Just in time, she caught sight of a Delta commando crawling out from under the vehicle that had transported her from the small airstrip a few miles down the road from the compound.

She spoke into her microphone. "Ace, I've got you on-screen. Proceed with caution to target."

Minutes later after making her way down a labyrinth of corridors, Regan met Ace on the back stairs leading to the holding facility where their informant had guaranteed that Ambassador Richards was being held.

"I'll take point from here on out," he whispered.

Dressed in black, his face darkened with camouflage paint, his body sporting a Kevlar vest, and an Uzi in his hand, Ace looked exactly like what he was—deadly. A cap covered what Regan knew was a head full of blond hair, and the grease over his face did nothing to darken his California-blue eyes. She followed the direction of his gaze and stood to the side of the door. Regan had acquired the knowledge of how to shoot from NSA instructors. However, after 6 weeks of Ace's expert tutelage, she'd learned the importance of timing. How to aim, fire, and kill in a split second.

His eyes bored into hers. "Stay low and right behind me."

She drew a deep steady breath and nodded. "On your mark."

"Let's go," Ace ordered, then threw in two low-powered sonic grenades. He slammed the door shut. A millisecond later, simultaneous flashes went off as the Delta commando reopened the door and shot his way in, dropping most of the guards before they could even reach for their weapons. Regan counted at least five bodies on her way to the locked door.

"You get on your way with the ambassador," the commando ordered. "I'll set the charges and make my way to the roof."

This would be the most daring part of their plan yet. Without the normal backup, she would get the ambassador while Ace laid explosives and cleared the exit route up to the roof. As practiced, Regan dropped to her knees and inserted the lock picks.

Normally, they would have breached the door with explosives, but without knowledge of the room's dimensions, doing so would put the ambassador at risk. One thing they did know was that he was in there alone.

Once the cylinder clicked open, Regan went gun drawn through the door and found him sitting in a chair. Regan scrutinized his face. Shaggy silver hair, hazel eyes, and a long nose. Ambassador Richards. One hundred percent match with the photos except for signs of stress and weight loss. Carlos Merona, one of the less-known members of the Medellín Cartel was believed to have been responsible for dozens of bombings, bribery, and hundreds of murders. When car bombs, murders, bribery, and attempted lobbying of the U.S. government had failed to get him what he wanted, he'd resorted to kidnapping.

One month ago, the president of the United States had received a letter from Merona demanding the release of his uncle, Colombian drug kingpin Fabio Ochoa, one of the ruthless and greedy founders of the cartel, in exchange for Ambassador Richards. At that moment, Ochoa was wearing an orange jumpsuit in the relative isolation of a maximum-security federal prison where he would serve out his sixty or more years on drug conspiracy and money-laundering charges.

"Ambassador," she announced calmly, "it's time for you to check out."

He closed his eyes, then opened them, the relief more than evident in his face. "Thank God. Where's your team?"

"It's just you and me for the moment. The rest of Delta Force is outside laying cover for our extraction." She bent down and began to work on the chains that bound his legs. "Explosives are being laid about the perimeter, and a helicopter is going to meet us on the roof."

She checked the display of her watch. She had three minutes to reach the first floor and check in. Eight minutes to get to the roof.

"Ambassador, can you run?"

"I think so."

"Good. Because when I say run, you run. And if something happens to me, do whatever it takes to get to the roof. Understand?"

He regarded her silently, and then nodded.

Regan checked the outside room, and finding it clear, motioned for the ambassador to follow.

"Hurry and put this on." She bent to pull off the guard's bulletproof vest, and then passed it to the ambassador. As soon as he'd strapped on the vest, Regan reached down again to pick up a discarded submachine gun the guard would no longer need.

While he pulled on the black vest, Regan checked the weapon. MP-5 automatic submachine gun with an easy trigger. Assured that the safety was off, she handed it to the ambassador, then met his level gaze and held it. "Just point and shoot."

She watched the way he handled the weapon and let her lips twitch up in a smile. This man would do his country proud.

They kept low and moved with deliberate speed up the stairs, skirting the kitchen and pausing on the landing leading to the second floor. Just as they ducked around a corner, Regan's earpiece came live. "People, be advised. Mr. Murphy has decided to pay us a visit. Snipers are reporting increased activity in the left wing. Patrols with dogs are closing on your left, Team Three."

Regan grimaced at the operative's weak attempt at humor. Murphy's Law had nothing to do with the success or failure of their mission. Planning and skills would determine the outcome. She tapped the Transmit button. "Taking secondary route. Ace, have you planted all the charges?"

"Yeah, sunshine. The roof is clear and I'm getting my ass bit to death by mosquitoes, so hurry up."

At 1958, over the sounds of machine-gun fire and explosives, Regan with the ambassador by her side stepped from the super-chilled interior of the mansion out into the thick humidity of the Bolivian jungle.

Making sure she had adequate cover and an eye on the entry points to the roof, Regan watched as a Pave Low, escorted by two Apache helicopters, rained down massive amounts of firepower against the mercenaries gathered in the courtyard and streaming out of the bunks. The flashing lights of the helicopters discharging advanced weaponry lit the night along with the small explosions from the forward rocket launchers. Regan's eyes teared for a moment; the world resembled a portion of Dante's Inferno.

"Ambassador!" she yelled over the sound of the helicopter rotors, the rush of air, and the sounds of fighting. "As soon as the ramp lowers, you stay low and run as fast as you can! I'll cover you."

"Young lady, I will not be leaving you behind."

Regan almost smiled at the hint of the north Texas accent she caught in the ambassador's voice.

About the same instant, the Pave Low landed and four commandos with black uniforms, night-vision goggles, and MP-5 Heckler and Koch machine guns jumped off and began firing.

"That wasn't a request, Ambassador. That was an order. So you move or I call in Ace to carry you. You have ten seconds to decide."

"Thank—"

Seeing the back door begin to cycle down, she cut him off. "Go!"

Her earpiece buzzed with Ace's voice. "Regan, follow the ambassador in. I've got you covered."

She strained her eyes to see Ace and found him taking aim at the door to the roof as the guards began to pour out. Obeying orders and with guns drawn, she sprinted across the open space and into the back of the Pave Low. "I'm moving!" she shouted into her headset.

Less than ten seconds later as the gunner sprayed the area, Ace jumped on-board. Even before the crew closed the ramp, they were airborne. The loud sound of the engine drowned out the ability to communicate without the assistance of specially modified headsets. Surrendering her weapons to one of the Delta commandos, Regan traded her communications headset for a helmet, and adjusted the volume so the nonstop chatter from the radio net wouldn't shatter her eardrum. Out of the corner of her eye, she caught the flash of bright orange light as the helicopter sped away at over a hundred and fifty miles an hour. One drug lord's mansion off the market, she thought.

"Thank God this is finally over." The ambassador's voice came through loud and in stereo into her ears.

Making sure to grab hold of the side nettings as the helicopter bucked to the right, Regan made her way over to the opposite side of the aircraft. Checking to see that a soldier had given Ambassador Richards a headset, she spoke into the mike. "I'm afraid this night is far from over, Ambassador."

She broke off her transmission and Ace's voice popped into her receiver.

"Nichols, do the introductions and fill the ambassador in while I report in to HQ."

"What does she mean it's not over yet?"

Regan motioned toward the Delta Force medic. "This man will check you out and help you get cleaned up."

"What?"

"Ambassador, there's an embassy social function tonight, and since it's your first day back from vacation, you don't want to be late."

"Vacation," Ambassador Richards repeated into the mike. "I've been held prisoner in a twenty-by-twenty concrete cell for the past month."

"And the top brass has managed to keep that information from the press. As far as your staff is concerned, you've been writing your memoirs at a friend's cabin in Canada. Your mother is the only person who has been apprised of your situation."

The man frowned. "Somebody actually bought that load of horseshit?"

Inadvertently, her lips twitched upward in a smile. "You of all people should know that the United States doesn't negotiate with kidnappers. Not only is this mission top secret, it never took place."

"And I guess I'm supposed to arrive back with nothing to show that I even left the country?"

"Not at all, upon your return to the embassy, you'll find a new stamp on your passport, some nice pictures of

Ottawa, souvenirs, maple syrup, and a rough draft of your autobiography in your suitcase." Regan paused as the helicopter dropped a few feet. "From what I've heard it makes for fascinating reading."

His brow creased and she caught the faint nod of understanding.

"Now." She gestured toward the medical officer. "Mack over there is going to give you a cursory examination and help you get cleaned up so you can change into your tux."

Unconcerned with the eyes behind night-vision goggles pretending to scan the ground cover instead of looking at her, Regan made her way to the left rear wall of the cabin that under normal conditions would have been strapped with litters to carry wounded soldiers. For this mission, however, the crew had cleared the small area of equipment for the expressed purpose of her use.

She turned her back on the soldiers and unzipped her top, then bent over to shimmy out of her pants. Combined with the South American humidity and the heat of the instrumentation in the state-of-the-art transport, it was hot and the night wind whipping in from the wash of the rotor blades felt good on her bare skin.

What she wanted more than anything in the world was a long hot shower. Instead, Regan settled for wiping the sweat and gunpowder off her skin with a cleansing cloth. She was slipping into the silk ivory gown by the time Ace made his way back to her. Grabbing hold of the wall webbing as the helicopter veered to the right, she motioned to the Delta operative. "Can you zip me?"

He lifted his hands and even in the low red light, she could see the black film. "Got something I can wipe my hands down with? Don't want to be getting residue on such a nice dress."

With one hand holding on to the helicopter's support and the other keeping up her dress, Regan pointedly looked to the left. "Grab a wipe. Over there near my bag."

When Ace finished cleaning his hands, she used her free hand to sweep her hair over her shoulder and out of his way. She couldn't control the shiver brought about by his cool fingers against her warm skin. "Thank you."

"Damn, Nichols. Even under the night goggles, you sure do clean up well for a spook."

Regan stiffened for a millisecond at Ace's use of her cover name, then ran her fingers though the long thick hair and fought the urge to scratch. Although the beautician had assured her that the hair extensions wouldn't come out even if she'd stood in a wind tunnel, she couldn't risk compromising her identity.

"Ace." She let the annoyance creep into her voice. Well aware that her every word was being transmitted and recorded, she maintained her alias identity. "I'm not with the CIA."

"Yeah, right." He took a seat closest to the window and strapped in. "Who signs your paycheck?"

Regan followed suit and strapped herself in. Reaching over, she collected her other clothing and stuffed it in the bag underneath the three-inch designer heels and makeup she would put on once they set down outside of the La Paz. "The State Department. I'm a diplomatic liaison, remember?"

"Sure." He nodded and Regan caught a flash of white teeth. "And I'm just some new recruit out of boot camp. Nobody moves like you did without a helluva a lot of training. Not to mention that I've never heard of an embassy clerk yet that can take down a target without getting all emotional and falling to pieces."

It took that one sentence to shake her, that single reference to the fact that she'd taken not one but four lives, to erase the thrill of success. She looked away from Ace and took a deep breath and held it to the count of ten, then let it out. On past intelligence gathering assignments, she'd never had to cross the line and use lethal force. "I did what I had to do to complete the mission," she stated more to herself than Ace.

"Keep telling yourself that and you might sleep okay tonight."

"What else can I tell myself?" she asked.

"That you did your job and in the end you'll save more lives than you take. Not just the ambassador's but those poor bastards forced to work in the poppy fields and the people dying because they'd do anything to get high on the garbage Merona was selling."

Regan mustered up a wan smile. "Thanks for the pep talk."

He shrugged his broad shoulders. "I've been where you are and I know it ain't gonna be pretty or easy to deal with."

"I get to go back to my desk job and get this behind me." She faked an excited tone.

"You don't have to. The military's looking for operatives and we're a lot less bureaucratic than the CIA."

Regan settled back into the seat and let Ace's comment fly over her head. "How's the ambassador doing?" Preferring to deflect attention from the subject of her background, Regan nodded her head toward the ambassador. The fewer lies she had to tell, the better. She wasn't a CIA operative, true. But the NSA gave her orders, and when her boss needed someone smuggled out of a foreign country or info on a potential threat to national security, Regan got the call.

Ace moved forward to look over Regan toward the cockpit, then he sat back. "Not bad. Some bruises and cuts, nothing much. Looks like Merona didn't have the stomach for torture."

"Or exercise," Regan commented disgustedly. Although Ace's commanding officer hadn't uttered a word about it, the possibility that she might have had to seduce the general had been inherent in the success of the mission. "He had the stomach of a walrus." Pushing the image of the dead man aside, she asked, "How's the team? Any casualties?"

"On their way in for debriefing. Not even a scratch. That's Delta Team Three for you."

"Yes, it is." Regan had only spent a few weeks with the team, and most of it had been under intense training, but she would never forget them.

"You ready for the next round?" Ace questioned.

"Are you coming?"

"Nah," Ace snorted, then proceeded to stretch his legs and put his hands behind his head. "I don't wear dress shoes and I sure as hell don't put on a suit and tie to suck down fifty-dollar martinis, and play patty-cake with a bunch of drunk-ass bureaucrats looking to talk crap about my country. I'll be heading back to base tonight and catching the first military transport to Fort Bragg."

Halfway wishing she could follow him back to the U.S., Regan turned her neck to take one more look at the ambassador. Somehow, even with the turbulence, the medic had managed to give him a close shave and a haircut.

"Ace, can I ask you a personal question?"

"You can ask, but I'm not guaranteeing an answer."

"Fair enough. Do you ever get tired of saving the world?"

He sat back and his large frame filled the rest of the seat and nestled into her side.

Ace sighed heavily. "I get tired of CIA desk jockeys trying to tell me how to do my job and journalists printing lies about my team and our missions." He rubbed his brow and spoke slowly. "I can't see doing anything else. I came from a small town in Idaho, with no prospects and little education. Now I can speak four languages, go into any situation, and get out alive. I've seen every paradise and hellhole this earth has to offer and I've earned a spot on Delta Team Three. I'll be a Delta until they kick me out or take my dog tags and bury me."

"I can see all the positives, but what about your family?"

Several moments passed before he spoke in a flat tone. "That's two questions, not one."

Regan met his steady gaze, and even in the dim light of the cabin, she caught a glimpse of sadness in his eyes before he turned away and looked toward the cockpit.

Careful not to turn away from the welcome body heat Ace provided, she settled back and closed her eyes. Yet her mind hummed along with the speed of the helicopter's rotor blades. She had spent most of her career working alone or in concert with independent NSA teams. No matter the target or the country, she had brought the foreign nationals—and in some cases their families—to the United States. And for the most part, she was happy.

Yet there were moments when the stress of leading a double life, the danger of possible capture, and the loneliness of secrecy crept up on her in the middle of the night or on a flight to a new assignment. But the adrenaline rush of danger, the triumph of success, and the knowledge that she was doing her part for her country made it all worthwhile. In fact, she felt in her heart that there was nothing else she'd rather do.

The rush of adrenaline, which had sustained her since the beginning of the mission, vanished. Regan welcomed the exhaustion as if it were a long-lost family member, and she pulled the dulling fatigue close to shield against the memory of Javier Merona's sightless eyes. Between one yawn and a breath, Regan soon fell off to sleep, not even rousing when someone tossed a light blanket over her shoulders. The hour nap she caught during the flight above the jungle and then over the rugged Andes Mountains was the best she'd had in weeks.

Chapter 2

"Thought you could use this. . . ."

Regan turned her neck slightly to the left careful to keep an eye out for Ambassador Richards. At the first sign of fatigue, she was under strict orders to put him in the guarded limousine and send him back to the embassy. Yet even after leaving the party, they wouldn't sleep for hours to come. The mandatory debriefing would require that they relive the night's events twice. Once with the military, and soon afterward she would have to submit a detailed report to the NSA. Regan swallowed back a sigh. The apartment given to her upon her arrival to La Paz looked appealing only because of the large bed.

"No drinking on the job, remember?" Regan met the sharp green eyes of her NSA senior officer. Neil Morgan with his silver-accented brown hair and mustache cut a dashing figure in both tuxedos and agency standard suits. Although the ballroom was filled with the cream of wealthy and influential Latin American families, she'd spotted him the moment she'd descended the grand stairway on Ambassador Richard's arm.

There were approximately two hundred guests, with half as many waiters, who were uniformed in black tuxedos and white gloves. Crystal chandeliers, a private orchestra, and handsome Latin bartenders to customize martinis. The attendants came from the cream of Latin American society and politics. In one glance, Regan recognized over a dozen foreign ambassadors, the city mayor, and the prime minister. The women wore exclusive designer dresses with low fronts and backs. Here, their husbands' wealth could be measured in the estate gems weighing down their fingers, wrists, and necks. Regan ended her survey of the crowd and returned her attention to Morgan Hewett, her NSA superior.

"Major Hanes just checked in. The operatives of Delta Team Three are already out in the streets finding the local bars and setting back the military budget a couple of hundred." He lifted the glass toward Regan. "Besides, you more than earned this."

"In that case." Regan took the glass of white wine from his hand and with a smile raised it up to her lips. The alcohol cooled her tongue while warming its way down her throat to settle in her stomach. "Thank you."

"Did anything happen on the mission you want to warn me about before we get into the debriefing tonight?"

"No." She shook her head slightly. "It went off just like we practiced."

"If I recall correctly, you practiced while wearing bulletproof vests. The ambassador made it onto the helicopter with a jacket, but Lieutenant Vance mentioned in his preliminary mission report that you had failed to put yours on."

"I had to choose between weapons and that jacket," Regan responded smoothly while looking around to ensure that no one could overhear their conversation.

Her insertion into the high-class bordello had been smooth and effortless. Replacing the drug lord's normal girl had taken perfect timing and required her to wear long black extensions to catch his gaze. But only being allowed a small overnight bag had forced her to rethink what she could or could not hide underneath the skimpy lingerie and sex toys.

"You could have chosen wrong," Morgan drawled after taking a drink from the glass in his hand. Even without tasting its contents, Regan knew it wouldn't be the requisite vodka and soda. Unlike her, Morgan didn't touch alcohol.

"Does it matter?" Regan shrugged a shoulder and began to sway to the music. When on a mission the key was to blend in with the surroundings. Despite the edge in her superior's voice, she would keep up the appearance of enjoying herself. "The mission was accomplished and no one got hurt."

"Giggle insanely and give me your glass," Morgan ordered. "People are starting to notice that we're not exactly looking like a happy couple."

"Are we a couple now?" Regan replied, doing exactly as he instructed. It would take more than one glass of wine to dull her senses, but he didn't have to know that. Her oldest brother, Marius, had taught her to appreciate the taste of their father's expensive brandy even before she'd graduated out of diapers. "I thought fraternizing with members of the staff was frowned on in the agency, and what would your wife think?"

She allowed him to lead her onto the already busy dance floor, and as she walked, the silk dress moved like a second skin over her body. Catching sight of the admiring glances from some impeccably dressed and undeniably handsome gentlemen, Regan let a feminine smile curve over her lips. If she had been in her official capacity as a political officer with the U.S. State Department, she would have met their glances with studied flirtation, then tried to pick up local intelligence information.

Her attractiveness owed much but not all to her beauty, or even the hint of sex she emitted. What gave her the edge was growing up with three brothers and numerous male cousins. Regan had a feel for how they thought, what they wanted, and how much they needed to be . . . men. And when necessary she used that knowledge to manipulate them like fine instruments.

"Since you've met Grace you should know."

She put her hand politely on his jacketed biceps and positioned herself so as to have a clear view over Morgan's shoulder. An amused laugh tickled the corners of her mouth. "Morgan, your wife is a CIA bureau chief. There isn't a hole deep enough on this planet that you could hide in if Grace ever thought you were having an affair."

"Yeah, well, you know I'd never cheat on my wife anyway." Morgan grinned.

Regan nodded and closed her eyes briefly and listened to the music. She calculated that she had less than two hours before every muscle in her body paid her back for the earlier rough treatment.

"We're getting you and Richards out of here in thirty minutes."

"Wonderful. No one suspects?"

"No."

She opened her eyes and stared straight ahead at the knot of his dark silver tie. "So I'm finished here?"

"You've got two weeks to finish up your work at the embassy."

"And then what?"

"You go home."

Her brow creased before she could control it. Her normal job as an NSA agent was to assist in the acquisition of foreign individuals whose knowledge was deemed vital for U.S. national security. She helped them defect to America and they helped her superiors gain valuable strategic political and military information. "What about the Turkish scientist?"

She looked upward, but Morgan's eyes didn't meet hers, and that was a very bad sign. "I've assigned someone else to bring him over. You're taking a vacation. Word is that a business-class ticket to Atlanta, Georgia, will be on your desk Monday morning."

"Why?" Even as her heart dropped to the bottom of her stomach, Regan kept her cool. She'd learned early on never to assume, just ask, and the answer had an over 50 percent chance of being the truth. Morgan had never lied to her, or at least she hadn't caught him in one yet.

"It's not my decision, this came from high up. Looks like you did too good of a job."

"Explain."

"Now might not be an appropriate time."

Lifting her head to stare into his hazel eyes, Regan did something that she hoped she wouldn't regret. She moved her body so every inch pressed against his, then leaned forward, positioning her face close to Morgan's, near enough she could see the tiny flecks of gold in his green eyes. So close that to all the undercover Secret Service, CIA, and Bolivian guards watching it would look as though they were a breath away from kissing.

"If you don't want rumors to put you in a very bad place, you'll tell me now."

"All right, back off." Her boss breathed a sigh of relief when she moved away, allowing a fraction of space between their bodies. "No one knows what to do with you. Lieutenant General Frank White has requested your top-secret records and psychological tests. I've been ordered to hand them over within forty-eight hours."

Regan moved back and plastered a smile on her face while inside, her stomach churned with anger at the mention of the four-star general. A balding wolf-faced man with all-seeing dark eyes, he had served time in all the wars after World War II. White had risen rapidly in rank and position because of his unorthodox methods and high success rate. She'd known going in that the all-male bastion of military elite wasn't going to be a cakewalk. Yet she hadn't expected him to be looking over her shoulder during the entire training operation.

She'd cut her teeth as an intern in the United Nations. The complex interrelationships between the U.S. security agencies and the military were a pit of political wrangling, a history of distrust and acrimony. The time she'd spent within the State Department had only served to highlight the cracks in the sharing of intelligence, resources, and knowledge.

She caught a glint of anger in Morgan's cold gaze. "There's more you're not telling me."

"Yeah, this is strictly off the record, Regan."

"*Everything* we say is off the record. My job doesn't even exist," she stated matter-of-factly. "Now talk."

"I've been hearing rumors that the Special Forces are looking to outside sources to add operatives for the Funny Platoon."

Regan was grateful that the music had stopped, because the surprise would have held her still. Combat-exclusion laws clearly barred women from serving as commandos in the U.S. Special Forces. The Funny Platoon had been an experimental unit within Delta that consisted of women only. The idea of having husband-and-wife infiltration teams had appealed to some sections of the Special Forces Command, but had been scrapped because of resistance to changing the status quo.

"What?" Her voice rose with surprise at the notion.

"Yeah, with the new threats to security they're leaving no stone unturned in their quest to be prepared and to get information. If what I've heard is true, then your performance today has put you at the top of their recruitment drive."

"You're going to let me go just like that?"

"Hell no," Morgan bit out. "You're one of the best agents I've ever trained. And I'm not going to let those commando SOBs poach. This is the NSA, not some damned FBI fishpond."

"What about my cover?" Regan let none of the fear churning in her stomach reflect on her face or in her voice. She'd spent years cultivating friendships, making connections, and doing everything possible to excel at her job and give her State Department identity solid credibility. And all the while laying stones to build a wall between her personal and her professional lives.

"Still holding. As far as General White is aware, you're Dominique Nichols. Damned if they didn't try to get past security protocols the other day. But for the time being all they know is that you're a highly trained intelligence operative for the NSA."

"Then there's no problem and I can book a flight out to Istanbul."

"Wrong, the problem is that I can't put you back out in the field until they back off."

"You think they're going to pull me out of the agency, don't you?" she concluded.

"I'm not giving you up without a fight. So, until this mess is straightened out, you're going on leave. I don't know what those sneaky bastards could pull, and I can't have them blowing your cover just to get back at us."

"How long?" She uncurled her fingers from his shoulder.

"As long as it takes."

"I can't be out of the game and come back that quickly," she reminded him.

"I'll pull you in for training if it looks like this is going to drag on. In the meantime, I've got the phone numbers for some people down in Atlanta. They'll provide you with the hardware and space you need to practice your skills."

"Remember, no dropping in unannounced." She pulled back and looked him in the eye.

"Duly noted. You just stay out of trouble until this blows over."

A smiled curved her lips and she slipped back into the southern accent of her birth. "What kind of trouble could little ol' me get into?"

"Plenty," Morgan said as he politely offered his arm. She

placed her hand on his forearm and they walked toward the ballroom entrance.

Regan laughed and her twinkling eyes met his as all of her anger at the forced leave of absence dissipated. Soon she would be home in the mountains of north Georgia. Home to see her family for the first time in over nine months.

Chapter 3

One month later

Thirty-four years was a long time to live without a home, Kincaid thought, as he walked underneath the arched doorway of his living room. He paused for a moment to gaze at a squirrel hunting acorns in the yard while the sunrise started to peek out over the mountains. He raised his coffee mug and took a drink of the fresh brew. Even inside, he could hear the wind rustle with the sound of autumn's falling leaves.

If a man's home was his castle, then he had found his own country and allegiance in the small city nestled in the foothills of north Georgia. In a month or so, the trees would be completely bare, the ground would harden with frost, and he'd be right there to see it. The architecture firm he'd hired to design the place had brought his vision of the house, studio, and stables into reality. In addition to his mother's generous contributions, he'd scouted out designers and shops to outfit every room, shipped items from his old loft, and pulled everything out of storage. Yet, as he tilted his head back and exhaled, the thought that something was still missing filled his mind.

Upon his hearing the sound of footsteps, a kernel of

understanding of what it was that seemed absent from his home blossomed.

"Good morning," Kincaid said without turning his head. Dana's trail of loud yawns and heavy feet brought a modicum of activity into the usual silence of the living room. "Coffee's ready and I'll have breakfast on the table by the time you get out of the shower."

"God, I'm going to miss you. Are you sure you can't come to Paris ahead of schedule?"

Kincaid smiled at his business manager and best friend's reflection in the window as she rubbed her eyes and yawned again. He turned toward her with a grin still on his lips. She'd never been a morning person, he thought. Her kind oval face as she smiled up at him was imprinted upon his mind just as much as his mother's was. As he moved away from the window, he had to admit to himself that he hated to see Dana leave.

It was just over a week ago he'd driven down to the Atlanta International Airport and picked her up. Now that the hour had come for him to drive her back, it might have been just yesterday.

"You've got cafés and restaurants up and down the boulevard. You don't need me there to baby you," he reminded her.

"Lie to me for once in your life, Caid," Dana tossed over her shoulder after making her way around the coffee table.

Kincaid grinned at the back of her below-the-shoulder locks and followed as she headed for the kitchen. "We have an agreement, remember? You handle the business and I supply the goods just like the other artists."

They'd formed an alliance on the first day of art class at Yale University, and it just kept getting stronger. She'd seen him through his first baby steps into the art world to the world-renowned sculptor he was today. And he'd given her away at her wedding and pulled her back from the edge when her much-older husband passed away from cancer. Now the once grieving widow turned savvy businesswoman had transformed his personal passion into a thriving art business.

She took a seat at the kitchen table while Kincaid pulled down a mug and prepared her coffee.

"Just the way you like it with loads of cream and sugar." He placed the steaming beverage in front of her.

Dana's narrowed eyes began to widen and Kincaid sat back to wait. He knew it would take at least five sips for her to come to complete wakefulness, and he wanted to be ready when it happened.

"I got up last night and went out to the studio."

"I know." He picked up his coffee mug and watched her over the rim.

"How could you know?" She sat forward. "I about froze to death walking out to that studio of yours."

His grin broadened at the overstatement. To Dana, who was visiting from California, any temperature under sixty-five qualified as a cold day. "I saw you through the window."

"And you didn't invite me in?"

Kincaid let his look of annoyance say it all.

Dana rolled her eyes to the ceiling. "Well, I wouldn't have to sneak if you'd just let me see what you're working on."

"You know the rules. No one sees the piece until it's finished."

"I've got to tell the art critics and your collectors something. I'm opening a new gallery in less than two months, and the centerpiece is sitting in the middle of this unmapped section of nowhere Georgia."

Kincaid threw his head back and laughed with Dana. The sound of their mingled laughter echoed through the kitchen and filled the room with more warmth than the September sun.

"Honestly, Kincaid, from what little I saw, I think this might be one of your best works yet."

"Thanks."

Dana tapped her fingers on the table. "Now, I said

might because you kept standing in the way so I couldn't get a better look at it."

"That was deliberate." He leaned forward and braced his elbows on the table.

"You can be such a little devil sometimes."

He tipped his head back and grinned. "Isn't that why you love me so much?"

"Maybe," Dana replied. He watched as her eyes slid past him to gaze out the window. "You know I've been worried about you."

"Why?" His brow wrinkled with confusion. His move from California hadn't been a surprise. He'd been itching to make a change for well over a year. The only reason he hadn't left sooner was due to business and the building of his new home.

She flicked her wrist and the tinkling sounds of her gold bracelets filled the air. "Don't get me wrong, the house looks fantastic and the city is something out of an all-American postcard, but I wonder if moving down here and building this place so far away from all your friends and family is a good idea."

Growing up the son of an Academy Award–winning actress and a film director had given him an appreciation for being alone and a yearning for a permanent home. He'd spent the first half of his life traveling with his parents and an entourage, which included his own personal teacher, to different parts of the world to shoot films. Kincaid thought of his mother and father, and for the life of him couldn't remember where they were. "By the way, where are my parents? New York?"

"Close. Washington, D.C. Your dad's been nominated for an achievement award."

"Oh." He snapped his fingers. "I knew that. Dad sent me an e-mail about it. Guess it slipped my mind." He didn't even try to hide the sarcasm humming through his voice. He spoke to his parents about once every few weeks, but their itinerary and flight schedule were too complex for him to be sure of their exact location.

"See? This place has already changed you."

"For the better," he countered, then took a sip of coffee. "I've never had so much inspiration, and for once I feel settled. Can you not look at the mountains and feel alive?"

"What about people?" she continued. "You can't cut yourself off from your family."

"Atlanta is less than an hour away. With its international airport, I can be anywhere in less than a day and New York in less than three hours."

Dana's mug stopped halfway between the table and her mouth. "What about your loft in San Francisco?"

"I've got a call in to a Realtor. If what the man says is accurate, I should get a nice return on my investment when I put it on the market. When I say I'm not going back out West, I mean it, Dana. This is the only place I want to be. I'm home."

"What about the business side, Kincaid? There's more to being an artist than creating art. People need to meet the man behind the work."

"You'll make sure I keep in contact with the gallery shows and the opening in Paris. By the way, how's it going? Are the arrangements suitable enough until you find a permanent replacement?"

She sighed as a soft smile lifted the corners of her lips. "Nothing can beat having a suite overlooking the Eiffel Tower. Your parents' apartment is fabulous. I just sent your mother a gift basket filled with heavenly chocolates. And I found your father's brand of Cuban cigars on a quick trip to Amsterdam."

"You know none of that's necessary. You're practically a member of the family."

"The one who submits weekly reports on how you're doing because you can't be bothered to pick up the phone."

He ignored her sarcastic comment and stayed on the topic. "So the living quarters agree with you. How soon do you think you'll be able to get everything up and running and return to San Francisco?"

"Well, I might not have to find a replacement. I'm thinking of making the move permanent to Paris and running the gallery myself."

Kincaid sat forward and moved his coffee cup to the side so that he could lean his elbows on the table. "What brought this on?"

"It's more along the lines of whom." Dana's lips curled upward and the natural spark in her eyes grew brighter. "I met someone. A wonderful someone who makes Paris and my heart come alive in ways I hadn't thought possible since Randall's death."

His gaze dropped to the table, and then he looked toward the window before returning his attention on his friend. All the feelings of being left behind resurfaced. When he was sixteen, his parents had felt it best to enroll him in Philip Exeter, a well-known boarding school in Massachusetts, in order to make it easier for him to matriculate into his father's alma mater, Yale.

Yet none of that mattered. His thoughts focused around the woman who sat across the table from him. She was an older sister to him in all ways except for blood. He'd given Dana away to a man almost twice her age, and then stood by to hold her hand during the funeral, and the thought of her being hurt again caused him to clench his teeth. Paris was eight hours away, but he still wanted her close.

"Kincaid?" Dana's hand reached over the table and settled atop his. "Are you okay with this?"

"It's a little hard since I haven't met the man yet."

"I know it's impulsive, but Jacques is good for me."

"Is he an artist?" Kincaid's frowned slightly.

"Good Lord, no," she snorted. "I can barely deal with you and you're like a brother. No, he's a businessman."

"I take it Jacques is French?"

"By way of the Caribbean." Dana waved her hand.

Several moments passed before Dana's soft voice cut the silence. "I really want your support on this."

"And you have it."

"Along with approval."

Kincaid released a pent-up breath. "Let me meet the man first."

"Fair enough."

They both stood. When Dana walked over to hug him, he pulled her into a friendly hug and rested his chin atop her soft locks. The familiar scent of cocoa butter wafted into his nose, and it made the thought of her leaving all the more difficult. "All right, you go and get dressed, I'll get breakfast ready, and if you hurry maybe you can feed the horses before we hit the road."

"You spoil me." Dana pulled away.

"Always." Kincaid reached out and ran a callused thumb along her cheek. "Now get a move on. You need to check in two hours before your departure, and the traffic getting through Atlanta is always heavy."

Much later, after he'd dropped Dana off at the Air France departure terminal, Kincaid crept up Interstate 75 with the heavy flow of commuters on their way out of the city. It wasn't until after he'd reached the outskirts of metro Atlanta that he noticed the flashing maintenance light. Leaning back and staring into the midafternoon horizon over the sea of cars and trucks, he tried to remember the last time he'd taken the car in for work, and the only time he could come up with was the day he drove it off the dealership lot.

When he looked down at the odometer of the Ford Explorer, Kincaid whistled. He'd bought the truck because it was tough, but a cross-country journey from San Francisco to Georgia would kick the hell out of any vehicle. The last thing he needed was to have his truck out of commission when he had to pick up a shipment of imported ebony wood in a few days.

The closer he got to Cartersville, the more the light

seemed to glow a brighter shade of red. Not taking any
chances, Kincaid moved the truck to the right and exited
the interstate. He made a quick U-turn and pulled into
Blackfox Automotive Service Center.

It wasn't until he'd located the car drop-off garage that
he noticed the hour. He'd arrived at 3:30 in the afternoon
without an appointment, and he hadn't bought the truck
at the same dealership. The fact that the Ford Explorer was
still under warranty seemed to be the only thing in his
favor. Turning off the ignition, he grabbed his leather
briefcase from the back and stepped down. Best he could
hope for would be a loaner vehicle and a guarantee to have
it fixed.

He stepped inside, relieved when the woman behind the
service counter flashed him a bright smile. After he'd ex-
plained his situation and answered a few questions, the
woman took his keys.

"We'll just have it pulled into the back and get a technician to take a look at it. We can't put you back out on
the highway and have you stranded, can we?"

"No, ma'am." Kincaid grinned. He'd only lived in the
Southeast for three months, but he'd picked up the importance of being polite.

"Just make a left and go up the stairs to the waiting
room. I'll have somebody come and update you on your
car as soon as I can. It might not be for a while, since it's
so close to quitting time and we've had people out with
this nasty stomach virus."

"Take your time," he replied, making sure that his voice
sounded as laid-back and relaxed as the California sunshine.

Kincaid followed the woman's instructions and went up
the stairs. As soon as he entered the waiting room, two toddlers attacked him.

"Whoa." He staggered slightly from the twin forces that
plowed into his legs.

"Wow, you're big."

Kincaid lowered his head to find two sets of large brown eyes staring up at him. He grinned down at the two little boys.

"Want to play?" the smaller of the two asked. "Henry fell asleep." He pointed a small finger at a tie-clad man hunched over in a chair.

"Sure." Kincaid put his briefcase and sketchpad on the round table, then looked around. "Are you sure it's okay with your parents?"

"Dad's upstairs in the big room and Auntie Regan said we can do anything we want—"

"No." The older of the two boys spoke up. "No, she said we can do anything we want as long as we don't touch the coffeepot, the phone, or the Coke machine. And we can't leave the room."

"Okay." The other boy sighed. "So, mister, can you play?"

"I've got a better idea." Kincaid pulled a chair back from the table, then motioned to the kids. "Take a seat."

He flipped back the cover of his sketchbook, ripped out two sheets of paper, and pushed them over to the boys. "How about we have a contest?" He looked over to see a children's book on one of the chairs and pointed a finger at the book cover filled with animals. "Let's see who can draw the best animal."

"Mr. . . ."

"Just call me Kincaid."

"Mr. Kincaid." The boy looked over at him with a wearied expression that looked out of place on his youthful face. "We forgot to bring our crayons."

"That's okay, I remembered mine." With that, he reached into his briefcase, pulled out a set of sketching pencils, and placed them in the center of the table. "We'll just have to share."

Half grinning with amusement, he picked up a sharp pencil and sat back in the chair. For a few moments, he just watched the boys bent over the paper with the colored pencils clutched tight in their tiny fists.

A little while later the woman from the courtesy desk tapped on his shoulder. "I've brought the kids some snacks, and something to drink. Feel free to help yourself." She busied herself arranging the snacks and beverages on the table.

"Appreciate it." He grinned broadly and reached over to grab the bag of pretzels.

"Sweetheart." She hummed the word with a southern flair and shook her salt-and-pepper hair from side to side. "You must be a miracle worker. This is the quietest they've been since their father went in to a meeting and Regan threatened to tie them up."

Kincaid stood and gestured toward the two boys. "They're not a problem."

"They are adorable. If I didn't have my own little devils, I'd fight Candace for them. Well, it's time for me to go home." She patted his arm. "It was nice meeting you. Regan should be out here soon to let you know about your vehicle."

"Regan?" Kincaid questioned as the unusual name caught his attention.

"Your service technician."

They said their good-byes and Kincaid went back to his seat and flipped open his sketch pad. Soon could have been minutes or hours, but it didn't matter to Kincaid or to the two toddlers sitting with him at the table. Time and art didn't mix, especially when he was inspired. With the charcoal pencil in his hand, he couldn't have cared less about his truck. His hand scribbled over the empty sheet. The charcoal lines were roughened in his haste to capture the childlike innocence and manlike determination of the boys as they drew the animals.

"Kincaid Sinclair?"

The feminine voice floated over his shoulder like a tropical breeze. When Kincaid turned around, he forgot about his plan to sculpt an abstract of the little boys' hands and promptly dropped his pencil. Even with the billed cap shadowing half of her face, the woman's bone structure begged him to sketch it, to chisel her likeness into marble, or mold her into clay and make it bronze.

"Mr. Sinclair?" she repeated.

Kincaid pushed back his chair, stood, and started toward her. "That would be me."

"Great." She gave him a direct look and her dark honey-brown eyes seemed to see through him. Something told him that the lady mechanic didn't miss much, and her aura of confidence only served to invoke his curiosity. Yet on the heels of his interest came the wind of déjà vu. Unconsciously, he frowned. For a split second, the watermarked image of his ex-fiancée hung suspended over her face.

"I'll be with you in a moment." She politely nodded her head, took three steps toward the bouncing little boys, and crouched down while balancing on the balls of her feet. "Tyler, Kevin, remember the drill I taught you this morning?"

The two boys scrambled out of their chairs and stood at perfect attention. "Yes."

"Good. Because your mommy's on her way and your dad's still in a meeting. So you know what to do, right?"

The taller little boy, who had to be Tyler, stepped up. "I get the toys and put them in the closet."

"What's your job, Kevin?" She looked to her clipboard and pretended to study it.

"I hide all the candy wrappers," the little boy piped up.

"Excellent." Regan poised her pencil on the paper and lifted an eyebrow. "Then what?"

"We go to the bathroom and get all cleaned up for Mommy."

"Perfect. Now you two get going and meet me back here at the table."

She turned toward him and when she smiled Kincaid's stomach dropped. Uncaring of her possible reaction, he examined her face as he would a piece of art. Feeling the hollows of her cheeks, the sharp edge of her chin, the smoothness of her dark amber skin, and the crests of her lips. The texture of her dark amber skin reminded him of the heartwood of a cherry tree. Kincaid had no business staring at her, but he did. Another man would have turned around to give some semblance of privacy, but his eyes never left her face.

When her expression remained unchanged, Kincaid thought maybe he had imagined the flicker in her eyes. But the sensual uptilt of her unpainted lips and the flush to her cheeks let him known his admiring gaze had not gone either unnoticed or unappreciated.

She looked down at the clipboard in her hand. "Apologies for that."

His gaze dropped to the name tag on her coveralls. "You're not David Blackfox."

"Very perceptive. This would be his shirt. David's my cousin and the father of those two angels you've been keeping out of trouble. I'm Regan Blackfox."

"Regan." He let the *rrr* sound of her name roll off his tongue and gave her his most charming smile while extending his hand. He was an artist, not a recluse. Growing up the son of a man who could talk Hollywood's leading ladies into giving the performances of a lifetime and movie executives into handing over blank checks, Kincaid couldn't have helped inheriting some of Alfonse Sinclair's charm.

In an automatic gesture, she reached out her own hand, but then pulled back. "I'd shake your hand, but I don't want to get grease on your fingers."

Instinct told him to take another step forward, and he obliged, getting deep into her personal space. Usually a man to take things slow and easy, he felt pushed by some unknown force to test her. He needed to discover if the instant attraction was mutual or merely a figment of his imagination.

Kincaid hardly had to lower his face to look at her.

Regan's height, like the rest of her, fit. In a flash of insight, he knew that they would be an even match in and out of bed. His estimation of her went up a notch further as she held her ground. "I wouldn't mind."

"But I would. My uncle likes to keep his customers happy, not splattered with transmission fluid, Mr. Sinclair."

"Please call me Kincaid."

Her lashes fluttered down, then swept up. "All right. Kincaid. I have your Explorer back in the shop. Been doing some powerful driving, haven't you?" She raised her eyebrows, making her eyes look even more intriguing.

"I just moved here."

"From San Francisco." She tapped her pen against the clip of the board in her hands. "That's a long way from Cartersville, Georgia."

"How did you know?"

Her smile as it crept over her lips and curved them upward reminded him of the beauty of the moon, and he so badly wanted to make it eternal. "Your front plate and there's a California address listed on the car history."

"So what's wrong with it?" Hell, the last thing Kincaid cared about was the truck. He'd needed something large to transport his more fragile art pieces to his new home, so he'd gone out and added an SUV to go with his Porsche.

"Nothing that a routine maintenance service and computer diagnostic couldn't fix."

Kincaid spotted a slight smudge on the side of her jaw and without dropping his gaze, turned his body, reached into his briefcase, and pulled out a Kleenex. "You've got something on your face."

"And on my hands." She smiled again.

Eyes riveted to the sight of her small white teeth, he raised the tissue. "May I?"

"Please." She lifted her face upward and closed her eyes. He placed a finger under her chin, then carefully rubbed away the mark.

"All done," he said, his voice husky.

Her lashes fluttered upward and her eyes stared into his. In that long moment something charged between them until she pulled away.

"Thank you."

"Anytime." Kincaid grinned. He liked the fact that, unlike most of the women of his past acquaintance, Regan didn't apologize for her appearance. In her stained mechanic uniform, her casual attitude let him know that she would be just as confident in any style of dress.

She cleared her throat. "Once I take care of the boys, we can settle the bill and get you home."

"There's no hurry."

"My cousins and I both appreciate what you did with my nephews. Kyle was supposed to be taking care of them, but he got called into a meeting and their mother had to be in Atlanta today."

He took a step closer to her, and the scent of flowers wafted to his nose over the smell of oil. "Least I can do since you took on my car this close to closing and without me having an appointment."

"Regan," a loud voice called. "I swear if he's had those boys under any of those cars that husband of mine will be sleeping in his office permanently."

Kincaid turned to see a tornado sweep into the room. "Candace," Regan started. "Calm down."

"Mommy!" the kids belted out in a chorus. The reunion was a sight to see as the boys crowded around the newest visitor, and Kincaid finally caught sight of her stomach and concluded that there would soon be another addition to the Blackfox family.

"My babies."

Each of them ran to the table and back to the nicely dressed woman. The older boy held up his masterpiece. "Mommy, look at what I did. I drew the best elephant in the world."

"And Mr. Kincaid helped me draw you a picture of Sparky."

"You must be Mr. Sinclair. Marilyn told me all about you." The woman held out her hand and he politely shook it, all the time aware of the two women's regard.

"Just call me Kincaid. Nice to meet you."

She smiled and he could see the resemblance between the mother and her sons. The kindly sloped eyelids and soft round faces the color of warm molasses. "I'm Candace, and if you ever need to borrow some kids, just let me know."

He laughed and nodded his head. "Will do. I'm always on the lookout for future artists."

She sighed. "If only they would always practice on the paper and not the playroom walls.

"Well, you two have probably been eating junk food all day. Let's see if we can say good-bye to Daddy and then head home for dinner."

"Regan." Candace looked over her shoulder. "Are you coming?"

"I need to close out the service bay and then I've got plans. I'll call you tomorrow night about the weekend."

Kincaid watched the interplay between the two women with unabashed interest.

Candace's eyes went from Regan to Kincaid and then back to her sons. "You take care, okay?"

"Will do. Now do I get some hugs or what?" Regan bent down and the boys both wrapped their arms around her. "You guys take care of your mom."

"Promise!"

Once the boys and then the mother departed the waiting area, Kincaid gathered his supplies from the table and followed Regan down the empty corridor. As she walked away, Kincaid's gaze slid down the short ponytail that hung to her shoulders, past the blue shirt to the enticing sway of her rounded behind, his ears detected nothing but the sound of his own footsteps on the linoleum floor. Once they entered the service area, Regan walked behind the tall blue desk, picked out a wet tissue, and wiped her hands. She returned her attention to him, then said, "Marilyn set up your service record in the system before she left. All I need is payment and your signature."

As Kincaid dug into his wallet for a credit card, he wondered if Regan was *really* a mechanic; she was certainly tall enough. But she had a delicate face and slender fingers. While they waited for the computer to process the transaction, he leaned on the counter. "Have you worked on cars long?"

"Practically all of my life. I started working on diesel trucks and graduated to Fords." She handed him the printed receipt for his signature but kept his card. "Kincaid Alfonse Sinclair. Why does your name sound so familiar?" Her voice trailed off.

He shrugged and picked up a nearby ballpoint pen. He'd been his parents' son for longer than he could remember. No matter how he much he'd tried to distance himself from his parents' fame, he couldn't and had long ago given up. The film director and actress whose names and genes he bore would always be an integral part of his professional and personal life. "Maybe you're into watching movies."

"No. That's not it."

When he looked up, he found her eyes on his and her pearly white teeth chewing on a corner of her lips. The small gesture kicked his already moving libido up another notch.

"The House of Slaves," she murmured.

Kincaid blinked in surprise. The name of the large slave castle built by the Dutch on Goree Island off the coast of Senegal made Kincaid's hand falter as he signed his name.

Regan continued. "There was a statue of a mother reaching for her child. The inscription bears your name."

"It was commissioned by UNESCO for the International Day for the Remembrance of the Slave Trade and its

Abolition." His voice lowered in reverence. "It was a deeply personal work."

She handed him his credit card. The touch of her fingertips on his palm sent a shock to his system that had nothing to do with static electricity. "Our city is very lucky to have such a talented artist in our midst."

Kincaid put the card back into his leather wallet. "Does that mean I get certain liberties?"

"Such as?"

"The key to the city?" he quipped. Yet he was half tempted to ask for the key to her heart just to see what kind of response he would get.

"Not possible, we gave them all away some time ago. But . . ." She winked at him. "Now that your bill's settled, I can give you the keys to your truck."

She turned to pull back the glass side door, and Kincaid called out, "I'll come with you."

"I'm sorry but you can't. Customers aren't allowed in the service center, as a safety precaution."

Kincaid waved around the empty office. Everyone else had left earlier. He was not a man given to impulse, and even his artistic temperament couldn't be the source of his actions. No, it was her voice. He wanted to listen to the modulated tone, which to his ears blended the best of the South with the lyrical intonation only the French seemed to have been able to master. "I won't tell."

"All right, but watch your step." She gave him a side-long glance, then dropped the set of car keys into the palm of his hand.

"So you're a traveling mechanic."

"And not only are you a world-renowned artist, but I do believe that you just happen to be the son of my mother's favorite actress," she tossed over her shoulder while walking past a toolbox. "I'm actually here on leave."

"Leave?" His brow furrowed with surprise.

"Vacation," she clarified.

Kincaid missed a step as he followed her deeper into the

service department work area. He took a quick glance at the succession of automotive lifts, workbenches, hanging metal parts, and tool drawers. "Looks like work to me."

"Looks can be deceiving." Regan stopped near his Limited Edition Explorer. "I like to stay busy and my cousin likes to keep his customers happy even when half of the service crew comes down with a stomach virus."

"It's good of you to help out." Kincaid continued to follow her closely. Vague thoughts in the back of his mind became more concrete. Something about Regan Blackfox made him think of time. His time. And how he spent it and more importantly, whom he spent it with.

"What can I say?" She shrugged. "It's hard to turn down family." She looked toward the large digital wall clock, then at his green SUV. "You have a great vehicle with a powerful engine. If you come back for the required maintenance services, your Explorer shouldn't give you any trouble for years to come. If you have any problems, don't hesitate to bring her back in."

She turned away and he looked down at the papers in his hand. Anxious to keep her from leaving just yet, Kincaid called out, "One question."

She stopped and turned toward him. "Yes?"

"What's this sheet?"

She took two steps and came to stand beside him. A short unpainted fingernail tapped the paper. "This is your emission inspection report. Should you decide that Cartersville is too small for your liking and move to Atlanta, you'll need that report to register your vehicle."

He lowered his voice. "Not a chance of that happening. I've discovered that I'm a small-town boy at heart." He paused and gave her a meaningful look. "And I plan on being a resident for a long time."

Regan cleared her throat and then aimed a glance at the digital clock on the far wall. "Good. I hate to rush you out the door, but I really need to lock up."

"Of course." His fingers clenched around the keys at the

briskness of her response. "Thanks for taking care of me, Regan."

"I aim to please. Thank you for your business."

He held out his hand and this time she shook it. Kincaid couldn't help but notice the softness of her palm, nor could he fail to observe that she didn't seem eager to pull away.

"Good night, Kincaid. Drive safely."

He let go of Regan's hand and moved to walk past her. Again as before she stood her ground. He started the truck and put it in gear, all the while keeping an eye on Regan.

The moment the Explorer cleared the service bay entrance, she pressed a button and the tall garage door began to lower. As inch by inch she disappeared, something clenched in his gut and he didn't want to say goodbye. Kincaid backed the truck into an empty space, cut the engine, and waited.

When she came out twenty minutes later, he watched her climb into a pickup truck before he cranked the engine and pulled out in front of her, effectively blocking her in. Without bothering to switch off the motor, Kincaid stepped out of the Explorer and shut the door behind him.

After a moment, she raised an arm to take off her cap so that he could see her face. Their eyes collided. Even without the bright inside lights to warm them, Regan's eyes were stunning. And the absence of the billed cap made his fingers itch to touch her bobbed hair. The artist in him imagined that it would be soft and thick, like the finest strands of a red sable paintbrush.

She stepped out of the car and all but stomped toward him and stopped. "What are you doing?"

He ignored her question and instead took a step forward. "Is it Mrs. Regan Blackfox or Ms.?"

She blinked in surprise and he enjoyed watching the rise and fall of her lengthy lashes. "I am not married."

Smiling inwardly, Kincaid released a compressed breath. "Have dinner with me tonight."

"I have plans."

"You can change them."

He watched her reaction and caught a whisper of something in her dark eyes. Then before he could identify what it was, she lowered her gaze.

"That's very presumptuous of you," she responded. There was a hum of amusement in her voice. If he'd thought she had a sense of humor before, this just about confirmed it. The corner of his mouth hitched up a little higher.

"Right alphabet, wrong word. It's persistence. I want to see you again."

She gave him a searching glance, and underneath the fluorescent light of the overhead lamps, her eyes gleamed like a cat's. Regan examined him with the perplexed expression of a woman who had suddenly realized that the man standing before her had the physical and mental confidence that makes him attractive. Kincaid didn't squirm under her scrutiny. He continued to watch her with a steady gaze that was mitigated by the slight upturn of his lips. He wasn't sure what was going through Regan's mind, but he knew what was going on in his. She had the most perfect lips he'd ever seen. Nicely full, smooth with a curvy bow, tasty. He could only imagine those lips pressed against his. Those long legs entwined with his.

She cocked an eyebrow. "You just met me."

"And I want to know more about you."

"Tomorrow evening." She turned her back to him and began to walk toward her car.

Flush with triumph, he rubbed his hands together. "I'll pick you up at seven."

"No." She turned her head back toward him. "I'll pick you up at your place. Five o'clock."

"What about my address?"

"I've already have it."

Kincaid rubbed his hands together. "What about your phone number should I need to contact you if something comes up?"

Finally, something got her attention; she put her hands on the top of the truck and crooked her neck to look at him. Regan met his stare, and he saw that the self-assured smile on her lips echoed in her eyes. "If you're as eager to get to know me as you say, then nothing will keep you from being ready."

"You're some kind of woman, Ms. Regan Blackfox." Kincaid let out a rumbling laugh.

"I'll take that as a compliment, Mr. Kincaid Sinclair."

"Please do."

"See you tomorrow. And . . ." She paused before stepping up into the truck. "Welcome to Georgia."

Chapter 4

Regan went home, took a shower, applied the barest minimum of makeup, styled her hair, changed into wool slacks and a sweater, and hopped back in her pickup in less than thirty minutes. She chanced a look in the truck's vanity mirror while waiting at a stoplight. And with her left hand, she ran her fingers through auburn-brown hair that fell below her chin, framing the delicate bones of her face.

She fought against a wave of embarrassment as her mind replayed the past two hours. Having been groomed from the cradle on the importance of making a positive first impression, she couldn't help but recall exactly how she'd looked in her cousin's work shirt and overalls. On any given day, she wouldn't have been bothered by her appearance, but today her feminine pride couldn't help but be more than a little out of sorts. Then again, if Kincaid Sinclair was attracted to her when she looked her worst, then when she looked her best, he'd truly be impressed.

The light turned green and she drove forward, but part of her mind dwelled on the events . . . no, the man she'd met only hours before. Nothing told more about a person than his mode of transportation. Kincaid's Explorer had come fully loaded but without all the flashy extras.

The interior, while far from a disaster area she'd seen when looking into some minivans, was far from neat. She could tell from the chunks of rock, pieces of wood, and an assortment of tools that he used his truck as more of a machine to get from point A to B than a social statement. Also, the Beethoven CD in the CD player let her know that he preferred classical to jazz. He didn't smoke or have friends who did. The last person who sat in the passenger seat had been either a woman or a short man.

Yet in all her thoughts, Kincaid's physical presence came through the strongest. It was almost too easy for her to recall with detailed accuracy everything about Kincaid Sinclair. From the rich walnut color of his skin to the midnight-black eyebrows to the rough calluses on the palm of his right hand.

Part of her job depended on knowing both the physical and mental characteristics of her targets. Nine times out of ten, she could memorize a person's face in such a way as to detail the exact likeness to a sketch artist. This time, however, she'd been wrong about the smoothness of his face. Kincaid had faint lines around his mouth and eyes. He possessed the best lines, those drawn by the repeated act of laughter.

"Peppermint," she said aloud. She blinked twice at the seemingly random thought until ten seconds later she made the connection. His breath smelled of the kind of sweet red-and-white-striped candy her mother always carried in her purse.

Why did I accept his dinner invitation? Regan reached over to turn down the radio, and then briefly slipped back into the role of Dominique Nichols, the persona that lived in a world of calculation, deliberation, and above all else self-analysis.

The simple answer surprised her. It was impulse and attraction. The light fluttering that had begun in her stomach and transformed to a sensual shiver along her nerve endings had influenced her actions. She had not reacted so strongly to a man's nearness in a long while.

"It has been a long time," Regan whispered. A very long time since she'd spent time with a man who didn't have a hidden agenda. A long time since she'd done something simply because she wanted to. And at that moment, more than anything else she wanted to indulge in the rush of getting to know a handsome and interesting man while reconnecting with her family.

Downshifting the pickup, she turned the corner and crept along behind traffic leaving the local shopping mall. The sight of a carpeting advertisement on a billboard was all she needed to remind her of her family's ties to the local business.

Blackfox Transport was one of the largest privately owned truckload carriers in the United States. The company was a legacy, passed down to her eldest brother, Marius. She'd grown up around trucks and had cut her mechanical teeth on a 250-horsepower diesel engine. When her father felt restless, he'd take over a shipment and she spent the entire Saturday either on the highway listening to the CB radio in the passenger seat looking down at cars passing by or with one of her brothers curled in the back sleeper cab.

Filling in at her uncle's car dealership had reminded her of how much she enjoyed using her hands. Her family's automotive and shipping businesses necessitated that all of the kids get involved with cars. There was nothing she didn't know about her automobile and nothing she couldn't fix. She just wished her skills extended to interpersonal relationships. Regan hit the switch to lower the window and then entered the code Savannah had given her to open the exclusive subdivision's automatic wrought-iron gates.

Not for the last time did she wish that she still possessed access to the NSA technology. At the touch of a computer key, she could log on to the NSA's intranet and within minutes download the latest intercepts, satellite imagery, defense analysis, and FBI reports. Whomever her cousin wanted Regan to meet obviously had money, but where had it come from? Better yet, with whom had Savannah had fallen in love? And why did she continue to hide his identity from their family?

Regan followed the streets past majestic homes and manicured lawns on top of the small mountain until she came to the one whose street numbers matched the address in her hand. She looked at the brick mailbox, blinked twice, then reread the name: Jack Archer. As surprise raced through her body, her fingers clenched on the truck's steering wheel.

Boston had the Kennedy family, but Georgia had the Archers. If "the Carpet Capital of the World" were truly Dalton, Georgia, then the Archer family would be its reigning family. As they rose to power and established themselves as the leading textile and floor-covering manufacturers, the Blackfox family came up right beside them. What the Archer factories produced, their trucks shipped. And that unholy alliance had been built on the ultimate betrayal.

By comparison with their family situation, Romeo and Juliet had it easy. Shakespeare's Montagues and Capulets only had a history of hate. The Blackfoxes and Archers had blood ties, history, binding family testaments, politics, financial interests, and entrenched mistrust.

After exiting the truck, Regan stepped onto the front porch, but hesitated to ring the doorbell. Before she could touch the pearly white circle, the large stained-glass door opened.

"Good evening, Regan. I'm Jack."

Regan couldn't do anything but blink as his cheerful voice resonated in her head. *Good evening, Regan. I'm Jack.*

For a moment, Regan wanted to look around for the hidden video camera, or search behind the bushes, because she knew that Savannah would jump out and tell her that this was one big joke. That she wasn't in love with the man whose grandfather had almost single-handedly destroyed their family. Instead, Regan kept her smile in place and her eyes steady with the man standing in the doorway.

Jack Archer was tall, about thirty-five, with boyishly handsome features: a strong jaw, blond at the ends of ash-brown hair, twin dimples, and eyes a shade lighter than moss green covered by wire-framed glasses.

Careful to maintain eye contact, Regan stepped forward and initiated a handshake by deliberately extending her hand. Years of training on the subject of politeness took over, and she smiled. "Nice to meet you, Jack." Remembering the bottle of red wine she'd procured from her parents' well-stocked wine cellar for the occasion, she held it out toward him. "This is for you."

He raised an eyebrow after examining the label. "This looks to be an excellent vintage. I'll go put it on ice." He took it from her hands and then gestured toward the inside of the house. "Come on in. Can I take your coat?"

"Thank you," Regan responded and turned around, letting him help her with the leather coat. Contrary to popular family lore, this Archer possessed gentlemanly manners. She had to admit he was not only handsome, in a wholesome way, but gracious and well mannered as well. She'd always known Savannah had excellent taste in men, just not common sense. This was playing with serious fire.

"Believe it or not, I've been looking forward to meeting you for a while. Savannah's told me a lot about the escapades you both got into growing up."

Regan stifled a snort. He had her at a distinct disadvantage because her beloved cousin had told her nothing beyond the mere fact that she was in love.

"Would you like something to drink? I have sparkling water, wine, soda, and fruit juice. Dinner should be just about ready."

"Sparkling water sounds good."

"Coming right up." He shook his head and a curl dropped

in front of his eyes. Regan watched him brush it away and
wondered for the second time what her cousin was thinking to be getting involved with Jack Archer.

"Please have a seat." He waved his hand and the gesture
encompassed the whole of the living room. She had her
pick of a leather sofa, love seat, or matching chairs with
ottomans.

"So where's Savannah?" she called toward his depart-
ing back. Instead of sitting down, she ambled in the direction her host had taken.

He stopped and turned around. "She won't be coming
until late. She called and mentioned something about a
PTA meeting running late. "I'm just relieved that she
didn't cancel." He opened a bottle of mineral water.

"What?" Regan called out. For the first time since
she'd parked her car in his driveway, she allowed her true
emotions to show by letting her bottom lip drop.

"Guess I should tell you why?" He chuckled.

"Unless you want me to call her on the phone, I think
you should."

"This meeting was my idea." He sighed heavily. "I've
been seeing your cousin for over a year and asking her to
marry me for the past four months. Savannah's afraid to
tell her family, and I'm sick to death of trying to get her
to change her mind. She won't marry me, won't move in,
and I'm too old and responsible to be sneaking around
town like a teenager."

"What does this have to do with me?"

"You're the compromise. Savannah feels that if I win
your approval, then there's hope for your family."

Regan let out the first laugh she'd had all evening, and
she laughed until tears came out of her eyes. *How many
more surprises will this day hold?*

Of all the possibilities running through her mind, this
hadn't been one of them. Despite a few instances of childhood mischief, her cousin had never outright rebelled
against her parents' wishes, while Regan had earned the

nickname "Rebel." Instead of refusing to take part in the debutante ball as she had, Savannah had taken four laxatives and spent the night in the bathroom instead of on the arm of her handpicked escort.

"Something funny?"

"I'm sorry." She wiped the moisture from her eyes. "But compared with the rest of the family, I'm a piece of cake."

"Please have a seat." He gestured toward one of the suede leather sofas.

This time Regan accepted the invitation and sank into the soft couch as her eyes scanned over the room. She liked the elegant, tasteful, and classic style. She could see her cousin's hand in the design of the room and its furnishings.

When Jack returned with her glass, she remarked, "Your house is fairly new, I take it."

"I lived at home until I met Savannah. All I had was work, so I didn't need a place of my own. She actually picked out the house."

"What about the interior design?"

"I couldn't tell an end table from a coffee table. I gave her a free hand."

"So what exactly is it that you do?" She crossed her legs and took a sip of water.

"I manage the information technology division at the corporate office. Excuse me for a minute, but I need to check on the soufflé."

Regan nodded and as soon as he left the room, she stood and walked toward the fireplace. She examined his family pictures first and noticed that Jack took after his mother in looks; she was willing to bet he took after her in temperament as well. There were photos of her cousin and many snapshots of Savannah and Jack. Her face and her temperament were delicate. Savannah had the kind of eyes and lips women paid large sums of money to achieve, and a smile.

With their arms intertwined, they had a look that she recognized well from seeing it in her parents' eyes. The intimate look of two people in love. She sighed aloud.

"I hope that doesn't mean what I think it means."

She turned to see Jack reenter the room. "Not exactly," she said wryly.

"So what's the early verdict?"

Regan placed her water glass on the mantel and then met his steady gaze. "I can't lie to you. The mess of anger and bitter mistrust that has lain between our families isn't something that can be easily crossed. Savannah has good reason to keep this relationship a secret."

He raked a hand through his hair. "Why is it that even though my great-grandfather tried to make amends to your family, they still hold a grudge? Actually, it's more than a grudge. The woman I love is terrified of telling her parents. And it was only after making my parents swear on a Bible not to tell anyone that we were dating that Savannah agreed to meet them."

"Those that were wronged, remember?" She gentled her voice as to not sound accusatory. "I'm not saying it's right, but it's a fact." The words echoed in her head. The last thing Regan ever wanted to do was tout the family line. However, the past could be neither ignored nor changed.

"Look." He raised his arms in a helpless confused gesture. "If I lost Savannah because I did something stupid like cheating on her or being dishonest with her, then at least it was something I did. Not because your family still holds a grudge against mine."

Regan had built her career on being able to read people. The NSA and life within the diplomatic corps trained her to see into their hearts and judge not only by body language and intonation but also by their eyes. And Jack, with the trademark Archer green eyes, was about as warm and sincere as they came.

For a multitude of reasons, a main one being the possibility of putting an end to the legacy of enmity between their families, she wanted him to win, wanted him in the family, and most of all she wanted her cousin happy regardless of the shock wave their involvement would cause once it became known.

"So how did the two of you meet?" Regan asked.

Jack's lips curled into an easy smile, and his already soft voice dropped to an almost reverent whisper. "I helped install computers in the school library. A couple of the technicians and I got too loud, and without so much as a warning, she clamped her hand over my mouth and in polite terms told me to shut up."

She chuckled. "Sounds like Savannah."

"You can't help but fall in love with a woman like that."

Regan delicately sniffed the fragrant aroma of food, and right on time her stomach growled to remind her that she hadn't eaten a proper lunch. "How about we put this aside and talk about more pleasant topics? I would much rather get to know the man that has my favorite cousin wearing makeup and smiling like she's won the lottery than rehash old family feuds."

"No wonder she calls you the diplomat."

Regan winked and put her hand on his shoulder. "That's because I know how to duck and hide. Savannah on the other hand will stand there and wait for the bullets to start flying."

Jack's eyes got big and round. "Bullets?"

"Not really bullets. Our family dinners can turn into war zones when my grandfather has a little too much bourbon on an empty stomach. He and Dad or Uncle Kyle will get into an argument about the company. Marius usually sides with Grandfather. My other brothers and cousins just put their heads down and concentrate on shoving the food in their mouths, so they can clean their plates and run off to the den to watch a ball game."

"What about Savannah?"

Regan chuckled at the memory of her cousin's theatrics. "She'll try to make peace by giving everyone an extra serving of something or trying to change the subject. Meanwhile all the other women in the family are minding their own business or making a beeline into the kitchen."

"Wow, that's not like my family dinners."

Regan shook her head. If he wanted to marry her cousin, he needed to know the truth. You didn't just marry a Blackfox, you married the family. And as much as she loved each member, from the old and stubborn to the young and spoiled, her conscience couldn't take the hit of having Jack Archer unknowingly walking into a minefield. "Ask Savannah to tell you about the time Marius proposed contracting owner-operated trucks to the East Coast division," Regan suggested.

Jack's left eyebrow rose and he nodded. "I'll do that after dinner."

"Good. Now could you please show me to the bathroom so I can wash my hands? I'll help you with the salad, and when Savannah gets here we'll work on your problems."

Later on that night, Regan unlocked the garage door of her cottage, flipped on the hall light, and kicked off her shoes. After securing the bolt, she walked farther into the house, dropped her keys on the foyer table, and was beginning to make her way upstairs when the phone rang. Smothering a curse, she took the stairs two at a time and ran into the bedroom in time to pick up the phone before the call transferred to the answering service.

Regan glanced at the bedside alarm clock and saw that it was already midnight. Her brow creased. Who would call this time of night?

Regan placed the phone to her ear. "Hello?"

"Finally!" the familiar voice on the other end of the phone exclaimed.

Instinctively she winced before pulling the phone away from her ear. "Hello, Mother."

"Regan Olivia Blackfox, why are you sounding all out

of breath and where have you been, sweetheart? I've been trying to reach you all day."

"One, I just walked into the house and had to run upstairs to catch the phone. Second, I've been working at the dealership and then had dinner with friends. You don't have to worry about me."

"Don't get cute with me, young lady. You might think you're a grown-up, but you are still my baby and I can be worried about you if I want to."

"I'm sorry."

"Well, I've got the perfect way for you to make it up to me. I'm going to buy you a mobile telephone when we get home. Your father thinks it's a good idea and so do I. He's been doing his research, and the newer models work in other countries."

Regan smothered an inward groan at her mother's honey-voiced comment. She'd had access to international phones years ago but had deliberately chosen to keep that information from her parents.

"I don't need a phone."

"Let's not argue, sweetie. You said you were out to dinner with friends. Was this a male friend?"

"Mother." Regan let the hint of annoyance creep into her voice before switching the phone to the other ear. With one hand, she unbuttoned her coat and laid it on the bed before walking into the bathroom. "How are things in Bermuda?"

"Your father's golf score is improving, I'm learning how to fish, and your grandparents have practically transformed the garden into a tropical paradise."

"Great. So when are you guys planning on coming home?"

"Well, your father wants to charter a yacht and come home by sea instead of air. I'm all for a little adventure, but I don't know if your grandfather can take being disconnected from the business for that long. He calls and checks on things at least twice a day."

"I'm sure," Regan agreed as she cradled the cordless between her ear and shoulder. Using both of her hands, she undressed and changed into her pajamas.

"Are you having a good time at home? I hope you're not spending too much time at the garage. Marius tells me that you've been working on your grandfather's birthday gift."

"I've stopped by the house. I'm waiting for the carburetor and water pump to come in."

"So that means you're going to be home for a while?"

She rolled her eyes toward the ceiling and looked right into a mess of cobwebs in the corner over the bath. Once she'd made a mental note to inform the cleaning service, she returned her attention to the phone conversation. "I can't tell you, Mother."

"If you're not, then I'm going to be on the first plane back tomorrow morning. I hate it that you came home just as we were leaving for our trip."

"We spent a lot of time together before you left." Regan plopped down on the toilet seat and hung her head. She still had unpacked shopping bags in her closet from their mother-daughter shopping expeditions in Atlanta and New York.

"Don't worry. We'll have plenty of time together when you get back," she said.

"You promise?"

Regan crossed her fingers behind her back and sent a quick prayer to God asking for forgiveness. "You bet," she replied.

"I did want to add a few paintings and a few art pieces to the cottage. It's just too impersonal. And now that you're back, we can see about getting some new tile for your kitchen. I saw a lovely rose color when I was at the design store a few months back."

"That sounds like fun."

"Oh dear. I think that's your father calling on the other line. I was supposed to meet him at the hotel for a late-night dance. And I really should let you get some sleep."

Regan nodded her head. "Give everyone kisses and hugs for me please."

"I love you, Regan."

Her heart squeezed at the slight thickness in her mother's voice. "I love you too, Mom."

Chapter 5

Wood and stone.

As the late afternoon sunlight streamed through the windows of his studio, Kincaid stood back and placed his chisel on the side bench. God, he loved his work. Everything he had, everything he knew, went into each nick, each curve, and each movement of his chisel. He recalled the days when his arms ached with the pain of carving wood or cramped with the repeated pounding on stone and shaping of metal. But he would do nothing else or be anyone else.

Without needing to run his hands over the piece, Kincaid could sense the marble stone with his eyes. He felt the crescents, the valleys, the sharp edges, and the round corners he had yet to create. The thousands of uneven veins of ash charcoal inherent in the stone, which made it even more precious.

Because of its rarity and extreme difficulty in carving, the black *portoro* marble, which had been quarried off the coast of Italy, would be his greatest challenge yet. Or maybe his second greatest challenge, he pondered as the fleeting image of a pair of brown eyes crossed his mind. After taking off his mask and gloves, Kincaid ran his hand over the cold uneven surface, and in his mind's eye he traced the smooth curve of Regan Blackfox's cheek.

He could have been more than halfway through with the sculpture, but thoughts of her smile had him stopping and looking out of the window instead of practicing his art. He still couldn't believe his actions from the other day. And he doubted that anyone who knew him would either. Asking Regan out on a date had been sheer impulse. And although many of his artist colleagues used their creative temperament as a blanket excuse to indulge themselves in anything and everything, he did not. Well, until last night.

Regan Blackfox. Kincaid shook his head as her name echoed through his mind. The woman hadn't even waited twenty-four hours to start distracting him. While his heart accepted the attraction with the ease and naturalness of a flower taking in the rain, his mind began to justify his actions.

Having grown up among the Hollywood scene, he'd spent half his life surrounded by the world's beautiful people, so he knew beauty in all its natural and man-made forms. But Regan had all of it, plus some. She carried a warm spark of life that hinted at fire. She was miles from the high-maintenance shells of women who lived for adoration, fame, and eternal youth. And miles from Kirsten, the one woman to whom he'd given a ring and his love, only to have it returned via international courier after she'd flown to parts unknown with an Argentinean playboy who could provide her all the excitement and jet-set lifestyle that he'd despised.

Shaking his head, he pulled the pair of goggles from his neck and stretched. His muscles protested from being in one position for an extended amount of time. Then try as he might to concentrate on the uncommissioned piece, he couldn't.

"Damn," he swore under his breath as his thoughts returned to yesterday, a day of departures and arrivals. Unlike in the previous times that they had gone their separate ways, the space brought by Dana's leaving hadn't been filled by his work. No, somehow the image of Regan wearing a cap with a small oil stain on her cheek seemed to have taken her place. There was something incredibly sexy about her mysterious eyes and the image of a woman holding a wrench and knowing how to use it. The absentminded grin on Kincaid's face disappeared at the sight of the clock.

It was a quarter to five. Regan would arrive in an hour and he had yet to change. Luckily, the cleaning woman had come earlier in the day, so the house looked presentable, unlike his present state. Dressed in ragged denims and an old torn long-sleeve shirt, he was the picture of a Bohemian artist, not a man going to dinner with a lady. He rubbed his rough chin, then drew the sheet over the sculpture and left the studio, making sure to lock the door.

Exactly one hour later, Kincaid leaned against the column of his porch tracking the progress of a pewter sports car rolling up the driveway. Nothing in the world could have kept him from letting lose an appreciative whistle at the sight of both the car and its driver. After expecting her to arrive in the truck he'd seen last night, he couldn't keep his gaze off Regan as she stepped out of the Corvette.

His eyes went from the powerful, smooth, and sophisticated machine to the woman who drove it. Long legs encased in dark blue jeans and a starched white shirt that just begged for his fingers to undo one of the buttons. "Like it?" she called over her shoulder while closing the door.

Kincaid's eyes never left hers and let his admiration show through. "Looks good, real good."

He took a step down the stairs and then another. Just a few feet brought him alongside Regan. "It's a world away from the truck you were driving last night."

"That was my work truck. This . . ." Regan patted the hood. "Is my baby. My uncle gave it to me for a birthday present. The catch was that I had to rebuild the engine myself."

"Which you did, of course."

Her twinkling brown eyes, which reminded him of the bark of an ash tree under a hot sun, grew brighter as her smile widened. "It took me two months. When I finished, I had her modified for racing."

"Her?" he repeated with a cocked brow.

She tilted her head to the side in a beguiling and mysterious smile as Kincaid moved closer. Close enough to get a good whiff of her perfume, and the image that came along with the scent and the sleek sports car sent blood rushing down to his sex. He couldn't help but notice the outline of her breasts underneath the jacket. Round and generous spheres that would fit in his hands with nipples that would harden in his mouth . . .

Kincaid cleared his throat and clamped down hard on his libido.

"She sounds good." He inclined his head toward the Corvette's hood. That was an understatement. The engine had purred like a lion on a tight leash. Kincaid closely examined the pewter Corvette and made note of the lowered suspension, Goodyear Racing Eagle tires, and chrome wheels. He'd inherited his mother's practical nature, but a weakness for fast cars from his father. The Porsche 968 sitting in the three-car garage hadn't been his first purchase and probably wouldn't be his last. "I'm guessing this has a 5.7-liter V-8 engine?"

She blinked with surprise at his guess. He'd bet his trust fund the car was barely street legal. "My, my, aren't you full of surprises?"

He looked her up and down, and the sight more than pleased him. Denim and boots, a blue jean jacket, and all she lacked would have been the cowboy hat. "I try, Rebel."

"Noticed the tag, huh?"

"Something tells me that your car's vanity plate is an accurate reflection of its owner."

She laughed. "I think I like you, Kincaid Sinclair."

"I'll remind you of that comment later." He placed his hand behind her back and began to lead her toward the doorway to his home. "Now, why don't you come on in while I change clothes?"

As he helped Regan take off her jacket, his fingers brushed against the back of her neck for an instant, and he caught her sharp inhalation of breath. The tattletale response crushed any remaining doubts. She was as affected by his presence as he was by hers. Only Regan Blackfox seemed to have the natural acting ability his mother also possessed.

"You are a little overdressed," she commented.

"I'm going to run up and change. Make yourself right at home. I won't be long."

"Take your time," Regan said absentmindedly as she took in the room. "The restaurant doesn't take reservations and never closes."

Forgoing the temptation to sink into the thickly cushioned sofa, she wandered around the living room space as a number of objects captured her attention. The exposed beams and tall ceilings with the heavy use of wood and interior brick seating areas and niches earned her admiration.

Definitely not a bachelor pad, she mused. The new house felt distinctly old and welcoming with its earthy tones and numerous works of art. Embroidered cushions and throws complemented the plush sofas and chairs. Even the floor with its chocolate-brown stone and area rugs matched the surroundings. Neutral walls and a multitude of windows rained the sun's light over the brick fireplace and wood mantel. The house combined the best aspects of a bachelor's abode and an artist's hideaway.

Regan compared the house to her two-bedroom cottage and grimaced. Even with pictures and knickknacks, her place resembled a corporate apartment, not a home. Then again, she didn't spend enough time in Georgia. A week or two a year to catch up with family and renew her driver's license didn't count as a permanent residence. She, who had the deepest of family roots, chose to leave the nest and roam the globe.

A sigh escaped her lips before she could stop it. Despite her cavalier attitude, the return home to all things familiar tugged at her heart and refused to let go. Deciding not to follow that train of thought, she continued to peruse the ultramodern kitchen before moving on to the dining room.

After examining all the tribal masks and exotic items that seemed to have come from all parts of the globe, she retraced her steps to the living room at the sound of booted feet coming down the stairway.

"Ready for the grand tour?"

Regan inclined her face toward the sound of his voice. Kincaid may have stood on the opposite side of the room, but the unabashedly full grin on his lips didn't lose its potency. Nor did the change of clothes lessen his masculinity. The dark navy blue corduroy shirt fit snug over nicely curved shoulders and tucked under a tarnished leather belt, which went well with broken-in cotton denim pants. Appearance-wise, living in San Francisco hadn't left Kincaid soft—not by a long shot. Her fingers once again felt the hard calluses on the palms of his hands.

Regan looked into his eyes and was keenly aware that he'd caught her staring. It had been ages since she'd last blushed, but she still remembered what it felt like and the warming sensation crept up her neck and into her cheeks. "I've finished with half of the downstairs, so how about we start on the second floor?"

He took her from the first floor with the majority of the living space—book-filled study and open staircase lit with recessed spotlights—then into the upstairs bedrooms with adjoining baths, and theme-oriented designs. A step-down den played host to a virtual exhibition of visual and audio equipment. The layout and personalized furnishing of each room confirmed her first impression of Kincaid's artistic talent. The home lacked for nothing, not even a woman's touch.

After they returned to the living room, Regan tapped a hastily manicured finger against her cheek. "Let me see if I've done the math correctly. Five bedrooms, six baths, a study, a professional kitchen, and a home theater. You're either planning for a large family or expecting relatives to descend upon you en masse."

"I guess you could say it's the former." Kincaid led her out of the family room and toward the main part of the house. "I grew up an only child and I want to have a lot of kids."

"Be careful what you wish for," she warned, thinking of her own large family.

"Spoken like a person who has in-depth knowledge of these things." He reached out, took her left hand, and held it up as though examining a rare treasure. "Is there an ex-husband that I don't know about or maybe you've hidden three kids in that sports car of yours?"

She shook her head and stifled a laugh. "No kids, no ex-husband, and no drama. The Corvette is a two-seater, just like my pickup truck. I have three older brothers and a bunch of cousins."

"Well, now that I've shown you the house, would you like to take a quick look at the stables?"

She tilted her head to look up at him as he politely held up her jacket. "I've been waiting for that invitation since I drove up."

They walked out of the front door and Kincaid locked it behind him. "Do you ride?"

"My father says I was born to ride. Cars, horses, motorcycles. Anything that moves, I guess."

"I always wanted horses. Couldn't have them when I was young, and now that I'm settled I decided to adopt these three from a ranch out in Arizona."

"Most men I know buy motorcycles."

"Anyone can ride a motorcycle. How many can control a horse?"

"Aha." Regan smiled. "So it's all about control?"

"No, the opposite," Kincaid replied. "It's about freedom. The closest I feel to being free is when I'm on Mercury's back."

Regan drew a deep breath and smiled as she looked off into the horizon. She raised a hand to block out the sun and stared at the horses deep in the middle of the field. A soft updraft, rich with the crisp tang of pine, brought a traveling rustle of dry leaves. Puffy clouds set off a pink salmon sky, and birds chirped as two lone figures trotted toward them from the center of the field. Without taking her eyes off the approaching horses, Regan queried, "Mustangs?"

"You know your horseflesh." The tone of approval in his voice was unmistakable, but she shrugged one shoulder while secretly thrilled that she could impress a man just by that small amount of knowledge. "We kept horses at my parents' place until I left for college. Dad felt they needed to be ridden more, so he donated them to a local riding school, which held a summer camp for underprivileged kids."

"Do you ride often?" Regan looked at Kincaid and studied the relaxed expression on his face. The black boots and blue jeans fit nice and tight over well-muscled legs.

"Not as much as I'd like. My work keeps me pretty busy."

She tilted her head to the right and looked past his shoulder. "I take it that's your studio over there?"

"You're two for two, Ms. Blackfox."

Her lips quirked upward. "I didn't notice any tools or paints in the house. It was either that building or the garage."

Unsettled by the effect his eyes were having on her, Regan turned away and focused on the horses as they began to trot toward them. When the smaller of the two mustangs came close enough, she reached out a hand and petted her. The horse's soft whicker brought a smile to her face as the mare nudged her hand. "Sorry, girl. I don't have any sugar cubes, but I can give you compliments." Regan laughed. "You are the prettiest filly I've seen in years. What are their names?"

He pointed toward the large white roan. "His name is Cloud. And the mare is Night Dancer."

Regan noticed the mare's strong legs and the pure midnight-black coat. The roan also had the beginnings of a handsomely full snow-white winter coat. From the corner of her eye, she noticed that Kincaid was looking at her, not the horses. Unconsciously, her smile grew wider. "You're staring at me."

"I want to sketch you. Then sculpt you. But first I'd love to see you ride."

It seemed playing with fire would become a specialty of hers. Impulsively, she met his gaze and ran her tongue over her lips as her pulse skipped up a few beats. "Maybe one day, you could invite me."

"Consider it done." He took a step closer. "You, Regan Blackfox, have an open invitation. But there's a small catch."

Into the small moment of question and response came the undeniable hum of anticipation and the unmistakable heat of attraction. Kincaid took hold of her hand and drew her away from the fence. "I want to be riding beside you."

Regan nodded and the modicum of tension she had been feeling left with his touch. "I can agree with that. Now I'm curious about all this." She waved a hand, indicating the house and the extensive grounds.

"What do you mean?"

"You're a well-known and vastly traveled artist, who would be welcomed anywhere in the world, yet you pulled up stakes and moved from California to Georgia. I'm curious as to why you chose this place."

"I came here as a kid during a movie shoot." His eyes left hers and drifted toward the mountains. "I never forgot the beauty of the mountains, the scenic views, or the southern hospitality." He shrugged. "I couldn't think of a better place to start over."

Drawn by something in his voice, the richness of his eyes, Regan moved closer to Kincaid and stared out over the Blue Ridge Mountains.

"And you?" he asked. She felt the rumble of amusement in his chest.

"I was born here, and the good Lord willing, this is where I'll be laid to rest alongside my ancestors."

"Your family owns the car dealership, right?"

Regan sighed and took a step forward, instantly missing the warmth of his body. Pivoting on her boot heel, she gave him a sheepish grin at the prospect of speaking about her illustrious family. "Something like that," she evasively responded. "Do you need help bringing them into the stable?"

Regan took a step away from the fence as Kincaid responded. "No, I'll bring them in tonight."

Her family's business employed many of the local residents and brought revenue to the area, yet to her it was business and not something she wanted to discuss with a handsome man whose eyes set her mind to humming and her stomach to fluttering. "You know, my stomach is about to demand dinner. So how about we continue this budding friendship over some good southern cooking?"

Chapter 6

After settling back into the buttery-soft leather of the passenger seat of the Corvette, Kincaid observed Regan expertly weave between cars and accelerate down the entrance ramp onto the freeway.

"Nervous?" she questioned while slipping the car from fourth to fifth gear.

"Not at all," Kincaid replied honestly. "Your car, you drive. My car, I drive. It's that simple."

"Most men are uncomfortable with a woman behind the wheel."

Kincaid stretched his legs out, and shrugged a shoulder. "I get nervous when I'm in the car with my mother. Not because she's a woman, but because she's a bad driver."

Regan's laughter filled the small confines of the car and Kincaid relaxed even more. "Really?"

"My father blackmailed her into hiring a chauffer after she managed to put two sizeable dents in his favorite BMW."

"Isn't that extreme?"

"This was after she rear-ended the studio director's Masarati."

Regan whistled. "Ouch."

Kincaid smiled remembering the incident. "It wasn't

nearly that bad. Dad screamed and yelled because I happened to be in the backseat."

Her slender hand never left the leather-wrapped knob of the gearshift lever, nor did the speedometer drop to under eighty miles an hour until they exited the interstate. What he calculated should have been a twenty-minute drive for a normal driver, Regan instead cut to it to ten. The woman took corners like a pro, and he imagined she would have no problems maneuvering the vehicle under any weather or road conditions.

After getting out of the sports car and opening the driver's-side door for Regan, Kincaid noticed that her Corvette resembled a collector's miniature next to the endless row of eighteen-wheel tractor-trailers. He looked around the area and chuckled at the surprise. The brown and white neon sigh flashed BISCUITS & GRAVY TRUCK STOP. Judging from the rows of eighteen-wheelers parked in back and minivans in front, the place was extremely popular with both the oversized and family-sized car owners.

Kincaid grinned after walking past tables filled with a blue jean and flannel crowd. They'd both washed their hands and waited less than five minutes to be seated. He would have expected whistles, stares, or something other than reverent respect. Working men, who spent more time on the road than walking on the ground, treated Regan like a daughter. A long-lost daughter returned to the fold. The place had a down-home feel to it especially with the daily special written on an old chalkboard and old-fashioned iron skillets decorating the wall. The jukebox seemed to belong in the corner just like an old record player sitting atop a collection of 45s.

The lighting and the smell of roasting meat could have been in what he imagined a real southern home would be like. Kincaid took off his jacket and slid into the leather-cushioned booth seat opposite Regan. It took him a minute to notice the laminated menu. A grin curved his lips and he nodded his approval.

"Surprised?" Regan inquired.

"And pleased," he replied honestly. "I had you pegged for a five-star restaurant in Buckhead type." Kincaid hadn't relished the thought of getting dressed for a night on the town in Atlanta's well-known nightspot. As the son of a Hollywood power couple, he'd attended formal events from the time he was old enough to tie his own necktie. Then after opening his first exhibit, he'd spent an average of two nights a week at galleries or dining with art patrons at exclusive restaurants.

The sound of her laughter trickled in his ears. "This after meeting me while I was wearing oil-stained overalls?"

"I could see that you'd be something else when you cleaned up a little bit."

"Really?"

"My art is to take a piece of wood or a chunk of stone and whittle it down to something wonderful. You see a dead tree branch and I see something that could be a work of art." Kincaid looked back toward the menu. "Now this"— he pointed to the pot roast—"is worth driving twenty-five hundred miles for."

Regan chuckled and Kincaid discovered that he enjoyed hearing her voice and looking at the relaxed glow on her face. He imagined kissing her generous mouth, and every muscle in his body tightened. Instead of backing away from his thoughts, he pushed forward and questioned himself. Maybe his intense reaction to Regan was due to the log absence of a woman in his life. No, he immediately discarded the notion. Regan Blackfox touched him as no woman had done before. She penetrated his defenses and caught hold of his interest on both physical and mental levels while inspiring his artistic muse.

"Glad you approve," Regan commented. "If Ruth's in the kitchen, you should tell her that. I've got to warn you, she makes the best fried chicken in the area."

Kincaid placed his menu on the table and turned his full attention toward his beautiful dining companion. "Why do I not find it the least bit surprising that you know the cook as well as the owner? Do you come often?"

"On the contrary, this is the first time I've been back in two years."

"Why so long?"

"Cartersville will always be my home, but my work takes me around the world."

Kincaid put the menu on the table and leaned in. "What exactly is it that you do?"

Regan took a sip of ice water. "I work for the State Department on special assignment."

"You mentioned seeing my art in Senegal. I take it you travel a great deal."

"I usually work at various U.S. embassies for a period of time from a few weeks to a few months."

"And you like living out of a suitcase?"

"I love my job and helping my country," Regan affirmed. Her dedication showed in the passionate tone of her voice.

"You don't get tired of moving?"

An affirmative response sprang to her lips, but she swallowed it. The temptation to pick up the menu and hide almost overwhelmed her. However, having known what she wanted to order before she'd stepped into the restaurant, she had no choice but to meet his penetrating stare and answer his question.

Gesturing toward the predominantly male restaurant clientele, Regan tilted her face. "More than sixty percent of the men in this room drive trucks for the carpet industry. When they come in to pick up a load, they stop here because the menu rarely changes and the southern food is the best they'll ever eat. They choose to do it because staying in one place would be like dying a slow death. They need the change and the possibilities of the open road. I need the challenges that come with my career."

"I see."

Regan tilted her head to the side and scrutinized Kincaid. In her answer, she'd deliberately left things unsaid, making room for mystery, and hopefully inviting his healthy sense of curiosity. But it seemed to have accomplished the opposite effect as the open hands that had once been inching in her direction withdrew completely to his lap and the glow of interest vanished from his eyes.

It was on the tip of her tongue to question his abrupt change of heart, but a waitress came over to take their orders.

The young woman cleared her throat. "Good evening. The specials for tonight are the fresh cornmeal catfish and chicken-fried steak. We have homemade chocolate pound cake, fresh brownie with ice cream, pecan pie, and peach cobbler for dessert. Now what can I get you folks?"

She stood silent with pen and pad ready.

"I'll have the chicken-fried steak with mashed potatoes and green beans," Regan replied.

The waitress turned her attention to Kincaid. "And you, sir?"

Kincaid closed his menu and grinned. "I'll take the smoked ribs, coleslaw, and baked potato."

Someone placed a quarter in the jukebox and an old-timey blues song poured over the murmur of diners and the clink of silverware. The tone of their conversation shifted from personal to current events, art, and food.

Regan snuck long glances Kincaid's way after the entrees arrived, and they both appeared to concentrate more on their meal than each other. She'd noticed not only his attire, but also what he hadn't worn. Unlike with her older brothers, the trappings of the information age didn't hang from his belt, nor did the chirp originate from his pocket. The silver-colored watch on his wrist, while expensive, fulfilled its true purpose as a timepiece, not a showpiece. Kincaid struck her as a man who guarded his privacy, and the fact that he hadn't brought a cell phone impressed her immensely.

She let the uncomfortable silence ride until dessert. The arrival of a generous bowl of fresh-out-of-the-oven peach cobbler topped with vanilla ice cream and Georgia pecans more than served to lighten the mood.

Her plan worked, and after dessert she celebrated her victory by trouncing Kincaid in a game of darts. In less than fifty minutes, Regan managed to fleece a group of truckers out of two hundred dollars that promptly went into a save-the-animals collection jar. Yet, as she concentrated on hitting the bull's-eye, half of her continued to ponder the cause of the artist's earlier withdrawal.

ASK ME NO QUESTIONS, I'LL TELL YOU NO LIES.

Later, after they'd left the restaurant, the phrase repeated itself as she turned into the driveway. Filing the incident into the back of her mind, she stopped the car in front of Kincaid's house and turned off the engine but kept the stereo on. She reached over and turned down the volume.

"You're not sore that I won our match, are you?" she teased, reaching to poke a finger into his muscled arm.

The intimacy of the Corvette's cockpit made Kincaid lower his voice. "Ahh, lady, you know how to take a stick of dynamite to a man's pride, but no, I'm not sore. Just aching."

"Anything I can do to help?" she cooed, and laughter rode her voice like a kite on the March winds.

"You could come in for a nightcap," he suggested.

Regan shivered at the husky undertone of his voice and the warmth of his hands, not from the increasing coolness of the car. Her heart decided to stop, then double-time.

"I don't think that would be a good idea," Regan replied warily. Just as she was about to figure Kincaid out, he changed from cool and impersonal to warm and approachable.

"It's pretty late for you to be driving home. You can sleep here if you like. I have plenty of room." His right hand left hers, and then his fingers stroked her cheek.

"True, but we both know that should I spend the night under your roof there is only one bed that I'll sleep on."

"That's a pretty confident statement, young lady."

Regan smiled in the semilight darkness. The porch light bathed them both in shadow. "Sugar, I can dance around a lie better than a world-class ballerina and skirt the truth like a fox being chased by hounds. But only when I have to, and believe me, Kincaid, right now I don't want to."

"Sugar." He seemed to taste the word and find it pleasing. "So southern, so sweet."

"Are you making fun of my accent, Sinclair?"

"No, I'm admiring the way you can adapt."

"You make it sound special." She drew back, startled by the unexpected response.

"It is. My parents are masters."

"And you're not?"

"Exactly. What you see is what you get. I can't change."

"Can't or won't?"

"Both."

"Yet you fit in well here. Marilyn at the dealership asked about you today."

"I think I was meant to come back to this place."

"Cartersville has that affect on people."

"But not you?"

"It did at one point," Regan answered after a slight pause.

"Not now?" he prompted.

Regan hesitated before answering, then let out a small sigh. "Maybe a little. There's something I want here."

"Something or someone?" Kincaid's lowered voice brought a flush to her stomach.

She tilted her head and looked into his eyes before telling the truth. "Someone."

"You want me." Confidence resounded in his voice as he held both her eyes and her hands.

"Just as much as you want me," she countered. The contact between their hands acted like a conductor while currents of attraction and anticipation cycled from her to him and back again.

"I won't pretend that I'm not itching to sketch you in the nude."

"Only sketch? No touching?"

"I like to sketch with my fingers too."

"And how is that done?" Regan's voice sounded husky to her own ears.

Kincaid reached over and lightly ran his fingertips down her cheek. Slowly trailing down to the nape of her neck, the curve of her collarbone, following down the V of her blouse, and then he grinned in pure masculine satisfaction at her indrawn breath when his index finger quickly skimmed the lace of her bra. "Like that."

Regan found her voice after several moments of searching, and the only word that made it past her lips was "Oh."

Kincaid cradled her hands within his own. "Have dinner with me tomorrow."

She shook her head to distract herself from staring at Kincaid's mouth, but the motion did nothing to stop the clandestine thoughts of running her lips over the hollow of his neck. Everything about the man appealed to her, even the sexy sandalwood and spice scent of his aftershave. But the logical part of her roped in her hormones and allowed common sense to surface. "Too much of a good thing can lead to ruin."

"Or lead to life."

Kincaid cupped her face with his hand, tilting her head back. She opened her lips to retort, but before the words could form, he brought his mouth down to hers.

First kisses are always the sweetest.

Apparently, no one had told that to Kincaid. The touch of his lips to her skin burned away all of her common sense as his tongue played with hers, teased the sensitive roof of her mouth. Then his lips slanted across her own, and his fingertips caressed the nape of her neck. Regan found his kiss held more heat than *harissa* sauce, one of the hottest sauces known to humankind, a fiery spice she thought would lead to her early death at an open vegetable market in Tunis. All the while, his fingers caressed the sensitive place behind her ear and tickled the soft curls at the nape of her neck. She released a gentle sigh of regret into his mouth.

The memory of the incident along with her reasons for being in the North African country broke the spell, and her hands that had been clutching at his shoulders lowered to work their way to his chest and form a barrier between their bodies. "I'd better go. I have an early day tomorrow."

"Working on Saturdays?"

"No, my brothers are coming over for breakfast."

"You can always reschedule."

Regan shook her head as laughter pealed from her throat. "I didn't invite them in the first place."

"When will I see you again?"

She stared deeply into his eyes and then moved quickly to turn on the overhead spotlight. Grabbing an old invoice and a pen from the glove compartment, she scribbled a note, folded it, and placed the paper into Kincaid's open hand. "You know where to find me."

She watched as he gave her a quizzical glance and then tried not to release another sigh as regret hit her square in the chest when he exited the vehicle. Having neither the time nor the inclination to play hard to get, she felt the urge to throw caution to the winds whispering at the edge of her mind. But she couldn't. Shaking her head, Regan keyed the ignition and headed toward home. Compared to the emotional knots the artist had begun unknowingly to tie her up with, tomorrow's breakfast with all of her brothers would be fast and easy.

Kincaid waited until the red taillights disappeared before letting himself into the house. He went straight through the house turning on lights, then unlocked and headed out the back door. All the while, he was remembering. The way Regan's tongue darted out to wet her lips as she concentrated on throwing the darts. The confident set of her shoulders each time she stepped up against an opponent. The taste of peaches and cream as his tongue explored her mouth.

Only when he'd entered his studio did he shrug off his jacket. He couldn't ignore the similarities between his ex-fiancée and Regan, but he could channel his emotions into his art. Unlike Kirsten, Regan had been honest about her intention to leave, but that provided him with little comfort. Reaching over to the table, he put on his goggles and his gloves. History wouldn't repeat itself, he vowed. He would allow Regan Blackfox to get under his skin, but he would fight tooth-and-nail to keep her from his heart.

Chapter 7

Regan finished putting the last of the silverware into the dishwasher. After wiping her hands on a dish towel, she checked her watch, then exited the kitchen and walked into the informal living room. Blinking her eyes in disbelief, she shook her head at the males occupying the over-stuffed sofas and chairs. Morning had passed an hour before, but her brothers showed no inclination to leave.

Three Blackfox sons lounged around in the living room of her cottage in various sorts of alert and relaxed postures. These were the crème de la crème of Georgia, she thought incredulously. Yet they all seemed to have come over to her place with the express purpose of hiding from their girl-friends, just friends, women on the side, and their aunt.

Regan put a hand over her mouth and struggled against the temptation to laugh. Marius, the future head of the family, was in dire peril of slipping off the love seat. Caleb, the emergency room doctor, had passed out on the sofa as soon as breakfast had finished. Not that she could blame him since he'd just finished the night shift. And Trey, the youngest, who happened to be one of the best veteri-narians in Atlanta, continued to flip though the sports sec-tion of the morning newspaper.

Her brothers. She exhaled slowly as a warm tenderness

filled her heart. God, she loved them so. But at the moment Savannah was on her way over, and the last thing her cousin needed was to encounter a small contingent of men who would rather take Jack Archer into the forest and leave him tied to a tree than marry a member of the Black-fox family.

"Okay, boys," Regan announced. "Playtime's over and you can't hide out at my place."

Trey shrugged his broad shoulders, and Regan examined her youngest brother from head to toe. Two years had changed them all, but him the most. A confident maturity had somehow gained a foothold on the comedian of the family. He put down the paper and sat back in the recliner. "It's not like you have company. Or is it *because* you have company on the way?"

Regan narrowed her eyes. "What kind of snide remark was that?"

This time Caleb opened a light brown eye and spoke. "This is a small town. And when one of the local drivers comes into the hospital thinking he's having a heart attack, which turned out to be a bad case of acid reflux, he tends to talk about little sisters and strange men."

Before she could hide it, a smile inched her lips upward. They'd only met for one dinner, but to the artist, though he was physically miles away from her two-bedroom cottage, the memory of Kincaid's eyes had become a continuous image in the back of her mind. "Kincaid Sinclair isn't a stranger, he's just new to the town."

"Hell yes, he is," Caleb answered after opening both of his eyes. He propped his head up with his hand. He'd progressed way past the four o'clock shadow and was in imminent danger of a roguish beard. "And that last name isn't ringing any bells."

"It would if you did anything but work, Caleb."

"I don't have time."

"You never have." She laughed, and just to make sure that he understood she was joking, she walked over and sat on his legs. "Well, to start, Kincaid happens to be a famous artist. I've seen his work during my travels."

Caleb sat up and pulled her into a bear hug. She put her nose into his neck and enjoyed the wash of memories and the sibling affection. When he let her go, she scooted off his lap and curled up on the sofa.

Her brother aimed a wide grin her way. "If I'm not mistaken, Rebel, you happen to be the only one in the family that doesn't even show up for Christmas," he scolded.

Inwardly, Regan winced. She'd managed to avoid this topic of her career since she arrived home. However, it appeared that her grace period had just expired. Making sure none of her thoughts showed on her face, Regan replied, "It's the job. I tried to fly back, but all the civilian and military flights out of South Korea were booked. The only other option was taking a boat, and you know that I'm not all that fond of water."

"Well, maybe it's time you started thinking about switching careers, baby girl."

Regan leaned her head back on the tip of the sofa, closed her eyes, and exhaled a long breath before turning toward her oldest brother. He sounded so much like their grandfather at times that if she closed her eyes she'd never be able to tell them apart. "Marius. Not now."

"Now is the perfect time. You fly in and fly out without thinking about what your absence is doing to our parents."

"Mom and Pop aren't thinking about me," she retorted. "They're probably out on the boat right now." At that moment, her parents were on their semiannual getaway to the family vacation home in Bermuda.

"Mom worries about you every day. I worry about you. The world's not a safe place."

"And when have I ever played it safe?"

"Never," Trey responded.

Regan winked at him. At least one of her brothers was in her corner. "Exactly."

Marius's deep voice interrupted her brief moment of triumph. "How much longer are you going to be home?"

Regan sighed. "I don't know."

"Couple of days? A week? Maybe a month?"

"I don't know," she repeated. "I have to wait on my next assignment."

"You'll wait until Mom and Dad get home." The statement sounded suspiciously like an order. Regan wanted to get off the sofa, curl her fingers around his muscular arms, and shake him until the carefree older brother of her youth came back. However, Marius was so entrenched in the family business and his role as the next patriarch that he didn't have time for fun, much less play.

"I'll try," she hedged.

"All right, my turn." Her favorite brother, Trey, jumped in, and Regan slumped with relief.

"Regan, I know how important your job is. We all do, but you need to be home more."

Her eyes narrowed as she stiffened at what appeared to be a betrayal. "I need to hit you on the head. Here are three responsible unmarried men with careers, talent, and ambition and you're sitting here trying to dictate my life. Don't you have better things to do? Some damsel in distress to rescue?"

"Nothing or no one is as important as you." Marius's voice took on the deep gravelly tone frequently used by their grandfather. "Now, who's the man you went to dinner with last night?"

"The same man you'll meet if you stop by the track tonight."

"You're not thinking about racing, are you?"

"I might take a few spins around the track. I want to test out the additions I made to the Corvette the other day."

"Mom will have a heart attack if she hears that you're racing again."

Those along with other reasons made Regan bite her tongue. Her mother had to be the strongest woman she knew. To help raise her brothers and still keep her sanity would be reason enough to admire her; they never would see eye to eye on the subject of how a female should behave.

Regan turned her head to look at Marius, and it was like looking at a younger version of their grandfather. He had a complexion of rich amber, piercingly light eyes, high cheekbones, and a dimple in his right cheek was the only sign of human weakness. They shared the same mannerisms, the same passion for winning, and the same ruthless arrogance. And that character flaw eventually led them to meddle in the affairs of others. Her older brother had never been-laid back. Mainly because he'd come out of their mother's womb groomed.

In a family where the second son began the business, it would always be the first son who would inherit.

"I can handle Mother."

"But can you handle Grandfather? Before leaving for vacation, he tore in to Dad and Uncle Robert about keeping a handle on the women."

Regan rolled her eyes upward. She didn't need to be in the hemisphere to imagine the conversation. Caleb continued, "He came down hard on Dad and on Savannah."

"Why Savannah?" she questioned while barely managing to keep the sharpness out of her voice.

"She's been seeing someone."

"Is that so? She hasn't told me about him." Regan widened her eyes in an expertly practiced look of surprise. Technically, she was telling the truth. Savannah hadn't told her the name of the man she was dating. No, Jack Archer's name on a certain mailbox had revealed that little secret.

Caleb rubbed a hand over his head. "She's been on cloud nine for the past few months."

"Okay, so what's the problem?" Regan questioned.

"Savannah won't introduce him to the family. Aunt Carrie wanted to have him over for dinner and he didn't show. We all think the brother must be into something illegal."

"Or maybe Savannah wants her privacy?" Regan responded, thinking of her cousin's illicit relationship.

Marius locked eyes with her, and she kept her gaze in-
scrutable. They'd both learned to play poker from their
grandfather. "You know something, don't you?"

"Sorry." She held up her hand and waved him off. "I
haven't talked to Savannah about men," Regan replied
honestly. She'd found out about Jack Archer from the
horse's mouth, so to speak. "But if you guys will get the
heck out of my house she might be inclined to talk when
she gets here in—" She looked down at her watch. "Thirty-
five minutes."

"This conversation isn't over." Marius's coal-black
brows drew together.

"Which one?"

"Kincaid Sinclair."

"We had dinner."

"In a very public place. If you'd wanted to keep him
under wraps, it's the last place you'd go."

"I don't like keeping secrets from my family, and if I
decide to spend time with him while I'm home, then you
should have the right to know about it."

"That's right. Everything is an open book unless it in-
volves your career," Marius responded.

Regan inwardly winced. She would have had to be
wearing an armored suit not to be cut by the sarcasm in
his voice. "Where is all this coming from, Marius?"

"Ever since those embassy bombings last year I've had
a bad feeling about you working with the State Department."

"The world is a dangerous place and it has always been
that way, Marius," she stated matter-of-factly.

"True, but you don't have to be in the line of fire."

She stood up and had to tilt her face upward to look into
her older brother's almond eyes. "I need to clean up
before Savannah gets here."

"This conversation isn't over," he stated for the second
time.

"I know. I love you." She smiled and gave him a hug.

"Back at you, little sis."

He strode toward his black SUV and sighed. It wouldn't get better. Once her parents returned, it would only get harder. Twenty minutes later, after saying good-bye to her other brothers, Regan stepped back into the cottage and closed the door. Part of her wondered if she'd made the right decision in coming home. Everything called to her here. The trees she'd claimed as a girl, the people she'd grown up with, the rush of memories brought about by the smell of diesel or the loud rumble of a truck.

Turning aside those thoughts, she went back upstairs to gather her things and prepare. Regan had a lot to get ready for.

Kincaid knew he shouldn't be turning his Porsche into the parking lot. Just like he'd known he shouldn't have tossed off his work gloves, left his studio, and showered before changing his clothes. Downshifting into first, he circled the gravel field.

Regan Blackfox had all the earmarkings of a tragedy. Yet the taste of her kiss, the scent of her skin, and the sparking challenge in her eyes called to the part of him that held his creative mood. She not only appealed to him as an artist but also as a man, and because of that combination nothing could stop him from wanting to get closer to her.

It took him another ten minutes to purchase a ticket and join the crowd streaming into the motor park. Kincaid walked along with the crowd. People of all different ages, genders, nationalities, and families filled the walkway and the stands.

Georgia Motor Sports Park. Look for number seven at seven o'clock.

Seven o'clock. Kincaid mulled the information in the back of his mind. He looked down at his watch and bit back a curse. He was over ten minutes late. According to the map in his hand, the fourteen-thousand-capacity grandstands counted off by the alphabet.

Where could she be sitting? Kincaid asked himself while his fingers clenched as the wind coming off the track threatened to rip the brochure from his hand.

Something out of the corner of his eye catching his attention, he turned toward the track and froze. While his peripheral vision took in the cars, motor homes, trucks, and concession stands piled into the infield by the hundreds, his eyes focused on the pewter color of a speeding Corvette. Even if he hadn't wanted to believe it to be a coincidence, Kincaid couldn't help but put two and two together. He'd witnessed the characteristic driving style from the passenger seat of the sports car with checked markings and a number—bold number 7 on the hood.

The track had cars of so many makes, models, and designs that Kincaid couldn't recognize them all. The souped-up American, Japanese, Italian, and German vehicles blurred with the speed of their movement. His heart shuddered as Regan's Corvette overtook another car by going deep inside the curve. He didn't know he was holding his breath until he felt the burning sensation in his chest. And it wasn't the scent of rubber that caused the metallic taste of fear in his mouth; it was the risk of what could happen to Regan because of a treacherous mixture of speed and aggression.

A deep voice interrupted his thoughts as a couple in deep conversation walked past him. "Damn it, Savannah. Regan has no reason to be out there without practice."

Changing his pace, Kincaid hung back slightly, but kept within listening distance of the pair. "Marius, what do you think she's been doing since she's been here, crochet and oil changes? No, she's been either here or at the garage."

"She shouldn't be on the track."

"Regan wouldn't be there if it wasn't for you, so why don't you just grab us some hot dogs and chill? Regan just took the lead," the woman responded.

Kincaid had no doubt that the man, Marius, was Regan's older brother. Dressed in a tailor-made suit and long wool coat, he stood out in the blue-jeans-and-boots crowd. The announcer's booming voice pulled Kincaid's attention back to the present. Kincaid made his way to his assigned seat, but didn't sit down. Standing along with most of the crowd, Kincaid couldn't keep eyes off her. And twenty minutes later as Regan sped across the finish line right behind the front leader, he cheered like a fan.

Chapter 8

"Are you so hell-bent on getting even with me that you'll get yourself killed?"

Regan's fingers tensed on the wrench in her hand, and then she consciously let go so that it dropped into the toolbox. Disappointment warred with annoyance at the way her night had turned out. She'd hoped to take home the first-place trophy and Kincaid Sinclair. Instead, she lost to her ex-boyfriend and had to rein in her temper at the finish line as Marius unleashed a hard scolding upon her head.

Having grown up shying away from all the attention and privileges given to her because of her family's money, she'd bent the rules and taken advantage of her father's generous sponsorship of the sports park and procured a private garage at the rear of the track. The last thing she would tolerate was another lecture from Trent Griffin.

She turned and leaned back against the table. "No." She spoke slowly, clearly. "I drive to win, not to play. And it may not have occurred to you, given your oversized ego that seems to have grown to even larger proportions with your acting career, but my life, my actions, and my emotions have nothing to do with you."

"I don't see it that way."

Regan gave a quick shrug, and then picked up a cloth

to wipe the oil off her fingertips. A car roared in the distance, answered by a second and a third as the next race began. "That's your prerogative," she said, deliberately dismissing him. "Now that you've said what you had to say, I need to get back to work."

"Damn it, Rebel." His voice came closer, but Regan didn't allow her attention to wander from the Corvette's engine. "I didn't intend for this to turn out so badly. How about we go grab a seat at the Waffle House and talk?"

She felt the strong band of his leather-encased arm wrap around her waist and turn her around. Regan stilled, then raised her face from looking at the ends of his black shoes, up his pants, over the unzipped jacket, to settle on his face. And for the first time in over a decade, she looked at him with eyes devoid of memories. She saw the taut cheeks, stormy upturned hazel eyes, sloped breadth of his shoulders, coal-colored hair, smooth lips, and pearly white teeth.

Women love handsome men, and Trent was loved by the moviegoing audience and critics alike. "This is not a fairy-tale reunion and you and I aren't on a handholding basis, so I recommend that you get your arm from around my waist."

When he didn't respond fast enough, she brushed his hands from her body.

Trent swore under his breath. "Rebel—"

No doubt, he expected her to fall into his arms like an actress or the way she would always lean on him when they were together in high school. But time had taken away the near addicting need to touch him. Unlike then, now she didn't care one whit for the man who'd succeeded in not only breaking her heart but also betraying her trust. She straightened her back and lifted her chin. Arrogance she had in abundance. After all, she was a Blackfox. "Go find a groupie, grab a fan, do anything but stand here and talk to me, Trent. You gave up all rights to having input in my life when you went to my grandfather behind my back."

Uncaring of the eyes boring into her back, Regan returned her attention to checking the oil as the sound of Trent's booted footsteps faded and the door slammed shut. She released a pent-up breath, reached up, and lowered the hood of the car.

At the sound of the door opening, she opened her mouth to make a rude comment, but the words stuck in her throat at the sight of Kincaid dressed in monochrome black. "You found the track all right?"

"After getting directions from the locals. When did you decide to race?"

"While we were playing darts at *Biscuits and Gravy*."

"Seems darts isn't your only game. Are you a champion markswoman or a professional thrill seeker?"

"Neither." She reached down to pick up a duffel bag to place it on the table.

"I have to admit you're a good driver."

She darted a sidelong glance his way. Oh yeah, she was a good driver. The kind of skills that came from the tutelage of her eldest brother and slipping through bumper-to-bumper aggressive testosterone-driven drivers at speeds of over a hundred miles an hour. "Have to?"

"I'm not happy seeing you risk your life, and for the most part you don't look like you're the second-place winner that trophy proclaims."

Regan touched the top of the trophy and then gestured to the front flat tire on her car. "What goes up must come down. I'm crashing hard."

"Is it always like that?"

"This isn't professional racing. No pit crew, announcers, spokesmodels, or autographs. It's just a couple of hours that normal people get to lose the fear of getting thrown in jail for pushing their cars to the limit."

"Is that all it is for you?"

"No, it keeps me on my toes."

"Do you need to be?"

"Normally yes."

"And now?" He took a step toward her and reached out to run his hand across her cheek. When she turned her face into his palm, a hastily expelled breath whispered through his lips.

"Now." Her eyes fluttered upward. The desire simmering in the midnight depths found an answering response in his. "Now . . ." She wet her lips with her tongue. "I want to be reckless."

His fingers traced the outer edge of her all-black racing suit and he toyed with the zipper. The temptation to pull it down and see the tender flesh underneath slammed into him like a physical blow. "Are you sure about that?"

Regan didn't answer. She flowed. With the speed and agility of a cat, she entwined her arms around his neck, bringing his face down toward her. Just as their lips met, her tongue darted out and she licked his bottom lip.

Kincaid didn't think. Hell, he didn't breathe, as the world tilted. Of their own accord, his hands moved to cup her behind and pulled her to him and covered her mouth with his. Wanting to taste every inch, he slanted his mouth to gain more access.

The feel of her leather-clad body against him, the softness of her breasts against his chest, the heat of her mouth. God, he could have drowned. Just let go and be submerged in the moan coming from her throat and the way her tongue curled and caressed, the way her hands rubbed the back of his neck.

"Excuse me," a honey-sweet voice intruded.

Kincaid opened his eyes and looked into hers.

"Sugar, if the two of you are going to burn, go for it. Just don't take my garage with you."

He raised his head toward the sound of the gravelly female voice.

"Sorry, Maybelle," Regan tossed over her shoulder before taking a step back.

Kincaid grinned. The lady didn't sound the least bit

apologetic or embarrassed. The deep flush on her cheeks was the one he'd put there.

"No problem. If I didn't have three ex-husbands and a mess of baggage, I'd give you a run for this one."

"He's taken," Regan announced quickly.

"Well, are you pulling out tonight, or will you come back for your car in the morning?"

"Got a flat. Is it okay if I take care of it tomorrow?"

"No problem," Maybelle said again and turned back to the door. "Just need to lock up."

Regan turned back toward Kincaid, grinning wickedly. "So can this second-place winner get a ride?"

"Only if you'll let me take you out for a private celebration dinner."

"I think I can agree with those terms."

"I have a bottle of wine in my car," he replied.

Regan playfully squeezed his biceps. "And I have a well-stocked refrigerator at my place."

"Are you inviting me to your house?"

"I need a shower and a change of clothes. You promised me a private dinner." She aimed a sultry look his way. "And when the adrenaline goes, I get hungry, Kincaid." She narrowed her eyes and delicately bit her bottom lip. "Very hungry."

By the time Regan finished her shower and changed clothes, it was after nine o'clock. She came downstairs to find the lights low. A long-sleeve A-line dress covered her body in midnight-blue silk. The smell of cooking wafted toward her nose, waking up her empty stomach, and the sound of jazz warmed the air. Regan allowed herself a more private and personal smile. Her cottage had never felt better than it did at that moment.

She walked into the nicely appointed dining room, and the smile on her lips faded at the sight of the champagne bottle in a bucket of ice and two empty glasses. The image of Merona's face flashed through her mind and she shivered. During her time at the academy, the more experienced agents who'd been in and out of war-torn countries said that you get used to the killing. But Regan doubted she'd ever be invulnerable to the horror of taking another human's life. Kincaid entered the kitchen and finished the steaks, while she tossed the salad. Ten minutes later, they were seated at a mission style table set with bamboo placemats and Asian stoneware.

Regan tilted her head back and smiled at Kincaid after he gave the blessing. "So how long have you been hiding the Porsche? Maybe we can race one day."

Kincaid paused before cutting into his tender steak. "I don't think my fragile ego can take that big of a bruising."

"I wouldn't be too sure that you'd lose." She took a bite of her salad.

"I've heard your engine."

"And I know for a fact that there's more to winning a race than what's under the hood."

Kincaid raised his wineglass to his lips. "Good point."

After finishing dinner and cleaning up the dishes, Kincaid refilled her wineglass and they sat down together on the coach. Kincaid pointed to a large family portrait that hung over a lowered bookshelf.

Replete with good food and enjoyable conversation, Regan sat on the sofa, leaned back into a solid chest, and enjoyed the sensation of being in a man's strong arms. No doubt about it, she mused. Kincaid Sinclair had gotten to her. In less than seventy-eight hours, she'd allowed him physical and emotional liberties it had taken her first and last boyfriend years to earn.

"That must be your oldest brother to the right."

"You're right. He's the one that looks like my grandfather."

"Yes, I saw him tonight at the track. He didn't seem too happy to see you racing."

Regan took a sip of wine, then answered, "We had an

argument about that before you arrived. He thinks I take too many risks."

"Are you surprised?" Kincaid asked.

"Marius was the one who taught me to drive. He's taken more risks on that track than I dared dream of." Try as she might, Regan couldn't keep her mind from wandering back to her childhood.

Before daybreak her eldest brother would sneak out of their large house, and by an unspoken agreement she would follow him into the Mustang, and for a moment in the front seat of the car on the empty streets, he'd turned up the music and hit the gas and they would ride. Sometimes she wondered if he'd turn around and go home. How easy it would be to keep going and escape their father's expectations. But some sign or the sight of a trailer bearing the Blackfox logo would remind both of them of their birthright.

"What happened so that now you're the one racing and your brother seems to be trying to keep you from racing?" he asked.

"He was young and invulnerable. When Marius was winning, my father turned a blind eye to his hobbies. But when it started taking him out of town and away from the family, my grandfather pulled in the reins."

"Yet your father let you get behind the wheel?"

"When he found out that I'd moved from just being the mechanic to putting together my own amateur race car, he cut my allowance. I had money saved so I didn't need his support. We fought and then my going away to college moved the grand battles to pitched arguments during the summers I came home. It all ended when I joined the State Department."

"Hence your nickname," he murmured, taking the empty glass from her hand. "How does a rebel like you make it in the strict hierarchy of government?"

She blinked as the question hit home. She did make it . . . barely. Maybe the NSA helped. During her assignments the political and bureaucratic nonsense disappeared in favor of whatever it took to accomplish the mission. Turning aside the thought, she answered Kincaid's question. "I don't accept. I compromise. There are ways around the bureaucracy. My challenge is doing it *without* running over people's toes and oversized egos."

"And it works?"

She laughed softly. "No. I get into my fair share of trouble."

"I wonder what it would take to keep you in line. To keep you here." His fingertips feathered over her skin, and Regan inhaled the faint wood and spice scent of his aftershave.

Sex. Desire. Passion. All the sensations and expectations she'd refused to allow in her world came crashing into her body and hummed through her blood. Yet, with all her impulses pushing her toward him, years of self-discipline pulled her back from the sweet entrapment of his words.

"Nothing."

"Are you sure?"

She caught his hand in hers and held it palm to palm. There could be no ambiguity between them. Regardless of what happened, she wouldn't be staying. "What is it you want from me, Kincaid?"

"You asked me that before."

"And I'm asking again. I don't like surprises and I need to know that we're on the same page as far as this attraction goes."

"As I said, I want the opportunity to get to know you better. Much better. This . . ." He drew her hand to his lips and placed a warm, moist kiss on the center of her palm. "Is a beginning of something far greater."

Regan cleared her throat. "I'm here on vacation, and when the time comes for me to go to a new assignment, I will leave, and there's a good possibility I won't be saying good-bye."

He drew back as if scalded and his brown eyes narrowed. "So what is it that you're looking for?"

"Emotional and physical sharing." To emphasize her point, she trailed her fingers over the hardness of his chest. "Friendship."

"That's all?"

"I work in a world of rules that can shift according to the balance of power. One of the rules that I play by is to be as upfront as possible. Another rule is that I keep my personal and my professional lives separate."

"And if I want more?" His voice held a nuance of challenge that both excited and frightened her.

Regan dropped her eyes. "Then you'll be deeply disappointed."

"I could take my chances."

"But I won't."

"So she has a weakness after all."

"I'm not sure I like the sound of that."

"Tough." He stood up. "It's late, I should be getting back."

"You can stay the night."

He raised a dark brown eyebrow, and she rose to stand in front of him. "You've had two glasses of wine, and although I'm sure you can handle the drive home, you don't have to."

"I'm not the kind of man who believes in one-night stands."

"And I'm not the kind of girl to indulge in them either." She tilted her head up toward him and continued in a businesslike manner. "You see, I like days and long nights. Regardless of whether or not we sleep together tonight, I have a guest room that you are more than welcome to use."

As Regan waited for his answer, her body tensed, belying her intended guise of impartiality. She wanted him to stay the night whether they spent it in bliss or in separate beds. The thought of having him under her roof added a tingle of excitement. She enjoyed the return of anticipation, an emotion that had long been missing in her life.

He stood over her. Solid and strong. His eyes locked with hers. She'd learned how to defend herself against men three times her size. And with Kincaid, although he was muscled and tall, nothing in either his expression or his demeanor would ever give her cause to fear him. Fear for him, yes. In essence, her job was to protect.

Kincaid reached out and gently fingered the soft strands of her hair, then followed the curve of her ears. A shudder racked her body at the serene intimacy of the gesture. The rough pads of his fingertips brushed over her sensitive skin at the nape of her neck. "You have the face of an angel, the body of my dreams given flesh. You are all that I could want."

"Then don't deny me," she whispered huskily and watched him with heavily lidded eyes.

"But I'm as selfish as they come, Regan. And until I can have all of you without certain emotional restrictions . . ." He traced his finger over her neck and stopped in the crease of the V over her heart. The warmth shot through her like an arrow while his wicked grin spurred her lips to curve upward. "I'll be staying close and sleeping in your guest room."

Chapter 9

"Did you have a nice jog?" Kincaid stood up from his place on the sofa as, freshly showered and dressed, Regan glided downstairs in a pair of beige wool slacks, and a thick black cable-knit sweater.

She reached up and tucked a stray lock of hair behind her ear. "I almost got sprayed by a skunk."

Kincaid blinked twice and laughed. "You're joking."

"No, unfortunately I'm not. I wasn't paying attention and it wasn't too happy to see me come around the corner. Luckily, I planned on turning around and coming back anyway."

Kincaid absentmindedly rubbed his jaw, and the rough sensation of his stubble helped distract him from the enjoyable sight of Regan's shapely legs. He'd been thinking about Regan since the day they'd met. And every thought was very visual. Very arousing and both of them had been naked. "I would have thought that all the animal life around here would have gone into hibernation by now."

Regan reached out and gave him a friendly pat on the back while turning them both toward the kitchen. "We'll have to wait until January. According to my all-knowing uncle, Georgia has had a mild winter, so the animal life is more active than usual. But in the meantime, how about you and I fix breakfast? I'm hungry enough to eat a small cub."

Kincaid's critical eyes scrutinized her body from head to toe. Regan's medium frame size coupled with an above average height made her perfect for him. "Don't they feed you overseas?"

"Not like home." She laughed as they made their way through the living room and entered into the kitchen. "Lucky for me I inherited my mother's metabolism, so I can eat what I want and not worry about the consequences until I'm fifty."

They worked side by side preparing vegetables, slicing fruit, toasting bread, and eventually cooking two southwestern omelets.

After pouring a cup of coffee, Kincaid casually inquired, "So do you have any plans today?"

Regan's hand paused halfway between her side and the glass of orange juice. "That depends on why you're asking."

"The sun is shining and I think a horseback ride with a picnic could do you well."

"You know what they say about too much of a good thing. . . ."

"I'm willing to risk it."

"I bet you are." She took a bite of toast, and Kincaid finished chewing a mouthful of his omelet, then placed his silverware on the table.

"Look, Regan, the fact is you're going to leave." A measure of his frustration leaked into his tone of voice. "When? You don't know. As you took great pains to make clear to me last night, the phone might ring and you'll pack a bag and disappear from my life. And until that moment happens and I have to let you go I want to spend as much time with you as possible, Regan Blackfox."

She cast her gaze upward and leaned her head to the side, seemingly in deep thought. Kincaid reached across the table and took her hand in his. He was about to say something more when the phone rang. Normally, he thought a telephone's electronic chirp an annoyance, but at that moment his gut filled with an emotion that stood on the borderline of hate.

He stood as Regan left her chair and moved to answer the phone. "Sit. This will only take a minute."

She was wrong. It took less.

"Sorry about that," Regan apologized as she took her seat at the table.

"Important call?"

"I'm going to have to take a rain check on that horse-back ride."

His jaw clenched as he waited for her to say more.

"I have to go see about the Corvette and get some things checked out for my uncle."

"And afterward?" he prompted, picking up both of their empty plates and heading over to the sink.

"We're going to be working on cars until well into the evening."

Kincaid bit back a sigh of relief as well as an offer to drive her. One thing he'd observed about Regan was the need for control, especially when inside a car. "This doesn't change my wanting to see you."

She drew next to him and opened the dishwasher. "So you're okay with my wanting a casual relationship?"

"Of course. A woman has the right to change her mind."

"And you think I'm going to do that?"

Kincaid dried his hands on a dish towel, then wrapped his arms around her hips and pulled Regan closer. "I'm an artist who deals with possibilities."

"And I'm a realist who needs to get ready." She smiled, placing her arms around his neck.

He kissed her gently, then pulled back. "Promise me you'll call me when you get home tonight."

When she didn't respond instantly, he kissed her again, and this time slanted his mouth to allow greater access to hers. The kiss ended, leaving them both breathless. Kincaid leaned his head against hers and stared down at her fingers as they toyed with the button on his shirt. "Call me."

"Keep that up, Sinclair, and you won't be picking up the phone, you'll be answering the door," she said, her voice thick with lust.

"I wouldn't mind a late-night visit."

"What am I going to do with you?" Regan smiled and pulled away.

"First you'll call and then we'll go to a movie tomorrow."

"I'm working a later shift at the dealership."

"I have a nice wide-screen television and a wide selection of DVDs," he tempted.

"Chips and salsa?" Her eyes sparkled with laughter and Kincaid had to put his hands in his pockets to keep from touching her.

"Anything you want."

Regan's eyes darkened and her smile, which had been teasing, took on a seductive pout. "Some things aren't on the menu, yet. I'll call you after I get home and shower."

"I have three bathrooms, Regan."

"Is that a hint?"

"No, it's a sign of greed. I want all of you, all of the time." She put her arm around his waist as they walked toward the door. "I'll come over straight after work."

"Good, I'll be waiting."

"But before you leave me . . ."

Kincaid grinned. "You want another kiss?"

"No, Romeo. I want to see what's under the hood of your car."

After putting the dishes in the dishwasher and washing up the pots and pans, Kincaid had wanted to sit back down in the little breakfast nook under the bright morning light and talk with Regan over coffee. He sat alone in silence as Regan went back upstairs to fetch her boots. The woman had a one-track mind, and for a moment it focused on his car.

"Ready?"

He looked up to see her leaning against the doorway. His eyes started from the tips of her boots and moved upward, over long legs, skimming the sleek figure in a black leather jacket, stopping on her eyes, but reversing downward to her lips. The sight of her tongue darting out could easily drive him crazy.

Her lips were naked with the slightest hint of lip gloss. He knew how they would taste. How the full, lush lips would open slowly and allow his tongue entrance. How her mouth would taste like nectar.

Their kisses would haunt him for the rest of his days, for he'd only felt that way three times in his life. Most recently, when he'd stood watching the sun come up over the Georgia Mountains safe within the comforts of his house. When he held her in his arms, inhaled the flowery scent of her perfume, and listened for the smooth lilt of her southern drawl, Kincaid felt as if he were home.

And he didn't like that feeling one bit. Kincaid flinched and stood up and emptied out his half-empty coffee mug into the sink. He was an artist and had learned from his teachers to embrace his emotions. However, the thought of Regan and the knowledge that no matter what he did she would leave touched his heart with blue flame, the hottest element of fire. And this time the pain of her leaving would burn deeper scars in his heart than Kirsten ever could.

He shook his head as a rueful grin pulled the corners of his mouth upward. *You never learn, Sinclair.*

"You know, this behavior could make a less secure man jealous," Kincaid stated as he lifted the back bonnet of the Porsche.

"It's good that you're a confident man." She leaned over to inspect the engine. "Good old German engineering. Confusing but comes together like clockwork."

"Looking for anything in particular?"

"I am looking for the fuel filter. I noticed a bit of drag last night."

"Be my guest. I key the engine, it purrs. I hit the gas, it moves. And when I touch the brakes, it stops."

"And you're happy." She laughed.

"As a clam."

"A girl's got to love a simple man."

"That's the hope." He stopped behind her and wrapped his arms around her waist, then leaned his chin into the crook of her neck and gave her a quick kiss. "Hmm, you're nice and toasty."

"And you smell like spring." She tilted her face toward him, and her eyes caught the sunlight. The sparkles of laughter warmed his heart and sent a burst of desire to the lower parts of his male anatomy. He leaned down to kiss her but stopped midway as he caught a movement from the corner of his eye. The sound of a car horn had them simultaneously looking toward a Volkswagen Beetle coming up the drive.

Kincaid straightened, and aimed a questioning glance at Regan. "Who's that?"

"One of my brothers."

"You have three?" Kincaid caught the look of exasperation on her face.

"That's correct."

"And which one is this?"

Regan's lips curled upward. "The youngest, Trey."

"Anything I should know before he gets out of his car? Maybe that he carries a gun or a big stick?"

"No." A wicked little glint shone through her eyes as she smiled at him. "He might have a tranquilizer dart, but never a gun. Trey loves animals, women, children, video games, and sweet potato pie. He's the veterinarian in the family."

"Overprotective?" he inquired. Kincaid didn't have a little sister, but he did have Dana. The knowledge of how he felt when a man came into her life coupled with the intensity of his feeling for Regan gave him a completely new perspective on the complexities of dating.

She winked, then patted him on the shoulder. "I'll keep you safe."

"Minx," he whispered and pressed a kiss to her cheek, before putting his arm around her waist.

"Hey, Rebel. How's it going?" her brother called out after slamming his car door. Tall and lanky, Trey still possessed both the Blackfox charm and arrogance.

"Good." Regan inclined her head toward Kincaid as her smile froze into place. The tightening grip of his arm around her waist prevented her from stepping forward to give her brother a hug. "Kincaid and I were just looking at his engine."

"Nice car. Little too small for my taste," Trey replied offhandedly.

Regan's eyes moved back and forth from her brother to Kincaid. The sight of the two grown men staring at each other to see who would blink first was so immature that she didn't laugh; she got irritated. As it continued on, Regan shifted her weight to the side and "accidentally" placed the low heel of her leather boot atop Kincaid's foot.

Glaring at her older brother, Regan spoke briskly. "Since I haven't forgotten my manners no matter how long it's been since I've been home, let me do the introductions. Kincaid, meet Trey, my favorite brother. Trey, this is Kincaid Sinclair. . . ." Her voice trailed off. For the first time in a while, Regan was unsure as to how to describe her relationship. He was far more than an acquaintance and a friend, though not yet a lover or boyfriend.

Kincaid took matters into his own hands and reached out to shake Trey's hand. Her older brother's grasp was strong, firm, he noted, but not painful. Measuring, instead of challenging. But none of that mitigated the assessing gaze in the other man's eyes. "I'm Regan's student."

"What?" The question sprang to her lips before Regan could hold it back. Her head swung toward the man at her side.

"She's teaching me about how cars work."

Trey's brow wrinkled. "Awfully nice, little sister. I've never known you to be so generous."

"Get that smirk off your face, Trey," she snapped. "It's a mutually beneficial arrangement Kincaid and I have worked out."

"And just what are you getting out of the deal?"

She aimed a sidelong glance in Kincaid's direction and almost bit her tongue to keep from cursing. He had a grin the size of Texas on his lips. "A chance to ride his horses. Kincaid has some at his place."

"Oh. *Really*?" Trey's voice practically sang soprano with disbelief.

"Yes," she replied firmly, then reached out and pushed the Porsche's bonnet down.

"Well, you've gotten yourself one of the best mechanics in town, Kincaid."

"What can I say? I'm a lucky man."

Regan's eyes narrowed on Kincaid's broad grin before she turned toward her brother. "Okay, Trey. I hate to be rude but Kincaid and I were—"

"About to finish up," Kincaid smoothly interjected. Then he glanced at his watch. "Sorry to cut the lesson short, but I need to get back to take care of the animals. We can fix my fuel filter some other time. Nice to meet you, Trey."

"You too." Trey nodded.

Before she could utter a word otherwise, Kincaid kissed her on the cheek, jumped into his car, and drove away. For a moment, Regan stood still in shock, and when she finally regained all of her senses, she glared at Trey. "If you're here to play the overprotective older brother, I'm not listening."

"That's not nice little sister," he said in a blatantly patronistic tone, "I'm just here to pay a brotherly visit and I get treated like a criminal."

His wide smile made the back of her neck itch even more. "What do you want?"

"See what happens when you leave the safety of home? You get paranoid." She let him pull her close into a hug and Regan sighed over his shoulder.

"I'm great, sis. How are you?"

"I'm great, Trey." She parroted his syrupy sweet tone.

"You don't look it. A man with a Porsche walks out of your house and you look as though Grandfather had summoned you into the study for a three-hour lecture."

Walking toward the cottage, Regan tossed out over her shoulder, "I'm just wondering why my lovely brother has shown up unannounced on a Saturday morning. You are a creature of habit, Trey, just like the creatures whose company you keep."

Regan glanced at her watch. "You shouldn't be crawling out of bed for another two hours. So what is it you really want?"

He shook his head, took off his coat, and hung it in the closet while Regan stood in the hallway. "All right. So I'm not here out of the spontaneous goodness of my heart. I'm here to help you."

"With what?"

"I've got inside information."

They walked together into the kitchen and Regan took a seat at the breakfast table as her brother went straight to the refrigerator.

"You didn't leave anything for me?"

"I didn't know you were coming. Why don't you keep talking about this inside information?" she suggested.

"I know when Mom and Dad are coming back from the Bahamas."

Regan's prancing fingertips went still. "When?"

"Where's the jelly?" he asked, pulling out the butter and placing it on the counter.

"Trey . . ." Regan called out toward the close-cropped back of his head. The hint of steel in her voice was unintentional. The delicacy of her relationship with Kincaid, the unknowns of her future missions, added to the threat of her parents' impending arrival back home, set her nerves on edge.

"I'll tell you for a price." Trey washed his hands, then placed two pieces of bread into the toaster.

Regan leaned back in her chair and let the tense silence speak for her. In her mind, she started a countdown. Her older brother broke before she passed six.

"I need to borrow your Corvette."

"No." She crossed her arms.

He grabbed the toast and slapped it on a plate, then took a seat opposite her at the table. "I promise on the zoo's new tiger, I'll keep it under seventy."

"Not good enough." She shook her head. "The last time I let you borrow my car, Caleb had to bail you out of jail and they put a dent in the front fender when they towed the car to the police impound. Not to mention the two speeding tickets from two different states."

Regan narrowed her eyes as he spread the butter and jam with a military precision. "Who is she?"

"Sasha Clayton."

"Wait. Not the celebrity animal researcher?"

"You know her?"

Regan nodded with an amused smile on her lips. In a word, Sasha Clayton was stunning, but that didn't make her memorable. No, the way she'd handled the Bahrain prince's pet jaguar had impressed the hell out of her. "We met at a birthday party in Tangiers."

Trey's eyes grew bright with hope. "So you'll lend me your car."

"No," she replied firmly. "My Corvette is a modified race car, not some pickup machine."

Trey took a bite of toast and far from slipping his arrogant grin widened. "I'll keep your secret."

"What secret?"

"Kincaid Sinclair."

Regan rolled her eyes toward the ceiling and counted to

three. "I'm a grown woman, Trey. It doesn't bother me if you or anyone else in the family knows about Kincaid."

"I'll take her to get detailed at Royal's Cleaners."

Regan hesitated. The body shop did some of the finest cleanup and bodywork in the Southeast.

"You could go out and buy two dozen high-end sports cars and not even put a dent in your trust fund. Why are you so keen to borrow mine?"

Trey shrugged and finished off the second piece of toast. "Sasha's smart and hip to the accoutrements of wealth. I've heard that she's dated millionaires, movie stars, and superathletes."

"So, you're rich, wonderful, my brother, and a sucker for animals." Regan toyed with a lock of her hair as the urge to give in and hand over the car keys tugged at her conscience. Not that anyone in her family would know, but she had a soft spot for romance, and Trey's efforts to impress the stunning animal trainer had her smothering a sigh of envy. Kincaid was just as charming and persistent, but while Regan Sinclair was free to be wooed and courted, her alter ego, Dominique Nichols, couldn't handle the commitment inherent in his dark gaze.

"Little sis." He tapped one finger on the table. "I can guarantee that if I arrived at her place in a new Corvette, she'd spot a play to impress her before getting a whiff of that new car smell or spot the double digits on the odometer."

"You can buy a used car."

He raised his hands and put his palms together in a semblance of prayer. "Pretty please."

"This means a lot to you, doesn't it?"

"I'll give you free passes to the zoo."

"And a private tour?"

He placed both of his hands down on the kitchen table. "Done."

Regan lowered her gaze and shook her head at the sight of Trey's excitement. *Will wonders never cease?* she thought.

Pushing back from the table, she grabbed his empty plate. "The Corvette's at the racetrack. You can have the keys."

"All right."

She grinned wickedly as they shook hands to seal the bargain. "After you help me rotate and align the tires on my truck."

After he'd driven back to his home and parked the Porsche in the garage, Kincaid forwent the temptation to walk straight from the garage to his studio. Instead, he changed his jacket and headed out the back door toward the stable. When he lifted the bar to the stable door and slid it open, the draft of air brought the familiar blend of alfalfa, dust, manure, and horse to his nose. The sound of the wheels moving roughly over the track set off a small chorus of stomping hoofs and neighs as his horses realized that lunch would soon arrive.

Kincaid stood for a moment in the doorway and closed his eyes. The sounds, which he thought of as a greeting, felt like an anchor. Something solid that would remain unchanged in his ever-changing world. He opened his eyes and scanned the inside of the barn, the deep mangers, the tall haystack, and the large yellow grain box divided into two for oats and feed. The cats woke and stretched on the hay, then seemingly fell back asleep. Moving to the left, he flipped a switch and the aisle lights buzzed and flickered before coming to life.

Taking a deep breath, Kincaid entered into the tack room and picked up his gloves. While his conscious mind directed his movements toward the waiting wheelbarrow and shovel, his thoughts remained fixed on Regan. The look in her eyes when they'd met in the hallway after he'd gotten out of the shower, the sound of her laughter, the heat of desire that made his skin itch. No way was Regan as unaffected as she claimed. He knew the signs of a restless night; he'd seen them in the mirror. God, he knew every inch of her guest room ceiling after last night. He'd tried his best to sleep, and all he got was the tempting vision of Regan dancing behind his eyelids. But he had drawn a line in the sand last night.

And now he asked himself why. It wasn't because of some sense of honor. No, he'd felt what was happening with Regan only one other time in his life. And that was with his art. The sense of peace, the anticipation. Maybe he should quit while he was ahead. But he'd never been a quitter. He wanted who and what he wanted. Like a kid dead set on one certain gift, he had to have Regan.

One at a time, he took the horses out of their stalls, tethered them, then scooped up shavings and manure, refilled the water buckets, and added hay and feed. When it was all over and he'd brushed their thick winter coats until both gleamed, Kincaid removed his gloves and then flexed his fingers like shaping clay. The first woman he'd loved went out for painting supplies one morning and never came back. His parents took him to boarding school, and from then on he only saw them two or three times a year.

Giving one last look to assure himself that everything in the stable was in order, Kincaid closed and latched the door, then put his hands in his pockets as he headed back toward the house. Afternoon had come and gone and the sun had begun to set. Sometimes he forgot how short daylight was during the southern winter months. Hours felt shorter and in the midst of his daily routine of caring for the horses or working with his art, everything including time seemed to stop. He reached up and rubbed the thick two-day stubble on his chin.

Time. The word sat on his mind as he removed his boots before entering the house. He had hoped to make light of the increasing amount of time he'd been spending with Regan. Hoped for once in his life that he wouldn't view a relationship as a commitment and the people in his life as constants. But something in him didn't like to let go, and at the back of his mind he knew Regan would leave at the end of it all. Yet he wanted her to stay, wanted to get her to the point where even the thought of saying good-bye cut. Cut like the thought of going without her smile. Somehow, she'd slipped in and filled the emptiness in his life he'd somehow managed to hide.

Kincaid took off his jacket and tossed it over the banister before making his way upstairs to shower for the second time that day. After a fresh shave and a change of clothes, he headed down to the kitchen and had just finished making a sandwich and pulling a bottle of beer from the refrigerator when the phone rang.

"Finally." The familiar voice from the receiver put a smile on his face.

"Dana." He cradled the phone closer to his ear. "To what do I owe the pleasure of this unexpected call?"

"Business never sleeps."

"Neither do you. What is it, eleven o'clock over there?"

"It's midnight in Paris, not that it matters. We need to get two things covered before I let you get back to work."

"I wasn't working."

"Eating then. That's all you do—eat, sleep, work, or horses. I bet that if you turned on that oversized television of yours, the Discovery Channel would pop up. How do I know that? Because I was the first and last person to turn it on."

"Are you advocating that I turn into a couch potato and spend the rest of my life with one hand curled around a beer and the other clutching the remote control?"

"No. I just think that you can take a little time to relax."

"Working with horses and creating my art is relaxing," Kincaid pointed out.

"Whatever."

He grinned and then cradled the phone between his shoulder and his right ear so that he could use both hands to put the cheese and lunch meat back in the fridge. "I see Paris hasn't changed you a bit."

"Actually it has and I can't wait for you to get here to witness it."

"I'll be there soon."

"It's the how soon we need to discuss. Would you like me to go ahead and book your ticket?"

"No, I'll do it."

"What?"

"I'll buy my own ticket," he repeated with a smile strong in his voice.

"Who are you and where is Kincaid Sinclair?"

"Very funny. Have you started a new career as a bad comedian?"

"Cute. So when are you planning to fly in so I can at least pick you up at the airport and let your parents' secretary know? She wants to know if you can return with them on their private jet. Your mother wants to spend some quality time with you, and she figures there'll be nowhere you can hide during the flight."

"I need to talk to someone first."

"Someone? Or a particular person? If it's that airline stewardess, I might have to get on a plane and make my way to that village of yours and slap you."

"She and I called it quits a while back."

"Then why is she still sending me hateful e-mails?"

Kincaid sighed. "I'll call Dad and let you know in a couple of days what arrangements I've worked out. Now what are the other matters you mentioned?"

"I've been approached by a corporation that wants to commission you to do a piece."

"You know I don't do those things."

"Normally, yes. But this is isn't for the chairman's mansion, it's for a park."

"And?"

"The park is in your new town."

Kincaid narrowed his eyes as a sneaking suspicion flared. "What's the company?"

"Blackfox Industries."

"You can go ahead and set up the meeting."

"Ahh, I can see the free publicity as we speak."

"Don't get your hopes up," he warned, then glanced at his watch. Regan would arrive in a few hours, and he needed to get some work done.

"Of course not. Well, back to business."

Five minutes later, Kincaid hung up the phone, exited the back of the house, and headed toward the studio. So he'd be meeting another member of Regan's family, he mused. A grin spread across his face as he pondered her reaction to the news of her family's interference. Shaking his head, he pulled a set of keys from his pocket and inserted one in the lock, then put the entire incident to the back of his mind. He would tell Regan *after* the meeting.

Chapter 10

"You can have all the time you need, Ms. Nichols, and if you want anything just hit the Call button and I'll be right down."

Regan bestowed a practiced smile upon the bald, multi-tattooed establishment owner. One of the advantages of working for the most powerful branches of the federal government was the benefits. After the heavy wood door closed and left the room in utter silence, she surveyed the grayness of the underground shooting range.

A chill crept over her skin as a blast of cold air poured over her shoulders from the overhead air ducts. Regan stepped into the shooting booth, and her hands automatically reached for and began to prepare the waiting semi-automatic Glock 35 as her thoughts drifted.

The last few weeks with Kincaid had been the happiest she'd spent in far too long to remember. Simple things like going to the movie theater and having his hand rest on her thigh, the touching of their fingers when reaching for popcorn at the same time, the coolness of his lips as he licked the remains of whipped cream from the hot chocolate off the corner of her mouth. These images and more threatened to overwhelm all the years of details from assignments that she'd gathered in her head.

It was ironic because she'd imagined returning home would be enjoyable for the short term, but a pain in the butt once her parents and grandparents returned. Yet rediscovering her hometown through Kincaid's eyes changed everything. Even the cold of winter seemed warmer.

Shaking her head to clear her thoughts, Regan put on the required safety goggles and ear protection, then slid the fully loaded clip into the gun. After positioning the target at the thirty-foot mark she closed her eyes briefly. Like magic, Ace, the Delta operative who'd drilled her for hours on the intricacies of firearms, stood by her side.

His voice came floating to her mind. "Just relax, Nichols. Take a few deep breaths, aim, and in between the last two breaths, pull the trigger."

After disengaging the safety, Regan raised the gun with a double-handed grip, lined up the iron sights with the target as she prepared for the preprogrammed target sequence.

Dominique Nichols. Her cover name seemed to whisper in her ear and remind her of the possible brevity of her homecoming. Regan bit her lip as a hot emotion akin to hate flared in her stomach. Once the targets began to move, she squeezed the trigger at a rate of one shot per two seconds, and the smell of gunpowder immediately permeated the air.

In less than five hours, she would arrive at Kincaid's doorstep and pretend that half her day had never happened. In two hours, her hand would cramp and her shoulders would ache from the gun's recoil. Even as the last of the bullet shells bounced on the concrete floor, Regan had already ejected the empty clip and put in a new one. Taking a deep breath, she pushed everything from her mind, and for the next sixty minutes, nothing else seemed to matter.

After an hour drive back from Atlanta she should have been at her cottage, preparing for a romantic evening, but at four o'clock that afternoon, Regan entered into her cousin's upscale town house not to the sounds of jazz, but to the unmistakable heaving accompanied by someone retching.

"Savannah!" she called after dropping her purse onto the floor. A panicked phone call from her cousin had brought about her change in plans.

"Upstairs in the bathroom," a faint voice called.

She took the steps two at a time and would have stepped on her cousin had she not been looking down. "Are you sick?"

"Isn't it obvious?" Savannah sarcastically snarled before she turned her face back toward the porcelain toilet. "Just leave me here to die."

Regan frowned at the out-of-character response, and she started to say something, then changed her mind. Instead of asking questions, she shrugged, turned her back, and began to leave the bathroom.

"Where are you going?" Savannah hollered.

"To get a drink," Regan responded sarcastically. "I need to get something to calm my nerves."

"You can't just leave me here," her cousin whined.

Regan aimed a sideways glance at the woman she considered a little sister, then without a word went downstairs and entered into the kitchen. It only took her a moment to search through the freezer and locate a bag of peas. On her way back to her cousin, she opened the linen closet and pulled out a few washcloths and a towel. Then after placing half of the supplies on the bathroom vanity, she kneeled down next to her cousin and gently placed the improvised ice pack on Savannah's neck.

"Now tell me what's wrong," Regan coaxed after Savannah rinsed her mouth for the third time. The dull pallor of her cousin's skin combined with the purplish color underneath her eyes had further increased her rising alarm.

"Everything," Savannah responded after flushing the toilet and moving to sit with her back against the side of the bathtub. Her voice wobbled. "I don't even know where to start."

"How about you start at the beginning?" Regan suggested. "First off, who or what has you kissing the porcelain goddess?"

The sight of pearl-drop tears rolling down her cousin's face made Regan regret asking the question.

"I gave Jack back the engagement ring. I'm pregnant," she sobbed. "And I'm having dinner at the country club with Mom and Dad tomorrow night."

Regan drew in a sharp breath. "How did this happen?" She shook her head as the old birds plus bees equals stork and baby came to mind. "No, don't answer."

"But I know exactly when it happened." Savannah blushed as a secret smile lit her wan features. "We were—"

Regan placed a single finger to her lips. "Don't tell me, tell Jack."

A worried look crossed Savannah's already harried features. The sixth sense Regan had developed to read people kicked into full force. "You're not planning on telling him, are you?"

Savannah opened her mouth, but the ringing of the phone cut off what she was about to say. In the silence of the bathroom, they waited until the answering machine clicked on. "That was him. He's been calling me every thirty minutes."

Her cousin broke eye contact and stared numbly at the floor. Regan pulled in a deep breath and let it out slowly. "Savannah, you have to tell him."

"He'll insist that we get married."

"And?" Regan's eyebrows shot upward. "Jack wanted to marry you before the pregnancy. The only difference now is you can't use the excuse of our family to stall him."

"Oh Lord. Regan, what am I going to do?" she moaned, and Regan fought back a grimace as Savannah's perpetually manicured fingernails bit into her skin.

"I think you've got to tell the truth. It's not just you and Jack anymore, you have a baby to think about."

"Mom and Dad will never forgive me."

"Bring them another grandchild to bounce on their laps and they'll forgive you for anything."

"Even marrying an Archer?" Savannah asked in a small voice.

The small look of hope in her eyes clinched it for Regan. Although she had serious doubts that the repercussions of the situation would blow over quickly, Regan nodded slowly as a horde of butterflies seemed to have broken loose in her stomach. A vision formed in her head, a sort of apocalyptic meeting of her family and the Archers. She wondered briefly if the location of her cousin's confession should be the family church with the reverend in attendance as a holy intermediary. "Even that."

Regan moved to stand up, but Savannah's hand flashed out and closed on her wrist. "Don't leave me."

"I'm just going to grab you a cola and crackers to help settle your stomach."

Savannah shook her head, then cleared the bangs from her eyes. "That's not what I meant. Don't *leave* again. Please."

It was only going to get harder, Regan thought. And quick on the heels of that realization came guilt. She let her body fall, then put an arm around her cousin. "Savannah, it's going to be okay."

"No, it won't. You left, Regan. You can leave again and I have to stay here surrounded by the men of our family who think they can run my life just because of a minor variation in age and gender."

It was on the tip of Regan's tongue to remind her cousin that she could stand up to them or leave, but she didn't. Time had changed Savannah for the better, but at the core of her very being, she remained utterly devoted to the Blackfox clan. Regan loved them, but she valued the freedom to live her own life more. "Cuz," Regan began with a soft tone, "my staying in town won't help."

"That's where you're wrong." As she watched, Savannah seemed to rebuild her composure piece by piece. "It's been like a vacation since you've been here. No questions at dinner, no comments on my dating life, no pressure to meet Dad's single business associates. Maybe they're afraid that you'll convince me to leave as well, or maybe they're waiting for Grandfather to come home and talk to me. But all I know is that I haven't had to lie about the time I spend with Jack."

Regan released a pent-up sigh and let her head fall back. Staring at the ceiling, she resisted the urge to rub her brow as the beginning of what could turn into a headache thrummed beneath her temple. "You love your job, right?"

"Of course, I don't think I'll ever tire of teaching."

"I feel the same about mine."

"But, Regan, there's a difference." Savannah's somber tone got Regan's attention. She turned to meet her cousin's gaze, and her heart sank.

Although half of her didn't want to know the meaning to Savannah's cryptic comment, the other more inquisitive side responded first. "What's the difference?"

"I would give it up for love," she whispered. "I would give it up for family."

Chapter 11

"When was it that Regan, the daddy's little princess, de-cided to become Regan the rebel?" Kincaid asked.

She smiled the first true smile she'd had all day. The two aspirins she'd swallowed before leaving Savannah's house had made her headache disappear, but it was Kincaid's presence that truly lifted her spirits. "When did you decide to become an artist?"

"Answering a question with a question could be taken as a sign of distrust."

Regan sighed slightly and curled farther into the hard protectiveness of his embrace. She'd loved eating pizza, snacking on salsa and chips, and watching a great foreign film, but what she'd enjoyed most was the simple act of re-laxing in Kincaid's arms. "Some habits are hard to adjust. I learned early that in diplomatic circles everything revolves around tit-for-tat. Only the goal is to get information before you give it." She deliberately formed her words. Being able to deflect and receive more information than giving was a tactic that had always served her well.

If everything went according to Morgan's plans, the Delta Force commander would soon grow tired of chas-ing down her alias and she would return to her post. In the past, the excitement of going on a mission would course through her body and fill her with anticipation. This time, however, the realization that she wouldn't be able to see Kincaid sat like a rock in her stomach while weighing heavily on her conscience. Unable to voice her true feelings, Regan summoned a semblance of a self-conscious grin. "My grandparents swore I was born a changeling child. My mother blamed my father because of his insistence that I was going to be a boy. Maybe I wanted to be a son to my father," she mused. "But I don't see myself as being anyone other than myself."

"I, for one, am glad of it."

"Really? My family wouldn't agree." She touched him gently on the shoulder. "The closer the time gets for me to leave, the less they'll pull their punches. I know they want me home. They can't help it. Ever since my great-uncle's birth, the men of this family have always been over-protective toward the women."

"You seem to have escaped," Kincaid observed.

"Or maybe I was given a temporary reprieve. Now, let's get back to the topic at hand."

"And that was?"

"When did you decide to become an artist?"

"You are relentless, aren't you?"

"Kincaid . . ." She enunciated his name in her best schoolteacher's voice.

"The day I made a life-sized model of Flipper, the dolphin, out of Play-Doh."

Her lips twitched up, then down, and then her mouth opened. "Flipper, huh? I used to love watching him as a kid."

"I actually got to meet her."

She watched as Kincaid's mouth curved into a broad grin. His thick eyebrows rose and created wrinkles in his brow. Her mind, like the shutter of a camera, clicked open, then closed, storing the image within her memory.

"Lucky," she said.

"One of the perks of being the son of a movie star. The head trainer had a crush on my mother."

"Was it all the stuff of dreams? Growing up in Los Angeles."

"To me L.A. was a place to visit during the awards ceremonies and the wrapping up of a film. I spent a majority of my younger days with a private tutor on the set. My parents decided before I was born that I would travel with them until I was old enough to enroll in high school."

"Were you happy?"

"For the most part. It was magical when my mother and father were on the same location and stressful when they weren't. They fed off one another in a way. My mother provided support to my father when she was in between films, and he to her."

"And Yale?"

"My father insisted. It was the only stipulation to my gaining control of my trust fund."

"So you were never tempted into the fast life of celebrity-hood?" she queried.

"Never is a long time, Regan." Kincaid shifted at the memory of his time with Kirsten. The one time he'd doubted his calling and lost his focus. "Once I almost turned my back on my art."

"Who was she?"

"Does it have to be a woman?"

"To the Greeks, Muse was a beautiful goddess, and a patron of all artists. Now what can steal a man from a woman if not another woman?"

"You're too smart for your own good." He laughed softly, then frowned. Of all the things he'd said and done after Kirsten left, laughing had never been one of them.

"If you don't feel like talking about it . . ."

"No, it's ancient history. Kirsten wanted the parties, the adoration, and the fame. I didn't see it at first, and I proposed only to discover weeks later that she found someone who could give her all that the wanted without reservations and left me."

"She was crazy."

Kincaid grinned. "Glad you think so."

"I know so," she affirmed, then tilted her head upward. "Her loss is my gain."

"That remains to be seen."

"What do you mean?"

"I want a home, a family, a chance to be a full-time father and husband. I want to grow old with love and art. I want to leave this world content with a fine legacy that lasts longer than pictures."

For several moments, silence lay between them. Finally after taking two sips of wine to wet her dry throat, Regan spoke. "You want promises that I can't make or keep, Kincaid. We—"

"I know. But I'm the eternal optimist, remember?"

During the movie, Kincaid had had a difficult time concentrating because of Regan's seemingly unconscious movement of her fingers on the nape of his neck. Now as she sat back and repeated the gesture, he placed his fingertips under her chin and slowly guided her head so that they would be face-to-face.

Bathed in the flickering glow of the TV screen, they stared at one another.

"I like optimists," Regan murmured, only half of her mind fully engaged and the other half buzzing with the anticipation of a kiss.

"Good."

Kincaid's voice rose husky and deep to her ears. Regan knew that wherever her travels took her, she would remember that moment, long for the heat of his fingertips on her skin and the sight of his eyes.

He reached over and pulled her into his lap, gently placed his fingers on either side of her face, and kissed her. His lips touched lightly as though asking permission, and then his tongue caressed hers and slowly entered her mouth.

Moments later when they both came up for air, he drew back and with a grin on his face asked a very trivial question. "What did you think of the movie?"

"It was nice. Very beautiful." Silently she added to herself that the time with Kincaid and the movie had been just what she needed. All day long the conversation she'd had with Savannah had gone around like a merry-go-round in her head. Having a baby should have been a happy and celebrated event, but her favorite cousin was miserable.

Kincaid placed his hand atop hers. "Herbert Van Salle is one of my mother's favorite directors. He's so good, he makes my father turn green with envy."

"That has to be a major feat."

"Easier than you think."

"The main character seemed very involved with his work."

"Most artists are. It's just me and the studio and the horses most days. I'm not very good at being sociable."

"Dinner, movie, and kisses?" She angled her neck to the side. "I think you're doing a great job."

"Thanks for the compliment. Would you like something hot to drink?"

"That would be nice."

She followed him into the kitchen, enjoying the sight of his tall strength and the way he looked in the polo sweater. "You happen to be the first artist I've known outside of a cocktail party or an embassy function."

"I'm honored." He took a kettle and held it under the filtered kitchen faucet.

"You should be," Regan replied as she trailed her finger over the kitchen countertop and then paused. "Are you obsessive about your work?"

"Only when I'm inspired."

"Is that often?"

"Since I met you, yes."

Kincaid flipped on the gas and placed the kettle on top of the blue flames. Regan met his stare with a sultry smile. "I still want to sculpt you," he said.

"Didn't you want to see me ride first?"

"True." He reached out and pulled her toward him.

Regan went willingly into his arms. "How about we go for a nice ride on Saturday and I sketch you on Sunday?"

"Were you always so dedicated?" Regan inquired. There was nosey and there was curious. Her brothers called her the former; her teachers, however labeled Regan as curious at an early age.

"I devoted my life to art even before I finished high school. My father insisted that I go to college before I made any drastic decisions."

"Did your parents disapprove of your chosen profession?"

"Actually they were proud. I think that they're being in film industry helped pave the way for my own independence. My father actually helped me move to Zaire after graduation. Even though it doesn't look it, with their busy schedules and the solitude of my art, my parents are the foundation of my career as a sculptor."

There was nothing but love in his voice, but Regan couldn't help but wonder if he'd always felt the same way. Kincaid hadn't talked much about his childhood, but she'd gleaned enough from his stories to know that it hadn't been his choice to attend boarding school.

"It's a blessing to have such a supportive family," she mused with understatement poignant in her voice. Not a day, week, or month passed without her wishing she could tell her parents about her real job at the NSA. She wanted them to be proud of her but knew that if they had an inkling of an idea about the dangerous situations she placed herself in, they would move heaven and earth to get her fired.

"Earth to Regan."

She shook her head to clear her thoughts and smiled apologetically. "Sorry about that."

"Where did you go?"

"A quick trip to fantasyland," she replied.

"How about a drink and you can tell me what happened in that faraway place to bring such sadness to your eyes?"

She leaned back against the counter as Kincaid brought out two glass mugs and a dark bottle without a label. He poured a measured amount of the mysterious brown liquid into each of the mugs. Biting her tongue to keep from asking about the contents, Regan waited. And it all paid off when he added the boiling water and the spicy scent of apples and cinnamon filled the kitchen.

"Apple cider."

"Only the best in the world," he assured her. "A fellow artist in Washington gave this to me. She picked the apples herself. Now, how about we go back into the den and you tell me about growing up as Regan Blackfox, the automotive princess?"

"That would be Savannah Blackfox, my cousin." She smiled, taking the glass mug from his proffered hand. "I'm the trucking princess who should have been a prince."

A giggle bubbled up from her throat at the look of confusion that spread like a wave over his handsome features. "My grandfather on my father's side of the family was given the opportunity to name my parents' fourth child. Because my mother had only had boys, Grandfather assumed I would be the fourth, hence the name Regan, which means 'little prince' in Spanish."

"Now that solved half the mystery."

"So you knew about my family?" Regan questioned as they resettled on the sofa.

"As of three days ago."

"How did you find out?"

"You mean how did I make the connection between the large logo on the semitrucks and the gorgeous woman in my arms?"

"Uh-huh."

"J.R.'s barbershop."

She giggled and laid her head back against his shoulder. "Must have been Henry. He got the first cigar at my birth. He and my father go way back. That man knows everybody's skeletons. Even some of yours, I bet."

"So your father is a trucking mogul, huh?"

"My great-grandfather started the trucking business, my

father is the chairman, and my oldest brother recently stepped in as the chief executive officer."

"I've seen many of those trucks on my drive from San Francisco."

"The company headquarters is in Cartersville and over half the fleet is dedicated to shipping flooring products for Archer Carpet."

Kincaid's eyebrows rose slightly. "You and your brothers would be great additions to the Black jet set society."

"All of us have trust funds and careers, but we don't eat from silver spoons or live off our inheritance. My second oldest brother is an emergency room doctor and you've met Trey. We all have very good careers and bring home paychecks." Regan kept her tone neutral. In the past, she would have immediately gone on the defensive. Money, or not, she'd never behaved like a spoiled rich kid and neither had her brothers.

"Point taken," he grinned. "So are you ready to tell me the story of your family?"

"It's a long one," she warned after curling her legs up under her.

"I have all the time in the world for you."

Regan wet her throat with a sip of the apple cider before beginning. "My great-grandfather, Abraham Blackfox, was an ex-slave and a mechanical genius. Most of his brothers and sisters went up North to live in New York and Philadelphia, but he stayed here. A very simple man, all he ever needed existed in a converted barn on the former plantation where he'd been most of his young life as a companion to the owner's son, Collin Archer. The only time he ever left town was to collect a wife who had been chosen by his relatives.

"No one knew the real reason why Collin went to Philadelphia with my great-grandfather. Some say to make sure he returned, others said he came as a friend and with the express purpose of keeping Abraham from be arrested by the sheriff, who wanted to keep the former slaves from leaving

Georgia. One thing that we do know is that something had changed. My great-grandfather received a clear deed to the land my parents' house sits on today, and moved off the plantation. Nine months after he married, his wife bore a child who had distinct Archer facial features and green eyes."

Regan took a sip of her warm apple cider and enjoyed the smooth feel of it sliding down her throat.

"Something tells me there's more to the story."

"And you are right. My great-grandfather continued to work in the converted barn and went on to invent many of the precursors to carpet mill machines still used today. And he did it all for the man who'd betrayed him and for the family that had once owned him."

"Fascinating."

"As I said when we first met, welcome to Georgia," she quipped. "The skeletons are deeply buried but never forgotten. In my great-grandfather's generation, Collin Archer was one of the wealthiest men in the Southeast, if not the wealthiest. His carpet products shipped around the world. When he died, the carpet industrialist left fifty percent of the company to Abraham Blackfox. Of course, there was uproar within the Archer family. Once the news began to spread that he left half his company to a Negro, most of the town took sides. The newspaper editorial comments would make your eyebrows curl. But you can imagine the shock at having an ex-slave as a business partner. The gesture didn't appeal to my grandfather either. You see, he blamed Collin Archer for his older brother's disappearance and hated that the man's actions had unrightfully made him to be second in a time when the firstborn son inherited. So they negotiated. And in the end, the deal led to the creation of Blackfox Trucking. My grandfather traded most of his stock in Archer Carpet for the money to money to buy a fleet of trucks and exclusive shipping rights to Archer Industries."

"That's a deep history."

"It would be nice if it were only history. On the surface,

everything's perfect. But to this day Blackfox and Archer work together, attending meetings and sitting on the same community board, but never speak. My grandfather is a wonderful man, but he's broken somehow," she mused. "And sometimes I wish I could fix him."

"What about bringing his brother home?"

"A while back my father tried to find him. No luck. We don't know if he's still alive. Lord, I wish he would come back."

"Something tells me that this is more of a problem than you'd like to think about."

"You're very perceptive." Regan leaned closer into Kincaid's chest and inhaled. The scent of his aftershave and the sensation of his strong hand kneading her shoulder sent her touch-deprived body into a euphoric state that made thinking extremely difficult. "Mistrust and anger still run deep in our family, which is why my favorite cousin lives in fear that someone will find out that she's involved with Jack Archer."

Regan absentmindedly drew circles on Kincaid's chest as she glanced through the open window and at the quarter moon hanging in a starlit sky. Even as she relaxed into the comfort of his arms, a small voice whispered, *why all the trust, Regan? You've known this man less than two weeks. He's not an old friend or an ex-boyfriend.* Yet sharing a part of herself that she had not given to the men she'd dated for months seemed to her as natural as breathing.

Her thoughts drifted back to her cousin's dilemma. Savannah and Jack didn't need help; they needed a miracle. Her grandfather hadn't changed a day in his life and he'd inherited more than his father's intelligence and Cherokee good looks, he'd taken in the bitterness of being a second son.

Regan felt his fingers in her hair and the brush of his lips on her brow. "If your cousin is anything like you, I have no doubt that she'll be a formidable champion for the man she loves."

"I hope so." Uncertainty rose to the surface of her

voice, and the arm wrapped around her waist felt all the more comforting.

"My father taught me early, where there's love, anything's possible."

"That was spoken with the romantic optimism of an artist." A slow smile curved her lips.

"That tone of voice sounded suspiciously cynical, Rebel."

The use of her nickname startled her into turning her face upward. Regan met his smiling eyes and her heart clenched because she actually believed him. In that moment, she'd have done anything in the world to be just Regan Sinclair and not Dominique Nichols. She would have given half her inheritance to wipe away the faces of the lives she'd taken and the people whom she'd lied to throughout her tenure with the NSA. "I'm not cynical. Just practical."

"Or maybe you're afraid?"

Her brows rose. "Of you?"

"No, of love."

"Isn't it a little early to be throwing out the L-word, Kincaid?"

"Love, Regan. You can say it . . . come on." He tickled her cheek.

"Love," she repeated while suppressing a shiver at the coincidence. Savannah had said the very same word to her earlier that day. "We just met."

"I'm not so sure of that. Who's to say that we haven't met in a former life?"

"That would be the incarnation where you abandoned me and our six kids to search for gold, only to return home with a cow, beans, and an overweight basset hound."

"And I thought I had an imagination."

She shrugged a single shoulder. "I get a lot of time on international flights with bad movies, bad food, and horrible company," she wryly admitted.

But the butterfly kisses he trailed down her cheek to land

upon her lips pushed everything from her mind. His lips moved up from her throat, rounded her chin, and when they came into contact with her mouth, she welcomed him. Kincaid might have been gentle in the beginning, but there was no softness in him now. He slanted his lips over hers, deepening the kiss, probing, exploring her mouth until she was breathless with desire.

Of their own accord, her arms rose to encircle his shoulders and her fingers worked their way underneath his button-down shirt to come into direct contact with his skin. He murmured something into her mouth, but Regan ignored it and gave herself over to the simplest pleasure of touching him. And her mind, like a sponge, soaked up the mingled sounds of their moans. And her body memorized the feel of his hands as they cupped her swollen breasts. Yet, in the end when she pulled away from the wonder of his kisses and the wonder of his touch, Regan sighed with regret. "It's getting late. I'd better go."

"You don't have to go."

His husky voice sent another wave of heat to the place between her thighs. "Your lips say spend the night and share my sheets, but your gentlemanly sense of . . ." Regan lifted herself from his chest but kept her hands nicely placed around his shoulders. *Damn, the man is handsome.* She shook her head to clear her thoughts as she fought the temptation to rub her hands over his close-cropped thick black hair.

"Honor won't allow me to sleep anywhere but the guest room."

"I'd be willing to put it aside for tonight."

"And a dozen mornings from now when you wake up and I'm gone, will you still be so agreeable?"

"This is a rare thing." He laughed and hugged her tight. "You're worried about my feelings."

She punched him lightly in his chest. Without a doubt, Kincaid's invitation was definitely better than a drive home and cold shower. "No, I'm more concerned about my reputation.

I have no plans for you to sculpt me into a modern version of the scarlet woman who left you heart broken."

"You're saving my heart now? I guess that's progress."

"The truth is I like you, Kincaid Sinclair."

"That I knew." He stood slowly and his powerful body came up less than three inches from hers. The confident upturn of his lips matched his deep voice. "Tell me more."

"I'm a rebel. And part of my personality is to explore."

His fingertips skimmed over her cheeks, across her chin, and down her throat, pausing at the V of her blouse. "I like exploring too, but I think that you're hedging, Regan."

"Wh-what?"

"Oh yes, woman. I bet you're probably one stop short of being terrified." He grinned.

Her eyes narrowed on his face. "What's that supposed to mean? I am not afraid of you."

"Prove it by spending the day horseback riding with me on Saturday."

Regan opened her mouth, then closed it as she thought better of snapping out a response. Damn it, he'd gotten her, she silently cursed. A mere novice had schooled her, who was supposed to be a master at the art of using words. She took two steps back and then nodded. "It's a date."

Kincaid stood and moved to her side. Before she could say a word, he placed a quick kiss on her cheek. "Saturday. I'll pick you up at eight o'clock."

Later, after cleaning up and helping Regan with her coat, Kincaid walked her to the car and closed her door. Watching the red lights slip away, he returned to his silent house with one sole comfort. She'd be back soon enough.

Chapter 12

"Mr. Blackfox." Kincaid rose from his seat on the leather couch and stood as Regan's brother walked toward him.

"Please, no formalities necessary. Call me Marius." He held out his hand and Kincaid grasped it in a firm handshake. And in that split second, his estimation for the man rose. He'd lived among the moneyed class for long enough to know the difference between those who did their own work and those who hired others. From the rough feel of Marius's palm, Regan's older brother didn't just crunch numbers.

Not by gesture or look did Kincaid betray the sense of unease that snaked down his spine upon entering the large executive office. Regan's older brother had come out to greet him after the man's personal assistant had offered him coffee, tea, or juice for the third time. Kincaid nodded. "All right."

"Kincaid, have a seat."

Marius Blackfox crossed behind his desk and took a seat in the black executive chair. "So tell me why I should let you see my little sister."

Frowning slightly, Kincaid crossed his legs and confidently sat back in one of the spacious office's twin leather chairs. Like his sister, Marius Blackfox cut to the chase. Too bad Kincaid wasn't in a more accommodating mood. "Would the piece you're thinking about commissioning be an indoor or an outdoor display?"

Marius Blackfox's assessing gaze never wavered. "You and I both know I couldn't care less about your sculptures, but if it's a means for getting you to tell me what I want to know, then I'll commission both."

"Both, huh?" Careful to keep his expression blank, Kincaid examined the man behind the large mahogany desk. Power rode over his broad shoulders, and where Regan's brown eyes held a warm twinkle, this man's gaze held chips of ice. Thick brows and a well-trimmed goatee made him look more like a fighter than a corporate leader. Annoyance fought with curiosity at the motives for Marius Blackfox's summons. Kincaid fingered his chin and relaxed into the chair, then named an outrageous sum. "One hundred and fifty thousand."

Marius didn't bat an eye at the dollar amount, but his fingers, which had been tapping the desk, froze. "Done. Now talk."

The smile on Kincaid's lips never made it to his eyes. He uncrossed his legs and sat forward. "That price is for each sculpture."

With his hands clasped and index fingers pressed against his lips, the man continued, "Tell me what I want to know and I'll cut you a check right here."

Then Marius proceeded to open up a leather portfolio, picked up a pen, and scribbled something on a piece of paper.

Astonishment held Kincaid still at the realization that the man would actually pay a quarter of a million dollars for information regarding his sister. The depth of brotherly concern was commendable, yet the Machiavellian ways gave Kincaid a hint of distaste. "Thanks for the offer, Marius." He placed extra emphasis on the man's name. "But I'm afraid I'll have to decline. As to my relationship with Regan, that's none of your business."

It wasn't in his best interest to irritate Regan's eldest brother, but if Marius had been the kind of man who offended easily, he would never have been appointed the CEO of the Blackfox empire.

Kincaid moved to stand, but Regan's brother had already risen and walked from behind his desk. "You speak your mind, don't you?"

"I wouldn't have it any other way."

"All right, Kincaid." Marius folded his tall frame into the seat next to him, crossed his legs, and sat back. "She's my sister, and in the absence of our father, I watch over this family. And I don't intend for her to be hurt."

"Really? Apparently you're not concerned enough to keep her from getting behind the wheel of her own race car, and it would seem to me that you weren't concerned enough to have kept her out of the passenger seat of yours."

Silence held for a moment, and then Marius's head rolled back and he let out a roar of laughter. It was at that time that Kincaid caught a glimpse the real man behind the corporate title and made note of his cynical sense of humor.

"Can I get you a drink?" The man stood and walked over to the discreetly-tucked-away bar area opposite the windows.

Kincaid stood and joined him, all the time wondering if the man was changing tactics or sincere. "I'll have what you're having."

"Bourbon it is." Marius turned over two glasses and picked up the decanter. "My grandfather had this specially ordered and sitting in the basement for a decade before he gave two bottles to me the day I took over the company. It's over a century old, but I swear I felt every one of those hundred years the morning after my celebration party."

Kincaid took the glass from Marius's outstretched hand. "Thanks."

"Just as a clarification. Regan spent weeks sneaking into the back of my car before I found out and let her sit in the front."

Kincaid took a sip of the smooth liquid and met the other man's measuring stare. "So what's this really about?"

"I have a thick folder in my desk with your name on it. After two hours of reading, I'm aware of everything there is to know about Kincaid Sinclair. On paper, that is. I have pictures of your parents, newspaper articles, copies of bank statements, and photographs of the inside and outside of your house. But what all that doesn't tell me is what I really need to know."

"You could have asked."

"Unlike the art world you inhabit, honesty is a rare commodity in business. And my father taught me on his knee that you never go into a negotiation without knowing what the other side wants and how far they'll go to get it."

"Is that what you call this, a negotiation?" Kincaid asked with all the casualness of inquiring about the weather. He'd passed through the glass automatic doors into the corporate center with the expectation of facing something more along the lines of an inquisition.

"Damn straight. I've seen the 8-digit figures in your financial portfolio. You're not after my sister's money and you couldn't care less about the family name."

"So you're still trying to figure out what I want?"

The man finished off his drink and placed the crystal glass on the bar counter. "No, I'm not. I know. You want my little sister."

"And what do you want?"

For the second time since he'd walked through the thick mahogany double doors, Kincaid saw an honest smile cross Marius Blackfox's face. It was a wide grin that showed two rows of pearly white teeth and transformed the businessman into an everyday man who cared about his family. "To give my father a long-awaited birthday present."

Kincaid allowed his confusion to show. "A sculpture for the park?"

"No." Marius shook his head. Kincaid wouldn't have thought it possible, but the man's smiled became even wider. "I'm giving him back his baby girl. He wants Regan home to stay, and I'm betting you're the man to do it."

"I wouldn't have pegged you to be a gambling man."

"And you'd be right. That's my uncle Raymond. He was the first African-American in the Southeast to own his own car dealership. Everyone said he would fail, and in the end he's one of the top sellers. But that doesn't help me with my current situation."

"Somehow I don't think that Regan would appreciate us having this conversation."

"That is an understatement. The last time someone tried to meddle in her life, she disappeared. I can't have that happen again."

"And what's to say that I won't tell her?"

"Self-interest, I hope. Because if you do she'll disappear. She won't get angry, which is what my grandfather assumed would happen the last time he tried this."

"Is it something in your family about people not learning their lessons the first time?"

"I'm not manipulating Regan."

"No, you're trying to do that through me."

"No, bro. I'm trying to help you." He reached down onto his desk and drew out an ivory-colored envelope. "Friday night, Regan is helping me host a small company function."

Kincaid didn't blink at the statement. "Funny she didn't mention it."

"She doesn't know about it yet," Marius replied. The other man moved forward to push an ivory envelope across the desk toward Kincaid. "I think it would make her night if you attended."

Kincaid let out a soft whistle as he stared down at the envelope, which just happened to be next to the quarter-of-a-million-dollar check. He returned his attention to Marius and shook his head slightly at the implication of the man's actions. "You're playing a dangerous game."

The grin slipped from the other man's face. "I don't have

a choice here. I started her on this path of rebellion and I'll do anything to get her back."

"Regan's a grown woman."

"Rebel is a spoiled brat. Our parents raised her as the baby of the family while I treated her like a kid brother," he replied wryly.

Just as Kincaid prepared to probe that line of discussion further, the intercom rang. "Mr. Blackfox, you have a video conference in five minutes."

"On my way," Marius responded.

Kincaid stood and then placed the glass, which had sat forgotten in his hand, on the desk. "Thanks for the bourbon."

"I'll see you Friday night."

"I don't take kindly to pressure."

"And I rarely take no for an answer. How about you take the invitation and the donation? Regardless of whether or not you decide to help me with Regan, I think the park could benefit from some art and our company could use the tax deduction."

"Hey, Regan, you've got company in the waiting room."

Reflexively Regan kept her arms raised and her concentration on sliding the tight rubber timing belt into position. Two days had already passed since the night of her second race, but she was still tired from the hours spent getting the Corvette back into proper form. With her hair pulled back and the cap's bill partially covering her face, she'd managed to hide the shadows under her eyes from both her uncle Max and the service team.

It had taken her longer than she'd expected to adjust the clutch last night. A few laps around the track had the sports car moving fast and shifting smooth. The car's great performance, with the purr of the engine, the lightning-quick acceleration, more than pleased her. Yet the truth be known, she should have been in bed resting, but who could turn down her childhood beautician, especially when her tresses would soon be in need of a deep condition and trim?

Regan pulled back from underneath the sedan's hood and straightened up, put her tools back in their proper place in the cabinet, and mentally made a note to inspect the transmission and spark plug wires upon her return.

Her hand automatically reached for the hand towel while her gaze locked on the service manager's smiling face. The tall balding man with a barrel chest and large hands stood by the car with his hands empty of everything but a clipboard. Regan narrowed her eyes as her brow creased in consternation. Daniel Rhone, or Dan, was more of an honorary member of the family than her uncle's right-hand man. She'd grown up seeing him at least once a week, and she could count on one hand the number of times she'd witnessed him smile for such a prolonged amount of time.

"Which brother is it this time?"

"None."

Regan's brow creased. "Then who is it?"

"You'll see. Maybe you can make a quick stop in front of the mirror before you go out."

"Why?"

"You've got oil on your cheek."

"And that's not stopped me from going out front to see customers before."

"This one's different."

Her heart gave a leap, and a smidgen of excitement ran up her spine. Kincaid. She took a deep breath and calmed her accelerated pulse. When did it start? she questioned herself. When did friendly attraction turn into affectionate attachment? Instead of letting her mind dwell on those thoughts, she allowed a growing smile to rise to her lips. Regan took a step forward and playfully tapped Dan on the shoulder. "He's seen me with oil on my face before."

"Well, when a man comes courting with flowers, you should at least try to look decent."

"Flowers?" Her mouth formed a surprised O, then curved up into a large smile as her left hand reached up to pull off her cap. When they'd parted company two nights ago, she'd thought that the handsome artist would pull away. This turn of events came as a shock since his reluctance to begin a relationship without a storybook ending had given her the impression that he wouldn't want to see her for a while. "What kind of flowers?"

"Pretty white and pink ones." He began to get flustered. "Same ones I buy my wife on her birthday."

Regan did something she normally didn't do because of the male environment of the service shop and because of her own reluctance to engage in public displays of affection. She took two steps, rose up on her tiptoes, and gave him a kiss on his cheek. "Thank you."

"Yeah."

"Just make sure you don't mess it up this time."

So excited as she was at the prospect of seeing Kincaid, Regan's normally sharp mind didn't catch Dan's parting comment. She walked straight through the service bay on a direct course to the bathroom. There was nothing she could do about the lack of makeup, but a splash of cold water on her face and a quick comb through her hair should help.

The NSA had taught her to always be prepared, but since she'd arrived home, the ingrained precautions and habits had slipped by the wayside. Regan finished drying her face and glanced in the mirror. Her eyes sparkled and the glow on her face had nothing to do with the adrenaline rush of driving or the danger of a mission. It was just the thought of seeing a man. A man who hadn't been far from her thoughts since the evening he'd walked into the dealership.

But you'll leave him. The analytical thought of her alter ego, NSA Agent Dominique Nichols, intruded upon her moment.

She balled up the paper towel and absentmindedly tossed it into the wastebasket. Yes, she'd leave and go back to that other carefully constructed life and identity. Regan closed her eyes and shook her head, then pushed those thoughts into the back corner of her mind. For the space of a few weeks, she would be Regan Blackfox, the rich single daughter of a wealthy family, amateur race car driver, and rebellious seductress.

She did a last final check and pinched her cheeks for color, left the bathroom, and headed for the dealership waiting area. After passing through the television area to the quiet room set aside for their more business-oriented customers, Regan spotted what she thought was a familiar back. She opened her mouth to call out a greeting, then stopped.

"Trent?"

He turned and the combination of orchids and lilies in his hands was indeed lovely. She inhaled and the perfumed scent tickled her nose. "What are you doing here?"

He came toward her with his signature grin on his face. The last time they'd met underneath the garage's dim overhead lighting, she hadn't noticed his looks. Now nothing, not even the bad memories of their breakup, could have kept her from recognizing that he had only become more handsome with maturity and age. The race car driver turned actor with his great bone structure and signature walk had come home a superstar.

"I was hoping I could talk you into having dinner with me tonight."

"I thought the loser was supposed to buy the winner dinner," she replied. It had been a tradition that she hadn't planned to exercise this time around.

"I shouldn't have said what I said, Regan." He started to apologize, but his next words negated the attempt. "I guess I'm not over some of the past yet."

"You make it sound as though I devastated you, Trent. And you know that wasn't the case."

"No man likes to be turned down for an offer of marriage."

"No woman likes to be manipulated by the man she's dating or by her grandfather."

"That night—"

She cut him off. "Only opened my eyes wider. I wouldn't have said yes because of school. Even then I knew there was more to life than pleasing my father by agreeing to be your trophy wife."

"Don't you think that's a little harsh, Regan?"

"No, Trent, I don't. Your ego took a bruising, but did you ever think about how I felt?"

She tilted her head to the side and chewed on the inside of her lip. "Let me answer that question. It probably didn't occur to you how betrayed I felt."

"Can't we forget about the past?"

"Forgive? Yes. Forget?" She paused and shook her head slightly. They'd spent hours talking about her family. At one point in time, he'd been an honorary member of the family. He'd known about her dreams of traveling and leaving home for a time, yet he'd traded her trust and affection for her grandfather's promises of marriage, money, and corporate racing endorsements. "No, I can't. Why would I want to? We had good times together, Trent."

He grinned. "Like the Wednesday night after Bible study when you convinced me to go skinny-dipping in the lake?"

Regan playfully swatted his shoulder. "How about the time you outran the state trooper only to get home to find the county sheriff sitting on the front porch?"

"Yeah. How crazy were we?"

"Very." She laughed, releasing a bundle of tension in her stomach.

"I brought these for you. I remembered your favorites."

She took the bouquet from his hand, lowered her nose to the flower petals, and inhaled. When she looked back up at Trent, Regan noticed that he'd used her distraction to move in closer. "Thank you. It's not every day that a girl gets such presents from a movie star."

Regan instantly regretted her words as the smile on his face melted away.

"It's not like that. I come home to get away from the

Hollywood hype and remember the boy I used to be. Makes me humble."

"I know how you feel."

His gaze narrowed on hers and his strong fingers removed the flowers from her grasp and placed them on a nearby table. "You do, don't you?"

"We diplomats have a tendency to grow large egos."

"Regan, we were good friends once." His deep voice grew husky. She looked into the eyes of the handsome man who stood before her and saw the image of the first boy she'd ever given her heart to. He'd been the easygoing rebel, academic jock, and steadfast friend. She'd liked him from the first day he'd arrived at her school and fallen in love with him the night he'd driven her down to the Atlanta Airport one summer night to see the airplanes arrive and take off from the comfort of his souped-up Ford Mustang convertible.

"And you were my first," she stated quietly, affection warming her own voice.

Trent took her hands within his own. "An honor that I will cherish to the day they put me in the grave."

He leaned in closer and before she could say a word, he kissed her full on the mouth. She kept her arms to her sides as his lips slanted over her own and his arms drew her closer. But it wasn't passion that flowed between them in that embrace, but the golden warmth of memories and faint longing of what might have been. It was then that she realized that in coming home, he not only wanted to remember the boy he'd been but also had deliberately sought to rekindle their relationship.

Regan pulled her head back and sighed, then rested her cheek against his chest. "It's not there, is it?" he asked, but she knew he already had the answer to his question. "I'd thought we could start over again."

"I know," she murmured. "You thought that by coming back, you could change back. You're not the boy you once were, Trent."

"And I'm not sure I like that."

"What's not to like?" She stepped out of his arms, then gave him a critical scrutiny from the top of his closely cropped sandy brown hair to the tips of his leather shoes. "If it's a pity party you want, you came to the wrong place. You're good-looking, talented, a great actor, you're famously rich, and have a wonderfully supportive family. Your mother, by the way, stopped by the house to say hello last week."

"But I still have to go back to Los Angeles, to the large house I bought on impulse and outfitted with every device known to man, and I'm alone. I have a garage full of cars that I don't have time to drive and an empty bed."

"I can't help you with the bed part."

"You sure?"

Her eyes narrowed at his cocky grin. "Very."

"Is there someone else?"

Regan waved her hand through the air and ignored the implication that there had to be someone else in her life. "I don't control my time, the State Department does. I move around a lot and that doesn't give me the privilege of commitment."

"Does he know that?"

"I've told him. More than once."

"Let me guess. The new man in your life isn't bowing down to the Blackfox princess?"

Regan aimed a sidelong glare his way, then tilted her chin. It should have alarmed her that Kincaid possessed characteristics similar to Trent's. The more she let the thought run through her mind, the more agitated she became. In hindsight, Regan realized that had she not overheard Trent and her grandfather planning her life, she would have eventually married him. She inhaled slowly and deliberately turned her mind to the matters at hand. "Just like you, he seems to be pigheaded."

"No, Regan." Trent's head moved wearily back and forth. "I'm hearing you loud and clear."

She blinked and her heart caught with sympathy. "I'm sorry."

"For what? Not falling into my arms and letting me sweep you off your feet?" He chuckled wryly. "Man, the rag sheets would have a field day with this. I can see the headline now. Hollywood Playboy Turned Down for the Second Time."

"Not true." Regan smiled and patted him on the shoulder as the handsome grin began to slip from his lips. "I've turned you down three times."

"My wounded heart."

"Try ego." She laughed. "Look, Trent, I have to get back to the shop."

"Yeah." He nodded, then gave her a big hug. "Say hello to your family for me."

"Will do," she said. He turned and walked out the office door, and as he turned the corner she started back toward the service bay. The past kept meeting the present, she thought. Hopefully this would be the last time. However, as soon as she had that thought, she dismissed it when another familiar face came through the door. Regan placed her free hand on her forehead and sighed aloud. "What is it?"

"Is that any way to greet your oldest brother? I thought Mom and Dad raised you better than that."

"Fine." She lowered her hand, then composed her face into a semblance of sisterly affection. "Hello, Marius. To what do I owe this pleasure of your company?"

"Forget that. What was Trent doing here and why are you holding flowers?"

"For an MBA graduate and CEO, you're not running on all eight cylinders today, are you, big brother? Isn't it a little obvious?"

"Don't even try it, Rebel. I know you're not getting involved with that guy again."

"And why not?"

"Because I know you better than that. You can take a

man like Trent and twist him around your finger so quickly that he'll lie down over motor oil and let you walk all over him."

Regan shook her head and for a moment longed for the simplicity of a car motor or the intricate planning that took place before a mission. Anything, it seemed, just to get away from the constant questioning and oversight of her brother. Yet instead of getting angry as she had done so many times in the past, Regan decided upon a new tact.

"You're right."

"What?"

"I said you are right." She raised her voice. "I am not getting involved with Trent. He just stopped by to say good-bye. Are you happy now?"

Marius's face relaxed and Regan watched as his lips curled into what could be identified as an honest smile. "Not yet," he replied.

She narrowed her eyes and the niggling sense that she had missed something popped up in the back of her mind. Careful not to be obvious, she examined her brother from head to toe, trying to pick up the visual clue her subconscious had found but her conscience had ignored. When her eyes paused on the envelope jutting out of his coat pocket, she grinned at Marius.

"It's not my birthday."

"I know that," he replied, pulling out the envelope. "I need a favor."

The smile dropped from her lips. "No."

"You don't know what I'm going to ask."

"Yes, I do," she retorted, taking a step away. "The only things that come in those envelopes are either money or invitations. As I said, it's not my birthday."

"I need you to help me host a corporate function tonight."

"Did you say tonight?"

"You've been around this place too long, little sis. I think your hearing is starting to go."

Regan cocked her head to the side and narrowed her

eyes. "Watch your step, big head. You're the one asking for the favors, remember?"

"It's just a dinner, some announcements, maybe a little dancing. You should be home by midnight."

"No, it means you'll be home by midnight, because you'll be too liquored up to drive."

"I'll take a cab."

"Whatever." Regan looked up toward the ceiling, then returned her gaze to Marius. At that exact moment, he hit her below the belt. Just as she opened her mouth to say no, she saw the special grin her brother had. The one that moved crooked across his mouth and wrinkled his nose. It was a smile she liked to think would only be reserved for her. Knowing that she was only fighting the inevitable, Regan still wouldn't make it easy. "What happened? Latest Atlanta socialite didn't pass etiquette inspection?"

"That wasn't called for."

"Well, you started it by trying to run my life again."

"Beats running away."

"Okay." Regan cut her hand through the air. "Let's call a truce."

"Agreed. You'll be at the hotel at five o'clock on Friday."

"I said truce, not surrender."

"Regan."

She cringed slightly at the way he said her name. Just like her grandfather. "It's time for you to pay your dues. We both know your government salary will never be enough to pay for your designer wardrobe, cars, house, philanthropic activities, and all the other things that you like to buy. It's time to earn a little of the interest you get from your trust fund."

Regan opened her mouth and then closed it. Without a word, she snatched the envelope from his hand, spun on her heel, and headed toward the locker room.

Chapter 13

Kincaid stepped out of the rental car and buttoned his suede coat against the damp breeze. For the third time since he'd woken at 5:00 a.m. to catch the first flight to Charleston, South Carolina, he hoped that he hadn't unwittingly set out on a wild-goose chase. He took a deep breath and filled his lungs with the tang of salt water. The ocean. A pang of regret and homesickness hit him square in the chest. He'd vowed not to miss anything about San Francisco, but nothing could have withstood the beauty of the ocean—infinite horizon of clear blue sky and amber-white waves.

Nothing except the thought of her. Kincaid closed his eyes and sighed. It had been less than forty-eight hours since he'd opened her car door and watched the taillights of her car disappear down his driveway. He'd gone back to his studio with the express purpose of concentrating on his art, yet he'd almost succeeded in smashing his work-in-progress to pieces.

What am I doing here? Running from thoughts of something, someone I can't have? Kincaid drew in a deep breath and remembered the way Regan had looked at him. Oh, he could have sex with her. He could have her between his sheets wrapped around his body, smooth and warm as the rarest of velvets. But in the end, he had to remember that she would leave. He'd been through that emotional hell with Kirsten. This time, however, no matter how much he avoided it, Regan's eventual departure would rob him of more than his sense of balance; it would take half his soul.

"Kincaid Sinclair?"

Unexpectedly, a feminine voice intruded upon his thoughts, and Kincaid's eyes opened.

"Yes?" He stepped from behind the driver's-side door and closed it. A tall slender woman with blond-streaked brown hair approached his car. The long black leather coat and monochrome colors, which would have looked normal in New York or Europe, stood out among the more color-oriented South.

"Beatrice Eaton," she announced while holding out her ungloved hand.

Kincaid gently took her hand within his own, only to be surprised by her solid grip. "Mr. Armitage recommended that I call you about the shipment," she said.

"It's very unusual for an importer to bypass the artist's guild and supply houses."

"Well, Mr. Armitage is unusual as well as very wealthy. He likes your work."

Without trying to be rude, Kincaid leaned against the car and stuck his hands in his pockets. Regardless of the innocent situation, something about Beatrice Eaton set off a warning bell in his gut. It took him a moment to pinpoint exactly what it was. Her accent. The mixture of upper-class New England and prep-school aristocracy accents in her voice reminded him of the years he spent in the Northeast.

As if he'd been thrown back in time, Kincaid stood next to the thick four-paned windows of his high school dorm. The snow pounded against the bare tree limbs as a lone body struggled to cross the open courtyard. No one had left the building that weekend and so classmates, friends, and mentors surrounded him. It had been his birthday and the day before a large box filled with paints, wood statuettes, pictures, and seashells had arrived with an Australian postmark. It had been the loneliest day of his life.

"Did I mention that I happen to favor your work as well, Mr. Sinclair?"

"No, you didn't, but please call me Kincaid."

Beatrice looked at him with a measure of curiosity in her hazel eyes. "Please call me Beatrice. The Ms. Eaton title belongs to my stepsister. This shouldn't take long. The shipping container is stored in a space just a few yards down the dock."

Kincaid looked down at the watch on his hand, then as if to make up for his earlier chilliness, smiled at the woman. "No rush on my part. The next flight back to Atlanta doesn't leave for hours yet."

"So it's true. The mysterious Kincaid Sinclair has become a Southern gentleman."

Kincaid shook his head. "Not exactly."

"I thought . . ." She paused. "No, I heard that you could be opening a gallery to show both your works and those of up-and-coming artists in Paris."

He shortened his stride and continued to look forward. As they walked, the dock seemed to come alive around them. Up until that moment, cranes that had sat still against the blue sky began to move. Narrowing his eyes, Kincaid could make out the orange vests of workers as they used hand signals to direct the crane operator. Forklifts started to slowly stream on and off the docked container ships.

Returning his gaze to Beatrice, he responded, "You are very well informed."

"I'm not an artist but I work in the arena. Plus, I love art."

"My business manager is opening the gallery in three weeks, as a matter of fact."

"You'll be there of course."

"That's the plan," he replied. Kincaid held in a grimace at the thought of leaving his home, and that brought him back to the motive behind his morning arrival in

Charleston. "You were rather vague about the shipment on the phone."

"It's fresh from a quarry in Greece. Not a large vein and what is left will go to a high-end tile designer in New York. Will Mrs. Sinclair be joining you for the opening?"

"It seems, Beatrice, that you know a lot about my work but not about my personal life, which is just the way I like it."

"I can understand. Growing up the only child of a movie star and an award-winning director doesn't lend itself to privacy."

Again, she caught him off guard. "You're right and the only Mrs. Sinclair now is my mother."

"Not for want of women trying, I'm sure. It would be quite a coup to be Kincaid Sinclair's muse."

Immediately Kincaid's thoughts flew to one such woman, and unknowingly his face softened.

"Gotcha." Beatrice beamed. "Who is she? A celebrity perhaps?"

Shaking his head, Kincaid thought about Regan. She was beautiful enough to blend with an appearance-obsessed Hollywood society, talented enough to do well in front of the camera, and confident enough to take center stage. But no, the woman who seemed to have made herself completely at home in his house and in his mind liked to race cars and travel from country to country without a thought of the family she left behind or her own personal safety.

"Not even close. She works for the government actually."

Beatrice stopped and pulled out a key ring. "Lucky woman. Will you be bringing her to your Paris opening? I only ask because Mr. Armitage is always curious about an artist's inspiration."

"I haven't thought about it. I'm not even sure she'll be in the country."

"Oh well, this is it."

Unsure of where the conversation was going and not willing to follow, Kincaid concentrated on helping Beatrice open the heavy warehouse door. Once they unlocked the large metal door and slid it back, he stepped onto the concrete flooring. Unmindful of his companion's movements, he peered into the darkness as the sound of Beatrice's footsteps echoed.

Only moments later fluorescent light lit the room and revealed row after row of multicolored steel and plastic shipping containers.

"All right, then." Beatrice returned to his side and he watched as she pulled a small device out of her purse.

"Locator?" he questioned, impressed.

"No. Palm Pilot. I never leave home without it. The trouble with paper is that I don't like to carry a purse and I never have enough room to list things. This small beauty, however, can take all the information I need and it doesn't take up too much space."

Several moments passed as she tapped on the digital device. "Now our target should be six rows left, five rows back, and placed on the first level to the right."

It took over five minutes for them to locate the right crate. Contrary to the coordinates listed in Beatrice's instructions, the crate sat farther toward the front of the warehouse. It took twenty minutes to open the shipping container, and ten minutes to identify and open the individual crate, but it only took one second for the sight of the contents to astound him. As Kincaid reached down and touched the rough-hewn piece, the images that flowed through his mind made his heart skip a beat.

"What do you think?"

Kincaid closed the top of the wooden crate, then turned around to face Beatrice. "How soon can all the containers be loaded and shipped to my studio?"

"Within forty-eight hours."

He turned back to look at the remaining boxes. "Are they all this good?"

She smiled. "I haven't opened them, but the supplier only sends quality."

"Can I get his name?"

"Sorry, that's confidential."

"And if I want more?"

"All I can promise is that if something comes along I'll give you a call."

"Sounds fair." Kincaid stepped out of the warehouse, swung the door closed, and locked it. "Now we need to talk price."

"Should I call your business manager?"

"Normally, Dana takes care of the financial details, but this is a special case."

"All right. Five hundred per case."

"Three hundred."

"You've seen the quality. I can get more by selling the marble as tile."

"Can you see something of that high quality lining a bathroom floor?"

She shrugged. "This is business."

"Need I remind you that you made that phone call? If this is a ploy to skim a little for yourself, I think that Mr. Armitage should be more careful of the people he hires."

Her jaw tightened and Kincaid could see that his point had hit home.

Beatrice looked down at the handheld device, then returned her gaze to his. "Four hundred and fifty. There were some hefty transportation costs involved here."

"Marble has a cost, but art?" Kincaid grinned before continuing. "Art appreciates even though its price cannot always be measured. Three fifty."

"Maybe I should talk to your business manager."

"I've got Dana's phone number in the rental car."

She snorted and then placed the Palm Pilot into her pocket. "Never mind. I'll call you later with payment instructions. You're a good businessman, Kincaid."

"Back at you, Beatrice."

"Now that we're done, how about grabbing some food?"

And a handshake sealed the bargain. Kincaid allowed the grin in his heart to reflect on his face. "My treat."

Chapter 14

First, when he left Los Angeles, and second, when he moved from San Francisco, one of the things that Kincaid strove to avoid was exactly the situation he would be stepping into at that moment. Dressed in his charcoal suit and tie, wearing obligatory leather Italian shoes, his hair sporting a fresh cut, all indications of his identity as an artist ended as he exchanged the keys of his newly detailed Ford Explorer for the valet parking ticket in his hand.

Looking up at the southern mansion turned corporate retreat, Kincaid rolled his shoulders and took his time going up the stairs. All the doubts receded as he joined the group strolling through the open double-door entrance. Just as he thought, Regan stood among the greeters, and the sight made digging through his closet earlier that afternoon worth it.

For a moment, the sound of murmuring voices receded and the piano keys faded as he focused on her. As he wondered about her. As his mind recalled all the stories his father had repeated about his walking down the sidewalk on a Sunday morning and seeing his mother for the first time.

Regan searched Kincaid's face before a smile curved her lips. "Fancy meeting you here."

"I was in the neighborhood and decided to stop by."

He watched as her eyes dropped to the bottom of his feet

and then leisurely strolled upward to pause on his face. "Dropped in . . . while looking devastatingly gorgeous in that suit?"

"Aren't coincidences amazing? I ran out of clean jeans."

"You're sporting a very handsome look tonight, Sinclair."

"And you seem to clean up just fine, Rebel."

"Thank you."

She smiled, then held out a hand. "Now back to the script. Good evening, may I have your invitation please?" Regan asked him.

Kincaid let a smile curve his lips upward before he could control it and he handed over two engraved invitations.

"Mr. Sinclair," she continued, "has your date not arrived yet?"

"Oh, she's here."

"Good."

"Regan, how long do we have to stand out here?" a soft voice, along with the scent of magnolia, wafted over his shoulder.

"Savannah, I'm greeting a guest."

Kincaid turned and smiled down at the woman who had come to stand at his side. Her soft cheeks and big brown eyes mimicked Regan's along with the annoyed look on her face.

"Guest?" he repeated. "For some reason I was under the impression that I was your date."

"Date?" Savannah's mouth transformed into a big O. "You didn't tell me you had a date."

Regan rubbed her brow before speaking. "Kincaid Sinclair, meet Savannah, my cousin."

"Pleasure."

"Why does his name sound so familiar?"

"He's an artist."

"No." Savannah gnawed her bottom lip. Suddenly, she snapped her fingers, and her features lit up with a bright smile. "You're the one who showed my nephews how to draw. They call you 'Mr. Pencils.'"

Kincaid nodded. "That would be me."

One minute, Regan's eyes twinkled with amusement. The next, Kincaid's own brow creased with concern as the smile on her berry-frosted lips disappeared and her gaze locked on something over his shoulder. Following his first instinct, Kincaid twisted his neck around and followed Regan's stare toward a well-dressed brown-haired gentleman exiting a silver BMW.

"Damn," Regan muttered so low that Kincaid almost missed it. He hadn't known Regan long, but in the small amount of time, he'd never heard a profane word leave her mouth.

She turned her cousin toward the entryway and urged her to go inside the hotel. "Hey, can you go check in with the caterer for me please? I was supposed to talk to Claude, but I forgot."

"But—" Savannah started.

"Thanks a bunch," Regan interrupted. "I'll be back there in a minute."

"Who is he?" Kincaid kept his voice low as he whispered the question into Regan's ear.

"Jack Archer."

It took a moment for the significance of the man's identity to sink in. It seemed tonight he would meet Savannah's Jack. In coming to know Regan, he had become very familiar with the Blackfox clan. His having come from a small close-knit family, the vastness of uncles, aunts, cousins, nieces and nephews, brothers, and sisters filled him with a sense of awe. And all or most of these family members would be in attendance at the anniversary celebration.

His train of thought came to an abrupt stop at the slight pinch on his arm. He returned his attention to the woman at his side. "I can't leave the door for at least another half an hour. So it looks like I might need your help to prevent a crime tonight, Kincaid."

"Always ready to help a lady. So how long will you be on guard duty?"

"Until Jack Archer is safely in the front seat of his car and five miles away from this place."

"I can stay out here with you."

"No. Please go inside and stay close to Savannah. She's going to need more support than I am."

"And what am I going to get out of all this, Ms. Blackfox?"

"My eternal gratitude?"

Kincaid fought to keep a grin from turning the corners of his lips upward and instead aimed a meaningful stare at the increasingly agitated Blackfox brothers.

"Not enough?" Regan guessed.

"Not by a long shot."

"So what's your price, Sinclair? And keep in mind I'm a government employee."

"Who happens to be one of the richest under-thirty-year-old women in Georgia, by absentee default?"

"That's not my money."

He gave her a pointed look.

"Technically it's my trust fund, but I don't really touch it." She blinked and shook her head. "Kincaid, why are we arguing?"

He took a step closer to Regan and placed a hand on the curve of her waist to draw her closer still. "Can you dance?"

She blinked twice and then focused all of her attention on him, which was just as he planned in an effort to distract her regarding Jack and to take the attention off the approaching family rival and focus it onto themselves.

"Can I dance?" she repeated.

He felt himself become aroused at the little hint of southern belle drawl in her voice.

"Mr. Sinclair. You do ask the silliest questions."

"Now that's not a good answer."

"Regan, is this man harassing you?" An unfamiliar voice interrupted their conversation. Kincaid slowly turned his attention toward the man who'd come an inch away from his face. Not recognizing the individual but having met the two people close behind him, Kincaid took only mere seconds to realize that this must be Caleb, the doctor. The middle Blackfox son. Not one but all three of the Blackfox brothers had abandoned their posts.

"No, you overprotective ogres. Kincaid, please excuse my brothers here for being so rude." Regan frowned a little, angry as always that her brothers' territorial nature still had the power to annoy her. She aimed a glare at Trey in particular because he'd already met Kincaid, yet now stood glaring daggers at her date. "You've met Trey. Here are my other brothers, Marius and Caleb."

Not by a hint did Kincaid betray that he had in fact met two of the three men.

He reached out a hand and waited as all three shook it. One thing he noticed was that none of them apologized. Not that he could blame them. Being overprotective was a brother's duty. Until their sister had a husband. When that time came and if that time came he would be more than a match for the Blackfox men and he would protect Regan from all harm, including if need be her own family.

"I'm afraid the introductions will have to wait for later." Marius took control of the situation as his attention turned toward the entrance gateway. "We've got work to do."

"Yes, Grandfather." Regan reached up and playfully saluted her older brother.

Her expression was all seriousness when she turned back toward him. "What was that all about?"

"Have you noticed that Jack Archer got inside the building without a scratch?" He smiled and looked down as her lovely brown eyes widened and went from him toward the last location they'd spied Jack.

"You're good."

"I aim to be great." He grinned and took a step closer to her. "So how about an answer to my earlier question?"

"Can I dance?"

"That would be the one."

Her smile broadened and she waved him inside. "You'll have to wait and see, Mr. Sinclair."

"I'm going to kill him."

Kincaid glanced to his left and looked down on the top of Savannah's array of curls. Soft jazz whirled in the background and handsomely dressed men and women milled around the room.

"Does Jack know that he's been marked for death?" Kincaid asked, amused by the way Savannah nervously tapped her foot ahead of the beat.

She drew in a deep breath as her eyes darted around the room, only to land on him. "Oh Lord, did I say that out loud?"

"Yes, you did."

"Regan told you."

Kincaid nodded. Although they'd just met, he liked Savannah. Regan's cousin had an air of spunkiness and vulnerability about her that made him feel like an older brother. "In the strictest confidence. She also asked me to stick close to you just in case."

"Just in case I committed murder, huh? I asked him not to come, but here he is." She took a drink from her glass and set it down. "Men, why can't you ever listen?"

"We listen. The issue is that we don't always obey."

Savannah rubbed a hand across her brow. "That would be, you never obey. I don't care if he had an invitation, the rules are that the Archers and the Blackfoxes don't mix at social events . . . ever."

"And I thought that the South had desegregated years ago."

"This doesn't have anything to do with race. The last time our families showed up at a charity en masse, the men nearly tore the place apart in a brawl, not to mention that Mama had to go and bail everybody out of jail."

"It doesn't look like anything's going to happen."

Savannah turned her head to stare at Jack as he stood next to the bar. "That's because my cousins haven't drunk enough bourbon yet and neither of my brothers has gotten here yet. Just wait."

Kincaid picked up a bottle of German beer from the tray of a passing waiter. "If you keep staring at the man, someone is bound to notice sooner or later."

"I can't help it," she cursed. "Part of me wants to walk over there, kiss him, and say to hell with what my family thinks."

"And what is your other half telling you to do?"

Savannah gulped down the rest of her soda, then gasped. "Run."

"Well, you had better make up your mind soon, because unless I'm mistaken, Jack is moving in this direction."

"Oh no. Oh no."

She turned to move away, and Kincaid grasped her arm lightly. "Every Blackfox in the room will notice, Savannah. If you leave, it will only invite further speculation."

"You're right."

"Chin up," Kincaid encouraged as he caught sight of the panicked expression on Savannah's face. Just as he took his arm from her shoulder, he caught the movement of someone's approach from the corner of his eye. Before he could turn, Jack Archer came to a stop in front of them.

"Good evening." Although Jack had addressed both Kincaid and Savannah, Jack's eyes never left the woman's face. "You look wonderful tonight."

"Thank you," she whispered, and for the first time that night a smile quivered on her lips.

Several seconds passed before Kincaid loudly cleared his throat. "Good evening."

"Sorry," Jack replied, then took a step back. "Didn't mean to be rude. I think I know about half the people in this room, but I don't think we've met yet." He held his hand out. "I'm Jack Archer."

"Kincaid Sinclair."

"The artist. It's great to finally meet you."

"You know my work?"

"No. I'm more into computers than art. Even in elementary school, I preferred math class to art class." Jack waved his hand and laughed.

Always a firm believer in first impressions, Kincaid decided then and there that he liked Jack Archer.

"So how do you know about me?" Kincaid inquired.

"My mother is a member of the Arts Council. She mentioned that you're going to be a new member."

"Kincaid, wouldn't you like a drink?" Savannah blurted out.

He looked down at the half-full bottle in his hand, then back to Savannah's pleading gaze. "Well—

Jack interrupted. "So how do you know Savannah? She and I went to school together."

"He's Regan's date. Now will you go away before my brothers get here?" Savannah hissed.

At that moment, Kincaid looked over Jack's shoulder and toward the entrance to the ballroom. "Would your brother happen to be six feet five and built like a linebacker?"

Her eyes grew round. "Oh no."

Kincaid observed another man, older but very similar. "And he's not alone. I think your father just arrived, too."

"Damn it, Savannah, we shouldn't run and hide."

"This is none of my business, but I don't think now is the time for you to make a scene, especially when you're outnumbered."

Jack looked Kincaid in the eyes, and the angry expression on the other man's face didn't faze him one bit. "You're right," he said slowly, "this is none of your business."

"Jack Archer," Savannah scolded. "You promised me that I could have as much time as I needed to tell my family about us. Are you going back on your word?"

"No, but—"

Savannah cut him off. "There are no buts to this. I'm

going to introduce Kincaid to my parents, and you are going to stay away from me."

She lifted her chin, and Kincaid fought back a grin at the familiar expression that he'd seen on Regan's face before.

"And, Jack?" Savannah continued grabbing hold of Kincaid's arm and pulling him away. "Don't bother to wait up . . . I'm sleeping at my place tonight."

"Ready for that dance?"

Instantly forgetting about the long list of things that she needed to check on with the caterer, Regan turned toward the sound of Kincaid's voice. A smile blossomed on her lips, even as she fought back a yawn.

"Maybe," she replied coyly, looking away.

A long, clever hand reached out and tugged her hand away from her side, guiding it to his shoulder as he stepped smoothly against her. She looked up at him, her other hand clutching automatically at his waist. Lips parting. Feeling his free arm slide easily around her back. Fitting her against him as if she belonged there in his arms.

Regan rested her head against Kincaid's shoulder and closed her eyes. For a few moments, she indulged in the spicy sent of his cologne, the warm presence of his body against hers, and the smooth sounds of music. Yet, try as she might, her mind returned to the potentially explosive presence of Jack Archer.

"Stop," Kincaid commanded softly in her ear.

Regan opened her eyes and drew back slightly to look up. "What?"

"I can feel you tensing back up."

"Is that why your fingers are playing along my spine?" The pleasant sensation stopped and Regan could have bitten her own tongue. Instead, she lifted her head and whispered, "Please don't stop."

"The lady's wish is my command."

"Then I wish you could get me out of here before the clock strikes midnight and disaster falls down upon our heads."

"Why so pessimistic? Your brothers are behaving themselves and Savannah seems to be in good hands."

Regan shook her head. "I don't know, it's just a feeling I have. By the way, did I thank you?"

"For?"

"Helping Savannah. I didn't get to see it, but I heard that you averted an incident."

"I was glad to help. So why don't you ignore that 'bad feeling' for a while? At least while you're in my arms. Deal?"

She pulled back and looked into his eyes as her body remained in close contact with his, and Regan began to appreciate the lean strength of him. All grace and sleek muscle under the stiff cotton shirt and wool trousers. Thighs hard against her own.

"Are you sure you're not a southern boy, Kincaid Sinclair?"

"Well, one of my grandfathers took his first breath in an Alabama cotton field, and the other spent a few years brewing moonshine in the Tennessee hills. Does that count?"

"I believe it does."

"Now, what's got your shoulders so tense besides a member of your family's archenemy sipping martinis in the corner?"

"Ms. Blackfox." A high-pitched young voice interrupted their conversation.

Regan sighed heavily and let go of Kincaid. When she turned around, one of the young hotel attendants stood chewing on a pen. "Yes?"

"They need you at the front."

Regan turned back to Kincaid and smiled softly. "Forgive me?"

He brought her hand to his mouth and kissed the back. "As long as you come back and finish this dance."

Steadying her nerves from the pulse of heat that crossed her skin from the touch of his lips, Regan crossed the ballroom floor, then took the stairs in the direction of the hotel lobby. Impulsively she stopped and retrieved a glass of white wine. Two sips and she was ready to go. As her high-heeled pumps echoed over the marble floor, she couldn't help but notice that the area was empty of people. Just as that thought crossed her mind, the hair on the back of her neck gave Regan a ten-second warning and the reason for her unease stepped from behind the lobby desk dressed in a hotel attendant's uniform.

"Looking good in that dress, Nichols."

"Morgan," Regan said slowly after coming to a stop a foot away from the desk. He might have dyed his brown hair black and grown a mustache but she'd recognize that face anywhere. "Didn't we discuss the 'no dropping in unannounced' rule?"

"You might have mentioned it. Maybe I forgot."

Regan's fingers curled into tiny fists. Her boss had a photographic memory. He didn't forget; Morgan had deliberately baited her.

"So have you fallen on hard times, or is this your second job, Morgan?" she asked sarcastically.

He seemingly ignored the comment and scanned the lobby entrance. "Nice hotel you've got here. What's it cost to rent out the banquet room, hire bartenders, waiters, and give out hundred-dollar gift baskets? Maybe thirty or forty thousand? Must be nice having been born with a titanium spoon."

Regan let the mockery of a smile slip from her lips. Skipping past the pleasantries, she took a step forward and placed the half-empty glass on the stained wood counter. "Whatever it is you want, the answer is no."

"Meet me at Stone Mountain National Park, two o'clock tomorrow."

"No."

"Hi, Rebel, I thought you might need some help. Everything okay?"

Regan slipped on her mask and pasted a smile on her

face before turning her back on Morgan. Now she blessed her lucky stars for the days of diplomatic training, which allowed her to appear calm, while her insides twisted into knots at her superior's presence.

"Did you think I might sneak out?"

"The idea did cross my mind, but you don't seem to be the type to run from a challenge."

Kincaid's words took the air out of her stomach. Not because of their truth, but because of the irony in the statement. Morgan had used that component of her personality when he'd picked her for the team.

"That's me. While some people run from fire I run toward it," she replied flippantly.

"How about I take you home?"

"Thank you, but I'll be here for a while. I need to make sure all the cleanup arrangements have been made."

"Well, how about another dance?"

"You're on."

As Kincaid placed his arm around her waist, Regan spared a covert glance back at the lobby desk, in time to see Morgan disappear into the back. Resentment flared in her heart at the control he had over her life.

Tomorrow at two o'clock. She looked at the man at her side, memorizing his face. It was time to say good-bye.

Chapter 15

The next morning with gloved hand holding tight to a lead rope, Kincaid led Night Dancer out of the stable and paused in the gate of the round exercise circle. The sun had only risen two hours before, but he'd woken up at dawn with the specific purpose of exercising the horses and fixing a part of the outer fence before the weather turned bad. After a few days of blustery winds and intermittent rain, the forty-degree temperature and sunshine seemed to be a blessing. His eyes first went to the bank of gray clouds over the horizon, and as they lowered, a flash of light off metal caught his attention. As he put up his gloved hand to shield his gaze from the sun's glare, his eyes went from the new Mercedes parked in his driveway to the man emerging from the shadow of his front porch.

"Who . . ." His brow creased. He didn't have visitors. Even in San Francisco, his colleagues and friends were well aware that they could not show up on his doorstep without warning. He knew that Regan had an appointment in Atlanta, and his brow creased. As the person walked closer, his surprise increased upon recognizing Jack Archer.

"Morning," the other man called out.

"Cold out," Kincaid responded after nodding.

Jack slowed his approach and took one step to the left

as if to stay within Night Dancer's field of vision. As he neared the horse, Jack held his hand out to the mare's nose. It didn't take Kincaid long to see that the man knew how to handle a horse.

"Mustang?"

Kincaid nodded, then watched the other man lift up the mare's lips and examine her teeth. Jack took a step back. "About four years old?"

"And I thought Regan was good."

"What's her name?" Jack asked as he reached up to rub the center of her forehead.

"Night Dancer," Kincaid answered while keeping a calming hand on the horse's neck.

A moment passed before Jack broke the silence. "I grew up with horses. Mind if I lunge her?"

Without a moment's hesitation, Kincaid handed him the lead rope and took a step back. "I have to warn you. She's full of energy, so hold on tight."

"Let me guess." Jack paused to run his hands over the horse's full haunches. "You've been feeding her alfalfa hay."

"Nope." Kincaid shook his head with slight bemusement. On the inside, he was impressed with Jack's knowledge of horse nutrition. While Alfalfa provided horses with an excellent source of protein, the grasses also gave them a lot of energy. "Weather's been cold and I've been distracted, so she hasn't been out of her stall in a few days."

"Thanks for the warning," Jack grinned. "So you don't just let them graze?"

"Not until the temperature rises. They haven't adjusted to this weather yet." The puzzled expression on Jack's face prompted him to add, "I brought them from Colorado."

"Original stock." Jack whistled and then looked back at the mare. "Are you going to breed her?"

"Haven't thought it out. Heck, I'm still new to this horse thing."

"My uncle's looking to get a horse for his grandkid."

Kincaid stepped back to lean against the padlock. He

stuck his hands in his pockets and watched as Jack led Night Dancer into the fenced-in circle. Under most circumstances when he'd brought the mare into the round pen, he'd have to raise his arms and yell to get her moving. This time, however, the minute Jack slackened the rope, Night Dancer set out into a trot. Kincaid rubbed his chin and allowed a grin to curve his lips upward. Cartersville, Georgia, just kept getting more and more interesting, and at that moment, although Jack Archer didn't know it, he'd just gained a friend.

Sometime later, after they had finished exercising, grooming, and feeding the two horses, Kincaid closed the door to the barn and took a deep pull of the bitter cold air. Although the sun had risen hours ago, his breath clouded the air while his ears stung with the cold wind. For the past thirty minutes, Jack Archer had culled every tangle and brushed the last speck of dust from the mare. The horse's coat had never looked better. And during that space of time, they'd talked about nothing but horses. And Kincaid left none the wiser as to the reason behind Jack's visit.

Without looking directly at Jack, Kincaid inclined his head toward the house. "I don't have much food in the fridge, but at least let me get you a cup of coffee."

"Appreciate it."

"So you didn't just come all the way out here to lunge horses, did you?"

"Wanted to apologize for last night. I took my frustration out on you and that was wrong." The southern drawl in Jack's voice increased. "You kept me from stirring up the mother of all hornets' nests."

Kincaid inclined his head toward the den and as he exited the kitchen commented, "The males of that family don't like you very much."

"For the past year I thought that Savannah was exaggerating. Regan wasn't that hostile."

"Regan seems to be the exception to many rules."

They both sat down on the couch. "I see that now," Jack said.

"So which is it, were you crazy or desperate?"

"Both. I love her like crazy and I thought by forcing the issue that maybe, just maybe she'd just go ahead and tell her parents."

"Didn't work?"

"Nope." Jack took a pull of the coffee. "Just the opposite. She won't talk to me. Went to her place before coming over and she wouldn't open the door."

"Guess she's a little upset."

Jack grinned ruefully. "She's pissed and I'm at the end of my rope. Most women I know would be jumping for joy at the thought of a ring and getting married."

Kincaid thought back to his brief engagement to Kirsten. The look of happiness on her face when he'd given her the diamond ring would remain etched in his memory only because of the beauty of her smile that night. At the same time, that moment of waiting for her answer had lasted an eternity, yet it had only taken him seconds to open the ring box and read her letter. "How many women do you know?"

Jack paused. "Including my mother, sister, and female cousins?"

"Sure."

"About nine, give or take some of the other system engineers in the Dalton office."

Kincaid shook his head and fought back the urge to laugh at the earnest expression on Jack's face. "And how similar are they to one another?"

Jack rubbed his chin. "Not very."

"That's my point. Women are all different."

"Including Regan?"

Kincaid inclined his head and grinned. "Especially Regan. Here's a secret my father taught me. Never try to understand politics or women."

"Sounds like a smart man."

"Yeah."

Jack stood, placed his empty cup in the kitchen sink, and then returned to his seat. "Thanks for the coffee."

"Welcome."

Kincaid waited a few moments before speaking again. "So you want to talk about Savannah?"

A look of frustration came over Jack's face, and Kincaid laughed before continuing, "Thought not."

"You want to talk about Regan?"

Kincaid shook his head. "No."

"Well, I noticed a section of fencing needed work."

"Cloud uses that spot as a scratching post. His backside ought to be rubbed clean of hair by now."

"Got an extra hammer?"

"Are you volunteering?"

"Guess I am. Beats going home to an empty house or an 'I told you so' message from my parents."

"I thought you were into computers."

Jack shrugged and stood up from the couch. "What can I say? Guess I was named right."

"Yeah." Kincaid laughed as he made the connection. "You seem to be a jack-of-all-trades."

Chapter 16

"I need you to go to France."

Regan looked over at the casually dressed man who'd taken a seat next to her on the empty sky lift, which at any moment would bear them to the top of Stone Mountain. Morgan's piercing green eyes regarded her in the shocked silence. Instead of arriving at the meeting point in her Corvette, she'd driven Trey's Beetle and arrived later than expected. Regan kept her expression neutral as she looked down at her newspaper and then glanced around.

Apparently, the attraction saw few visitors in autumn. As a crisp draft snuck through the open cable car doors, Regan fought the urge to huddle into the warmth of her goose-down jacket. Her eyes stopped on the four teenagers waiting to enter the vehicle. The uniformed attendant stood in front of the rope and called out, "We apologize for the delay, but this car will be going out of service. The next departure for the top of Stone Mountain will leave in five minutes."

As soon as the attendant said those words, the double doors slid closed. Deliberately not responding to his previous statement, Regan coolly asked her boss, "Why are we meeting here?"

He shrugged. "I've never been here before and I thought

I should at least check out some of the sights before I fly back to Maryland."

Morgan had a sick sense of humor in his choice of a meeting point. No matter what he said, they both knew he would never be an ordinary tourist clamboring to get a better view of the Confederate Memorial carving. Annoyance played havoc with her normal cool detachment. She'd lied to Kincaid when she said she would be in Atlanta to visit an old high school friend. And unlike all the evasions and deceit she'd practiced since joining the NSA, the act of dishonesty to such an honest man whom she'd come to care for didn't set well with Regan. Soon after that thought came the unsettling realization Morgan was back in control and he could potentially order her to any place in the world at less than a moment's notice.

She angled her head toward him and planted a polite smile on her face while the muscles in the back of her neck stiffened. "Repeat what you said a moment ago."

"I need you to go to France. Paris to be exact."

Regan made a conscious effort to slow her breathing. In the space of a few heartbeats, she mentally went through all the preparations necessary for her departure. It wouldn't take her long to pack two suitcases of clothes, return her cars to the main garage, and write notes to her family. The cleaning staff would take care of the cottage. "All right. Have my orders and papers delivered to me tonight and I'll leave in the morning."

"No. I need you there as Regan Blackfox, not Dominique Nichols."

Her fingers tensed for a moment and she forced herself to relax as dread trickled into her stomach. "Why?"

"The military's still all over your file. The use of that identity will set off flags the minute you show your passport."

"Then get me another identity."

"I can't do that right now."

Her eyes narrowed. "What kind of game are you playing, Morgan?"

"The one that can cost me my career if it gets out that I'm using you against the express orders of my boss."

"Why me?" Because she was watching for any sign of what exactly was going on, Regan saw Morgan don his poker face.

"I can't tell you that, but it's essential that Regan Black-fox and not Dominique Nicholas complete this assignment."

Her eyes narrowed slightly, and then she reached down to clutch the edge of the bench as the lift lurched out of the bay. Sunlight filled the space, giving Regan no choice but to narrow her eyes against the glare. "When and where?"

"Three weeks. The target will be at the opening of Kincaid Sinclair's gallery. After that you'll have four days to get him out of Paris."

Regan inhaled her breath sharply, but the mechanical whirring of the rotating wheels atop the lift covered the sound. It took every ounce of discipline she had not to go at her boss with accusations. Instead, she loosened her jaw and focused on the issue at hand. "Who is it?"

"I can't tell you."

"I know the target, don't I?" Regan surmised. The blank expression on her superior's face all but confirmed her suspicion. "I don't like this."

"Look. I don't know anything but the fact that this person needs to get a new identity and we need him to disappear."

"Who is it?" she repeated as the lift slowed to a stop in the middle of the trip between the ground station and the top of Stone Mountain.

"The brass is playing this close to the vest and no one can get near him. My best guess is that he's some political liability they need stashed away."

Her mind locked on the small but telling word, *he*. At least now she had a gender. "And you expect me to do it?"

"Along with a little help. You'll need to take this."

She took the case from his hand, turned, and placed it on the adjacent bench. When she released the suitcase locks, her entire body went completely still. The array of weapons inside could have helped neutralize a small army. Regan pursed her lips and let out a soft whistle. "There are other just as capable agents stationed in Europe. I ask you again, why me?"

Morgan rubbed his brow, then raked his fingers through his hair. Regan's bottom lip almost dropped to the floor. She'd never seen her boss openly express his frustration. "All right, Regan. In a nutshell, you're the only person I can trust to get him out."

"If you're giving me this much weaponry. . . ." Her voice trailed off. She'd gotten targets out of the country without breaking a fingernail or a sweat, but most of her assignments hadn't been that easy. It looked as though this mission wouldn't be a walk in the park. As the cable car rose farther and farther from the ground, the speed decreased. Regan had taken the same trip many times as a child and realized that the slowing of the ascent was a deliberate tactic to give them optimal time to talk.

"Yeah, it's dangerous."

"Does the target want to come, Morgan, or is this force?"

"All I know is that he's protected."

"You know I don't want my identity to be compromised."

"I won't order you to do this. I'm just asking a favor."

"A large favor. For me to disregard you having me watched, to use a civilian, and to lie."

"You've lied before."

Anger crackled in her voice as every muscle in her body tensed. "Not to friends and never to family."

Mason leaned back against the window and sighed. "On second thought, maybe I shouldn't assign this to you."

Regan blinked twice at her boss's abrupt about-face.

Then she narrowed her eyes on his unsmiling face. He knew better than to try some amateur reverse psychology to gain her cooperation. "And maybe you should clarify that statement."

He released a loud sigh. "If you can't keep your personal feelings about Kincaid Sinclair from interfering with the mission, then maybe this isn't a good idea for you to go to Paris."

Regan's harsh laughter echoed in the empty cable car. "I don't believe this. Where do you get off? You were on assignment when you met Grace."

"That's different."

"Please, spare me the 'I'm a man who can separate his emotions' crap." The sarcasm in her voice could have cut through steel. "Remember, I was there when you thought Grace had been killed."

Morgan met her stare, and the intense green eyes held a suspicious twinkle of mirth. "Look, will you do it or not?"

"You wouldn't have asked if you weren't sure I'd take the mission," she pointed out through halfway clenched teeth. If she let it, the life of lies and deceit could get to her. It had taken her too long to get to the point where she could separate her professional duties from her personal feelings. This mission could bring down that house of cards, and they both knew it.

Mason sat back and crossed his legs at the knee. "There's always the chance."

She eyed him closely. "How do you know Kincaid will invite me to the gallery opening?"

Morgan shrugged. "Because he's a smart man and you're a beautiful and charming woman."

"Don't give me that."

"Let's just say I have it on good authority that he's not planning on attending his own gallery-opening party alone."

"You tapped his phone." Her cool tone hid the underlying accusation.

"My mother would adopt you if you could get Juliet

Sinclair's autograph. His parents will be at the opening, by the way."

"Morgan, stay away from Kincaid," she warned in a quiet voice. "I'll leave the agency before I let you hurt him." Never in the course of her career at the NSA had Regan thought of leaving. But they both knew that she would do it. That she would leave behind the danger and excitement.

"Opposites attract and all that," Morgan commented offhandedly. "But he doesn't seem to be your type, Nichols. Sinclair's profile suggests that he's more of a homebody."

Regan clenched her teeth to keep from saying something she was 100 percent sure she'd regret later. Instead, she took a deep cleansing breath and stated calmly, "When this is over, we're going to sit down and have a long discussion."

"Just bring him back in one piece."

Regan turned her attention back to the weapons as the sky lift began to move forward again. She looked down at the weapons. One high-powered stun gun, modified pistol, laser-sighted rifle, low-level explosives, and a mixture of bullets and darts. An envelope containing credit cards and Euros. As the cable car approached the docking bay, she closed and locked the briefcase placing it on the floor.

"Are you coming out?" he asked.

She waved a dismissive hand. "I've seen it all before."

Morgan nodded before pushing off the bench and standing. "Suit yourself."

She continued to sit as her boss moved toward the doors. "One more thing, Regan."

She gave him a sideways glance. "Yes?"

"Wear white to the gallery opening and try to keep this quiet as possible. The French are still pissed off with us about that Algerian cleric we grabbed under their noses a few months ago."

Chapter 17

The trickling sounds of a piano covered the sound of his entrance into the main house's car garage unit. He slipped his hands from his gloves and flexed his fingers in the dry heat of the room. First, his gaze landed on a new-model Jaguar, then trailed over a late-model Thunderbird parked next to a Mercedes.

Finally, after lingering over a four-door Cadillac, his eyes landed on the pleasurable sight of Regan's blue-jean-encased derriere. The well-formed curves lifted Kincaid's already high spirits. He watched as she turned to the side, and he caught a glimpse of her intent expression as she examined the engine, her white teeth gnawing her bottom lip, and a sense of unexpected lust sprang to life.

When she'd invited him over for lunch and a matinee movie, he'd jumped at the chance to spend time with her. In his old life in San Francisco, nothing short of an earthquake could have pulled him from his studio in the middle of the day, but now that he'd moved to Georgia, it had become easier for him to separate his life from his art.

"I stopped by the cottage and got your note off the door." Kincaid leaned up against the door while Regan turned around, then took a step toward him before pulling a rag out of her pocket and wiping her hands. "Since the movie doesn't start until later on this afternoon, I thought we'd get some work done."

Kincaid aimed a glance over her shoulder toward the antique Chevy truck. Her request that he come over in the middle of the week had been a welcome surprise. He couldn't place the model or the year, but he'd seen enough old movies to know that the vehicle had probably rolled out of the automotive plant about the same time his own grandfather came of age.

"New car?" The grin on his lips inched upward two notches.

"My-my, aren't we the comedian today?" Her lips curved into a smile. "This is a 1948 Ford F5. In its heyday, this baby could haul over a ton of carpet stock. I'm working on the truck for my father. It's my grandfather's birthday gift."

"Looks good for its age."

"It should." Regan patted the oversized grille. "Daddy had it loaded on the back of one of the trucks and delivered it personally to one of the best body restorers in the Southeast."

As if to defy the very bounds of logic, Kincaid's blood warmed. An artist's eye always remained fixed on beauty and aesthetics. Yet, standing under a stream of pinkish gold from the setting sun, dressed in worn overalls, a backward Atlanta Braves cap, with smudges on her fingers and her face, Regan Blackfox's smile would remain fixed in his memory as a perfection rivaling Leonardo da Vinci's Mona Lisa.

Kincaid drew a deep breath and took three steps forward, coming to stand inches from Regan. The scent of her perfume gently edged out the metallic smell of the truck's open engine. "Fixing cars is a lot like painting."

"The creative process at work, huh?" Her teasing smile matched his own.

"No, more like you get interesting stains of color all over you."

"Not very flattering, huh?"

"On other women, maybe not. You, Regan Blackfox, are an exception to many rules."

"I can say the same about you, Kincaid."

Kincaid moved to stand beside her as she pulled out the drawer on a large red tool cart. "I noticed your truck outside. Is the Corvette in the garage again?"

"Nope, loaned it to Trey again."

Regan shook her head while her fingers ran over the various silver sockets to settle on one, and then attached it to the wrench in her right hand. "My brother wants to impress a visiting colleague, so he borrowed it."

"That's pretty trusting of you."

"Believe me when I say that trust has nothing to do with it. Trey knows to bring it back with the gas tank full of high-octane, the wheels shiny, and the paint gleaming to perfection. Plus a pair of personal passes to the Atlanta Zoo."

"Planning a trip?"

"Ouch!" Regan yelped as the rough edge of an old wrench caught her finger and drew blood.

"Let me see." Kincaid took her hand and cradled it within his own.

Both sets of eyes watched as the blood welled up and trickled over her skin. Regan tried to stick her finger in her mouth, but Kincaid held her hand still.

"Where's your first-aid kit?"

She gave him a curious look. "It's just a scratch."

"That can get infected."

"It's just a minor scrape."

"Humor me, Rebel."

She turned her head and aimed a glance toward the first-aid kit hanging on the far wall. "Are you always this cautious?" she questioned toward his back.

"No."

"Is it because I'm lucky or because I'm a woman?" she asked after he returned with an antiseptic pad and a Band-Aid.

"Both," he replied.

Regan wanted to say more but found herself distracted by the deep brown of his eyes. That was until the pain hit. "Ouch." Her hand automatically jerked back.

Unmindful of her glare, Kincaid meticulously cleaned her wound, then wrapped the Band-Aid around her finger. "Have you had a tetanus shot recently?"

"Two years ago."

"Good."

Regan wiggled her finger experimentally. Looking from the Band-Aid to Kincaid, she gifted him with a smile. "Thank you."

"You're welcome."

For several moments, they stood facing each other. And into that space grew something warm and sweet. An invitation to bury her head in his shoulder, to feel his arms wrap around her. In the deepest part of her heart, which remained untouched by her life as an NSA agent and an independent woman, beat a rhythm that just wanted to be helped, longed to be taken care of.

She dropped her head and then returned her attention back to the conversation they were having before her minor accident. "I've got some time off and I thought I might convince a certain artist to spend a day with wild animals."

"You don't have to ask twice. Just name a date and time."

Kincaid caught the teasing glint in her eyes and it hit him again, how much he liked her sense of humor. How much he appreciated her ability to make him smile. "What makes you so sure I meant to ask you?"

"This." He moved and, before she could laugh, cradled her face in his hands and brushed his lips across hers. Kincaid took his sweet time, exploring the corners of her mouth, tasting the strawberry of her lip gloss, before availing himself of the temptation to deepen the kiss. When he pulled away, the sight of her passion-dark eyes, the satisfaction of being the source curved his lips into a pleased grin.

Regan took in a deep breath. "Hmm, I should have had you as an assistant a long time ago."

"Something tells me we wouldn't have gotten too much work done." For a moment, they just continued to stare at one another. Until the sound of the central heating unit clicked on and broke the spell.

She moved to pick up her forgotten tool. "Yes, we would."

"I have to be honest, I'm not mechanically inclined. I drive a car until there's a problem. Then I take it into the experts."

"You should have thought of that before telling Trey that you were my student. Now, let's get started."

"Yes, ma'am."

"Funny. Could you hand me the angled pliers over there?"

He raised his eyebrows.

"It's the length of your hand, has jaws and a red handle."

"Ahh, I see it."

He took his place by her side and blinked at the sound of her humming. "You really get into this, don't you?"

"I'm happy doing something. It's that sense of accomplishment, just like your art."

With half her body still bent down into the massive jigsaw puzzle of the truck's parts, she asked. "Do you miss San Francisco? We have an art community, but I'm sorry to say it's pretty loose-knit and tiny."

"I miss the water, the architecture, and the easy access to my gallery, but I don't miss the competitive atmosphere. I don't judge or do comparisons."

"What about your family?"

"My parents' main residence is in Santa Maria, a valley just north of Santa Barbara, but Mom and Dad are heavy travelers and visit less than three months out of a year. I expect they'll drop in to check up on me some time soon. Speaking of parents, yours seem to be suspiciously absent."

"No suspicion about it. My father was a borderline workaholic, so Mom built a clause to the wedding vows. Every anniversary, they spend two months with my grandparents at the house in Bermuda."

"You seem pretty cheerful about it."

"I am. Don't get me wrong, I love my parents, but we have opposing viewpoints as to how I should live my life."

She turned to take aim at him. "Now bring that sexy body closer and hold this gasket while I slide under."

"Sexy, huh?"

"Don't pretend, Sinclair. I'm still amazed some California socialite didn't follow you here."

"I covered my tracks well." He laughed while following Regan's progress as she pushed herself under the truck and half of her disappeared.

"You sure?"

"Positive. The field is wide open for that perfect southern lady to steal my heart."

"Move it a little to the left . . . good. Now press down."

He felt the tension of the engine part Regan tightened into place.

Moments later Regan reemerged and stood up. Kincaid turned and leaned back against the truck's grille.

"Southern lady." Her teasing eyes mesmerized him. "Guess that rules me out."

"How so?"

"I lost my lady certificate the day I decided chassis were more interesting than makeup."

"You're going to make this hard, aren't you?"

"Extremely."

He twisted her cap back and grinned down into her laughing eyes. "It's good that I like challenges." And he stole another kiss.

Chapter 18

Without opening her eyes, Regan reached out and blindly hit the Snooze button on her alarm. Snuggling back down into the blanket and pillow, she tried to hold on to the wonderful images of her unconscious mind. For the first point in time since Ambassador Richards' rescue, she didn't dream about Javier Merona's face as his cheeks went slack and his eyes turned glassy with the slow dripping of blood, or wake up shuddering from the image of the guards she'd killed.

No, she'd had a dream about the sweetness of a first kiss and the tender arousal brought about by a man's fingers running up and down the gentle valley of her back. Regan wrapped her arms around the pillow and inhaled sharply as her body hummed with desire.

Kincaid

Her sleep-blurred eyes opened slightly as a smile played at the corners of her mouth. The man in her dreams wasn't a fantasy; he walked, talked, laughed, sculpted, and kissed. The ringing of the doorbell abruptly cut off her pleasant train of thought. Regan looked over at the digital readout on the clock, and two things simultaneously occurred: a polite Belgian curse slipped from her lips and she got out of bed.

Who would be dropping by her place at seven o'clock

on a Saturday morning? She slipped on her house shoes, then pulled on her velvet robe and tied it. Her slippered feet moved soundlessly over the Berber carpet. Regan rubbed her arms to ward off the morning chill as she left her bedroom and headed downstairs. Long used to living in countries without the luxury of central air, she never bothered to set the temperature control.

The closer she got to the door, the more her heart began to race. It occurred to her that there had been many instances in the past when a change in mission orders was delivered by human means versus electronic means. Her boss could have changed his mind about sending her on the Paris mission.

But when Regan peered through the peephole to see Kincaid's impatient frown, her heart slowed and excitement tinged with relief spread through her body. But soon on the heels of her happiness came the realization that sooner or later, she would have to leave him. If it had anything to do with her, it would be later, she vowed. Regan reached up to finger-comb her sleep-tousled hair before turning the dead bolt and pulling back the door.

Before she could say good morning, or invite him inside, an oversized yawn brought tears to her eyes and made her ears pop.

"Good morning, sleepyhead," he said once he stopped laughing. She wiped back the wetness from her eyes and tried to frown at his amusement at her expense. Her lips, on the other hand, had a mind of their own and twitched upward. "Good morning," she responded, her voice slightly husky with sleep.

"Forget to set your alarm?"

This time Regan did frown as her mind was distracted from taking in the sight of Kincaid's nicely rugged good looks. Why would she set her alarm on a Saturday? Then her eyes caught a tiny movement over Kincaid's shoulder and focused on the horse trailer hitched to the back of his truck.

"We're supposed to go riding today, aren't we?"

"That's right and this beautiful morning is being wasted. So why don't you shower, get dressed, and pack a bag while I make some coffee?"

She yawned again and like a robot made her way back into the great room. Regan stopped on the first stair as her brain shifted into first gear. Secret agents needed sleep too, she thought resentfully, then pushed the annoyance aside and recalled her southern manners. "Make yourself at home."

"Not a morning person, are you?"

It wouldn't take a rocket scientist to figure that out, nor would a crime scene investigator need to be called to put together the who, what, when, and where to the cause of Kincaid's death. However, the why would be difficult. Who would think that someone could kill a person simply because he had the audacity to be among the small percentage of cheerful morning people?

Regan shoved her hands in the robe's oversized pockets and glared at Kincaid, but he ruined her sarcastic response by leisurely looking up and down her body, then grinning. And that grin had the force of a hundred whispered flirtations. Her cheeks grew warm as her skin prickled.

"Okay if I fix us some breakfast?"

Sleep cleared from her eyes and with her vantage point of being on the first step, she was eye to eye with Kincaid. The sight alone coupled with the remnant of her dreams would wreak havoc on any woman's self-control. Not to mention that the idea of a sexy man serving up a fresh cup of coffee and food almost had her jumping into his arms and kissing him despite her morning breath.

Some of her thoughts must have shown on her face, for Kincaid's grin widened. Blinking twice, Regan nodded numbly and then turned to go back up to her bedroom.

"I'll take that as a yes," he called out.

Not bothering to respond, she kept going and the warm tendrils of his laughter followed her down the hall.

* * *

Dressed in her black leather-riding boots, sheepskin gloves, heavyweight denim pants, and a soft lamb's wool sweater with a jacket, Regan lifted her face to the breeze and tasted the crisp air. The overhead sunlight made the sight of Kincaid's profile even more handsome.

"Ready?" he asked.

She stood alongside the mare and waited for him to finish adjusting the saddle and stirrups. "Is there anything I should know about Night Dancer before I get on her back?"

He stood up and she met his stare from across the saddle. Then she watched, as if it were in slow motion, as his lips curled upward in a grin and his eyes narrowed. Right then and there, all unused muscles in her chest tightened, and if she hadn't been paying so much attention to the melting sensation his look had caused, Regan would have sworn she was having a heart attack. The sight of his laughing eyes lifted her spirits even further.

"Just like all women, she can be feisty, until you show her a firm hand."

She breathed as his comment broke the spell and she registered the slight against her sex. Deciding against giving him a piece of her mind and starting the ride off on a contentious note, Regan looked skyward and pretended to ignore his slight chuckle.

Half an hour later, Regan let Night Dancer choose her own destination over the field toward the woods. The horse's steps never faltered as they made their way up and around the small mountain. Sunlight sparkled through the tall pine trees as Regan relaxed into the horse's rhythm. Apparently, though Kincaid's Cloud was lacking certain parts, Night Dancer was still going to follow her male.

Her grip on the reins tightened slightly as Kincaid dropped to a slow trot beside her. "You ride like you've been born to the saddle."

"There's a trick to it." Her lips curled upward. "You move with the animal. Follow its rhythm."

"I'm surprised that you follow anything or anyone, Rebel."

She grinned wickedly. "I'd follow you to the shores of Antarctica for the chocolate in your pack. And you're not that bad of a rider yourself."

"My mother had to ride a horse for a historical documentary. She thought it would be a good idea to spend some quality time with me."

"You don't seem so sure."

"We both kept getting dropped on the ground. My father always talks about the fact that Mom and I had matching bruises. But that horse trainer they hired was a tough woman. She never gave up on us."

They broke out of the forest canopy and entered into a grassy knoll. She snuck a lingering glance at his profile, then turned her attention back toward navigating the small grassy incline. So easy, her gloved fingers tightened on the leather reins. So easy to fall into the rhythm of being with the man; day by day, falling in love with him. Just as soon as the word entered her vocabulary, Regan pushed it away. Love was for people like her grandparents, parents, aunts, and uncles. Love meant years of sacrifice and commitment. She had only met Kincaid and had no thoughts of settling down any time in the next few years.

"Wayne Holt," Regan said after a little while. "He was the first man I ever fell in love with. He rode broncos and tamed stallions. My grandfather hired him to teach all of us how to ride."

"Did the object of your affection reciprocate?" Kincaid loosened his grip on the reins as the horse protested the mishandling of his bit. Jealously reached its rough tendrils and grabbed a spot in his gut and started ripping. He'd grown up sharing his parents with the world. As an artist, he put his heart into every piece of his work; that creative expression went on display for the public and his critics. However, a primitive part of him didn't want to share Regan's past or present affection with anyone.

She laughed loudly and the musical sound enveloped him with warmth. He wanted to keep the sound to himself, too.

"Wayne was old enough to have been an original cowboy, had four ex-wives, was devoted to riding, beer, his Chevy pickup truck, and smuggled Cuban cigars."

Kincaid led the horse down the makeshift path, not far from one of the area lakes, just north of Canton, a place where he'd spent time as a child watching them film his mother. Looking out, she could see nothing but the cones on the trees and the splashes of sunlight through the branches, hear nothing but the crunch of the underbrush underneath the horses' hooves.

And as the forest passed by, they reminisced, laughed, and shared. Rabbits broke from the underbrush, squirrels froze on the sides of trees, and the sun climbed steadily in the sky. When the trail widened, Kincaid stayed beside Regan, and when it narrowed he took the lead but steadily looked back. All the while, a small voice warned him of a promise he'd made to himself about not allowing her into his heart.

Later that afternoon after unsaddling the horses and tethering them about twenty feet from their makeshift campsite, Regan laid down a blanket as Kincaid prepared a circle to build a fire. He crouched down to place the small dry sticks in a pyramid configuration.

"I would love to do this more often." Regan smiled.

"Horseback ride?"

"That and being with you on a beautiful day."

"I only get the beautiful days, huh?" Kincaid questioned. "Rainy or overcast days are excluded."

She sat down close to him. "No, I think I'd enjoy being with you under any circumstances."

"You can spend all your time with me. Especially if you stay here." He didn't turn but instead struck a match and started the campfire.

"I like my job, Kincaid."

"But do you like the lifestyle your job requires you to keep?"

"Sweet potato," Regan blurted out. The subject of her career brought up thoughts of her job, her mission. The clock continued to tick and Kincaid had yet to mention his upcoming trip to Paris, much less invite her to accompany him.

"What?" He paused from putting down the dry leaves around the small flames.

"Any time we asked Nana, my grandmother, about something she didn't want to talk about, she'd distract us with the promise of sweet potato pie. The summer I asked where babies came from and could I order a little sister, Nanna hustled all four of us into the kitchen and we all baked our own pies."

Kincaid laughed before striking a match and lighting the fire. "You can bake?"

"As we say in Georgia, I can burn and decipher a wine menu. My father married my mother for two reasons. He loves her and she got him addicted to her stuffed pork chops. Lucky for me, I learned my way around the kitchen before I decided to rebel. What about you?"

Kincaid took off his gloves and warmed his hands with the growing fire. "Why don't you hand over the picnic basket?"

Her brows rose and he wanted to kiss the quizzical expression on her face. After Regan placed the large wicker basket between them, Kincaid shifted to his knees and began to take out container after container.

"You made all this?" Regan asked after arranging the paper plates and silverware and pouring the warm apple cider.

His eyes shifted from the feast spread out in front of them to her wide eyes and he shifted his shoulders as though a devil hopped up and down on the right and an angel stood calmly on his left.

"Impressed?" he asked, stalling.

Regan dipped a cracker into the smoked salmon pâté, then took a bite. "Very."

"I'm glad, but I didn't make it. I ordered it from a new gourmet shop in town."

"So you can't cook?"

"Let's just say I won't be winning any awards, or getting my own cooking show on cable television. I try to concentrate on doing what I do best, and that's sculpting, sketching, or painting."

"Good point. I'm very pleased you're so honest. All of my brothers know how to cook, but they never tell the women in their lives because they always want to be cooked for."

Kincaid finished off a small sandwich and took a drink of cider. He almost wished he'd added some alcohol to the beverage. A little Dutch courage never hurt. Shifting to the left, he placed another piece of wood on the fire before turning his attention back to Regan. Things always had a way of coming out, and the last thing he wanted was for her to find out about his meeting with her older brother from someone else.

"Speaking of your brothers."

"Must we?" A bundle of sparks arched from the fire as she tossed in a dry twig.

"Marius didn't just invite me to the dinner party, Rebel. He offered me a quarter of a million dollars to do two sculptures for the local park."

"And?"

"He asked me to keep you home." His brow lowered as he studied her face. Her expression gave nothing away; not even her eyes gave him a clue as to what she was thinking. For a split second, a prickle of unease ran over his skin. It felt as though he were looking at a stranger. "You're not surprised?"

Regan shook her head from side to side. "Sadly no. Marius is a chip off Grandfather's block. My grandfather called in enough favors to get my State Department offer rescinded. Only Nana's intervention kept him from going through with it."

"He must love you a great deal and want to keep you safe." Kincaid watched her hands as they curled into small fists in her lap.

"I know and I understand what drives both of them. It's not just love. It's the need to control, and the constant fear of losing someone. If something were to happen to any of the Blackfox wives or daughters, my grandfather would blame himself and so would all the other men in the family. And that's the only reason I'm not furious right now."

"I'm going to create the sculptures for the park, but the money will go to a nature preservation foundation."

"That's good."

He pushed away all the things between them and pulled Regan into his arms so that they were both staring into the fire. "The thing is, I didn't need to hear his offer and in a way I'm just as guilty as your brother. I want you to stay here for my own selfish reasons."

"And what are those?" Her tone took on a seductive warmth.

"I'd rather show you than tell you."

She halfway turned around in his lap and cradled his face between her palms. "No one's around." She smiled, then brought his lips close to hers. Regan's tongue traced the corners of his lips and then delved inside, seeking his. Kincaid pulled her close for a moment and closed his eyes while basking in the feel of her hands on his chest and her tongue leisurely exploring the inside of his mouth.

When Kincaid broke the kiss a few seconds later, it took him a few moments to get his breathing under control. He wanted her. Wanted to take her right there in the middle of the woods on the plastic tarp. But he hadn't come prepared and when they did make love, not *if* they made love, he wanted everything to be perfect. The surroundings, the mood, the moment. He imagined Regan warm and soft in his bed, her skin touching his as the firelight flickered in the room.

Kincaid cleared his throat. "It would be better to show you back at the house."

Her lips quirked as she shifted in his lap. "Really?"

Kincaid bit back a groan at the delicious feeling of the friction of her behind on his ever-hardening erection. Although he was long used to riding on the back of a horse, the thought of taking a trip back in his aroused state was as effective as jumping in an ice-cold lake. He removed his hands from around her waist. "Oh yeah."

She leaned forward off his lap and began to gather up the Tupperware, plates, and utensils, then stopped and looked at him over her shoulder.

"Hey."

It took Kincaid more than a few moments to drag his eyes from the tempting sight of her rear end and focus on her face.

"The faster we get this cleaned up, the sooner we can get back to your place," she prompted.

Kincaid caught her well-intended look and stood up. Together they cleared the evidence of the picnic, put out the fire, and mounted the horses.

They raced back to the truck like two fierce competitors in a death match, each taking the lead, and in the end Cloud led by a nose. He knew he would pay for it later, but the sheer enjoyment of seeing Regan bent over the saddle laughing as they weaved between the trees and then went from a gallop into a flat-out run once in sight of the horse trailer set his heart to pounding with both exhilaration and anticipation.

The sun had just begun to dip below the mountains as they led the horses down the small ramp and into Kincaid's barn. Smells of hay, leather, earth, and horse filled the room. She took her time and thoroughly brushed her mare once Kincaid finished checking her hooves.

Out of the corner of her eye, she caught a movement and she watched as two hefty barn cats, both all black but for white racing stripes over their hind legs, sauntered across the floor. "You have cats."

"More like long-term tenants," he responded. "They moved in soon after I built this place, and since the horses seem to like them, I added cat food to the supply deliveries. I call them David and Goliath, but they don't answer to any call except dinner."

"They look adorable." Regan smiled. She gave the mare's side a gentle pat and was rewarded with a soft whicker she could have sworn was the horse equivalent of a thank-you. Walking past the stall where Kincaid worked on his animal, she put the brush back in the supply room, then returned to lean against the railing next to the occupied stall.

She watched mesmerized at the play of muscles in his shoulders as he vigorously brushed the horse. "So the artist has a soft spot for strays," Regan teased.

No matter how many new things she discovered about him, the countless times she'd gazed upon his face and seen some new aspect of his features, one truth would always rest in both her heart and mind: Kincaid Sinclair was a truly remarkable man. "Your soft underbelly is showing."

He straightened, rubbed the roan on his haunch, then left the stall and closed the door. Wordlessly, her eyes followed the confident stride of his progress to and from the supply room. When he at last came back to where she stood, Regan's heart clamored in her chest.

"Soft underbelly, huh?" He grinned and pulled her into the circle of his arms. Before that moment, there had been a slight chill in the air, but as her blood coursed through her veins, she placed her cheek against the soft suede of his jacket. He smelled of wood smoke, horse, and pine. Happy childhood memories resurfaced, adding an extra glow to the moment.

In the lens of her heart, she watched the scene and recorded the slow uptilt of her face, the building rush of his lips lowering atop hers. His mouth closed over hers and she opened her lips.

An unconscious moan worked its way up from her throat and echoed in the silence of the barn. When he released her mouth, time moved again and all the sounds that had previously vanished due to the pounding of her heart rushed into her ears. She returned her cheek to his shoulder and listened to the thudding of his heart.

Unexpectedly something rubbed against her legs. Regan opened her eyes and looked downward at one of the cats. The oversized feline walked like a runway model on the catwalk wearing its shaggy thick fur like an original Versace gown. Regan giggled as he started at her ankles— working with his whole body. He rubbed, nudged, and eased with back and flank and cheek and chin against her jeans, all the while purring like a well-tuned diesel engine. "Bold thing, isn't it?"

Kincaid followed her gaze and laughter rumbled in his chest. "Rebel, I think you've collected another admirer," he said, his voice a husky rasp.

And he couldn't blame the animal for staring, since the woman in his arms had the same effect on him. Each time he touched her, each time they kissed, laughed, or made contact, he wanted more. He had never had a one-night stand, never had casual sex because his respect for women and devotion to his own moral code precluded sharing his bed with any woman who hadn't engaged his emotions as well as his physical interest. Not for the first time had he found a woman he wanted to keep. Only in this instance, his heart sank as he knew ahead of time that she would leave.

Chapter 19

An hour later after he'd locked up the barn, taken a shower, and changed clothes, Kincaid examined his face in the bathroom mirror. "You can do this, Kincaid," he told his reflection.

Once they'd finished with the horses and returned to the house, he hadn't needed to but he'd led Regan upstairs to the guest room down the hall from his. He'd carried her small duffel bag and placed it on the bed. Made sure fresh towels were in the bathroom closet, then for all intents and purposes ran out of the room.

Kincaid took a deep breath before exiting his bedroom. He quietly slipped into the guest room and noticed that her bag still sat unopened on the bed. He told himself that he was just checking on her. But that was far from the truth. He really wanted to catch a glimpse of her.

Pausing next to the door of the adjacent bathroom, he listened for a moment and the splashes of water interspersed with Regan's humming made everything in his lower body grow heavy and tight.

Taking a deep breath, Kincaid knocked on the door.

"Come in."

He opened the door wide enough to stick his head in. In the soft light, he had little difficulty making out her form in the large bathtub. "I came to see if you needed any assistance."

Her soft laughter echoed through the steam-filled bathroom. Kincaid inhaled as a wave of longing pierced his gut. "My body's seemed to have forgotten the aftereffects of four hours on a horse. Would you mind washing my back?"

Kincaid hesitated for a moment before taking a step forward and closing the door behind him. Natural sunlight diffused through the room from the frosted cube windows. Solid chunks of handmade soap contrasted with a collection of old bottles as they sat perfectly placed on glass shelves. "Would you like me to turn on the lights?"

"No. This is perfect. I love this bathroom. Your designer did a wonderful job."

"I appreciate the praise." He grinned.

Regan glanced over her shoulder and a surprised smile spread across her face, making her look like both a seductress and an innocent cherub as her hands covered an obvious characteristic of her femininity. He dragged his eyes away and instead looked down at the floor and concentrated on rebuilding his self-control as his pulse throbbed to keep up with the beating of his heart.

"You designed this room?"

"And purchased everything in it. Except, of course, for those neatly stacked clothes over there. I believe they belong to you."

"Very impressive, Kincaid."

He rolled up his sleeves while approaching the bathtub, and a bead of sweat trickled down his brow. Luckily, Regan had already turned from him and couldn't see the desire plain on his face. When Kincaid kneeled down behind her, she went still and he took the sponge from her hand and dipped it into the warm water. Then he reached out and beside her, picked up a bottle of lavender-scented shower gel, squeezed a small amount onto the sponge, and rubbed it into a fine lather. The rich floral scent perfumed the room and made him painfully aware of the droplets of water on her skin, the moist-heat-filled air, and the glow of the fading sun.

"Are you sure you're comfortable with this?" Regan asked.

"With what?"

"Washing my back?"

Instead of answering, he began to wash her shoulder, using enough pressure to send the warm soapy water running down her skin in bubbly rivulets. Overly aware of the softness of her skin, he applied just enough force to massage her muscles as well as clean. When the sponge ran dry, he dipped it into the water and began his ritual again.

"You're . . . very good at this," she said after a moment. Kincaid hadn't missed the slight quiver in Regan's voice.

"It's genetic. Dad would read me a story while Mom took a bath. She couldn't tolerate showers. If we were in the Los Angeles house, she'd call out over the intercom for my father and he'd mumble something about to be continued, then disappear into the bathroom."

Her head fell forward, inviting him to explore the curve of her throat.

"Are you falling asleep on me?" Kincaid asked.

"No, quite the opposite. I've never been more . . . awake," she responded, letting out a throaty purr.

He dipped the sponge into the water for the last rinse of her back. And when he finished, Kincaid put the sponge to the side and gave in to the temptation that had gnawed at his stomach from the moment he'd opened the bathroom door. He reached out his hand and ran his fingers from the nape of her neck, over the curve of her shoulders, then down her spine. Regan's harsh intake of breath made him rock-hard. The more he thought about making love to Regan, the better he liked it.

Silence reigned for a moment, until Regan pulled away and turned to face him. "I guess it's good that I brought a change of clothes."

She dropped her hands, and the sight of her fully erect nipples robbed him of speech.

"I'll need them in the morning," she continued, smiling languidly and raising her brown eyes to meet his. "I'm finished with my bath now, Kincaid." Regan curled her fingers around the sides of the tub and stood up. Water ran down her stomach, over her legs, and he barely managed to smother a curse as she reached for the bath towel on the stand next to the tub. The room, which already felt like a sauna, got even hotter.

"You don't have to look away."

"Regan, are you trying to seduce me?" he asked, but he already knew the answer. They both knew the answer. Each had spent the latter part of the past month trying to seduce the other.

"That depends. If I were, would I be succeeding?"

"Beyond your wildest dreams."

Her face wore a confident expression. "Then the answer to your question is yes."

"You have a very competitive streak."

"Does that bother you?"

In answer to that question, he leaned in closer, wrapped the towel around her body, and nipped her on the neck with his teeth. The reward of her shallow breaths gave him a spurt of satisfaction.

"So, you wash and dry." Her voice hummed with amusement.

"And you somehow manage to keep your sense of humor when I'm a hairbreadth from taking you right here on the marble floor."

He wrapped her in the towel as soon as she stepped out of the tub and onto the thick cotton bath mat. But just as quick, he turned her around so that her back was to him. For some reason he thought it would be easier that way. They would make love, no doubt about that. But he wanted to take his sweet time and make sure her pleasure met or exceeded his own.

Standing behind Regan, he looked downward, his eyes following the trail of droplets of water from her shoulders down to the swell of her breasts until it was absorbed in the ivory towel. Her bath-warmed skin glowed underneath the fading natural light.

He took the towel and gently ran it from her shoulders down, patting away the moist droplets, only to pause at the slight swell of her hips.

His pupils dilated and he let the towel fall away from her body as the fingers of his right hand traced the insignia he'd discovered on her skin.

"It's the Chinese symbol for protector."

His eyes moved away and he looked upward to lock with Regan's brown eyes. "Why?"

"I was out on the town partying with a group of Japanese diplomatic counterparts. They believed women were the softer of the sexes and I wanted to prove them wrong. When they took us to an esteemed skin artist, I went as well."

"You picked the symbol?" Kincaid rose upwards.

"No. The man who drew the tattoo believed that the Chinese character chooses its owner, not the other way around. By the time he finished, I really didn't care."

"I bet it hurt."

She nodded. "A lot."

Kincaid reached and took the oversized clip from her hair and ran his fingers through the damp strands, delighting in its softness. He removed his hands and wrapped them around her waist, pulling her even closer, burying his face in the neck and inhaling the fragrance of her skin. His strong fingers slipped over the curve of her breasts and the softness of her stomach with leisurely enjoyment.

Then as he reopened his eyes and watched one last droplet of water give way to the lure of gravity, he gave in to the sweet allure of his body's hunger; he turned her around, lowered his lips to hers, and feasted.

Their shadows moved across the wall. She needed nothing. Just the feel of him, the smell of his skin, and the pleasure of his mouth against hers. She couldn't resist the pull and didn't try. Regan closed her eyes as he gently licked his way down her neck.

He was good at making her want him. So good she locked her knees to keep from sliding to the floor. Arcs of pleasure trembled over her skin at the sensation of his lips on her skin, the heat of his tongue, the gentle scrape of his teeth on the crescent of her breast while his fingers roamed her backside. To keep her balance, her fingers clung to the fabric of his shirt. The hard evidence of his arousal pressed against her stomach. "Do you know what you do to me?"

"No, tell me," he whispered, and eyes as mysterious and dark as obsidian bored into hers.

"You make me weak in my knees, Sinclair."

"Afraid you might fall?" his roughened voice taunted.

The double meaning in his question returned a little bit of sense to her passion-filled mind. "I know you'll catch me."

He looked up and their gazes locked. Her breath caught as his fingers explored her inner thigh and inch by inch crept upward. Her hips arched against the palm of his hand as he touched her secret spot, tested, and found her more than ready.

"You're wet, Regan."

She reached out and drew his hands upward toward her, molding her body into the cotton of his shirt, and the softness of his pants felt wonderful on her sensitive skin. "I need your clothes off and your hands on, Kincaid."

"Bossy, aren't you?" The grin in his voice came through loud and clear. He seemingly ignored her request, bent down, and without her permission rewrapped the bath towel around her body. "I started a fire."

Her fingers toyed with the collar of his polo shirt. "I know."

"In the master bedroom and you can join me, or the guest room is fully prepared."

She surveyed him from head to toe, taking in the wet

patches on his shirt and pants. Her eyes lingered on the concrete evidence of his arousal. In Kincaid Sinclair, she'd found a friend, an artist, and a gentleman. Her heart shuddered with an unidentifiable emotion that overwhelmed every survival instinct even as she was so wonderfully close to getting what she wanted. Him, his smiles, his lips, his hands, and his body touching her, the way his presence had haunted her since the first evening they'd met. "I said once that the only way I would sleep in your house would be in your bed."

"Yes, you did."

Willing her heart to slow its furious pace, Regan placed her arms around his neck. "I was wrong."

"This has to be a first."

The firm lips she alternatively wanted to savor and taste like fine wine and greedily drink as though she were at a pool in a desert. Pulling his face down until it was less than an inch from her own, she whispered, "I want to be in your bed, and the last thing we will do in it is sleep, Kincaid. I want us to finish this and then start all over again."

Not giving him a chance to response, she went to her tiptoes and kissed him, took his mouth, and sucked on his tongue. Regan wanted there to be no mistakes in communication, and as such put all her erotic dreams and fantasies into one deep kiss.

While their mouths met and their tongues danced, her hands explored, running over every inch of skin she could touch. She touched his maleness, savored the naked strength of his arousal while the knowledge that she pleased him as much as he pleased her increased her pleasure.

He moved his hand and gently cupped her breast, pulling his head away from her long enough to look up and catch her gaze; then he slowly guided the cocoa-tinted nipple into his mouth. The sensation of his teeth skimmed her skin at the same moment his fingers delved into her center, sending her body arching toward him as a harsh moan escaped her mouth.

Everything stopped as the first of many climaxes rocked through her body and her entire being focused on Kincaid. Focused on the magic of his hands and lips. Yet, as her shudders began to subside, the pleasure didn't stop and just kept building as his lips moved from her nipples to the sensitive curve of her neck, down the valley of her breasts, and then lower still. As he prepared to administer the most intimate of kisses, her fingers gripped his shoulder. "Kincaid."

"Hmm?"

"I don't think I can take much more of this."

"I have a lot more to give, beautiful."

"Tonight, tomorrow, next week, but not now. Finish this. . . ."

He drew away and moved to pick up another lotion. "Stand still."

"Kincaid. . . ." Her voice trailed off and ended abruptly as her eyes fastened on his hands. In particular, the way he poured the contents of the bottle into his palm and then rubbed them together.

Every thought left her head at his touch. For what seemed like an eternity, Kincaid massaged her with scented oil; he smoothly rubbed every inch of her skin, and squeezed every muscle as though he would sculpt her body like wet clay.

But all of it didn't end when he placed the plastic bottle aside. No, Kincaid kissed the hollow of her breasts tenderly, and his tongue gingerly caressed the tips, drawing them into his mouth and nipping them with his teeth. Regan's fingers locked onto his shoulders as her knees threatened to buckle. And when he finished imparting equal treatment to her nipples, every nerve in her body quivering with an ache so strong it closed her throat and made speech difficult, Regan opened her eyes and moaned. "I need you inside me . . . please."

That sentence had to be the best he'd ever heard in his life. And he spared no time in wrapping Regan in the towel and leading her from the bathroom to his bedroom. And just as he had imagined a thousand times since he'd first seen her, he laid her on his bed and never took his eyes off her while he took off his clothes.

Somehow, Regan ended up watching from the tangle of sheets as Kincaid rolled across the bed and dug into the nightstand. The rational part of her mind appreciated the sight of his hard, firm backside while most of her succumbed to out-and-out lust. Moments later after he had covered himself with a condom, her skin jumped with anticipation. Yet instead of pulling her into his arms, he hesitated.

"Kincaid, now is not the time to hold back."

"I want this to be perfect for you."

Her response was to pull him closer for a kiss, and before he knew it, Regan had wrapped her legs around his and pulled him close. "I don't want perfect. I want you."

He complied by pushing himself up with one hand and using the other to guide himself so that he slid inside in one smooth, shallow thrust. The gentleness of his entrance, the care, and the concern with giving her pleasure caused in her a cascade of tenderness. Regan wrapped her arms around his shoulders and her legs around his hips. The heady feel of his mouth on her breast caused her to close her eyes as the intense and sudden rush of desire made her light-headed.

As they moved together, she released all her thoughts, instead concentrating on the friction of him sliding out of her, then back in. Kincaid made a soft, strangled sound, his fingers squeezing her rear, and she gasped and opened her eyes at the hypnotic grinding of her hips against his.

She trembled violently, crying out with an almost painful ecstasy. Then, seconds later, he released her legs, sinking back against her as they joined, arms wrapping around each other as he hid his face against her shoulder, a long, trembling groan escaping his lips. He went over and pulled her with him.

"So sweet . . ." was all Regan had strength to say as her climax hit and she tightened around him.

Much later, after they'd made love for a second time, silence crept back into the room. A breath of cold wind rattling against the window and the hiss of the gas fire were the only sounds in the room beside the soft, slowing pants of their breath. Regan lifted a hand and gently touched Kincaid's skin, stroking it with her fingers as he tightened his arms around her waist.

Naked and entwined in his arms, Regan closed her eyes even as her mind worked to make sense of what had just occurred. She wondered if she should say something, but changed her mind. Words meant very little without actions. And the wonderful sense of peace that infused her body would prompt her mouth to make promises she couldn't keep.

"Rebel?"

"Yes."

"Are you okay?"

Her lips curled into a smile and she placed a soft kiss on his shoulder. "Very."

"One thing . . ." He paused. And in the pregnant moment, Regan fought the urge to tense as she imagined what he could say.

"After tonight, you can drive any time you like."

Regan closed her eyes as a giggle formed in her throat, then progressed to an outright laugh. "Thanks," she said and reveled in the way Kincaid hugged her closer. As the possible consequences of her actions began to knock on the door to her consciousness, Regan pushed them away. Yet, she could not keep out one voice.

There is always a price to pay, her alter ego, Dominique Nichols, whispered. Regan snuggled closer into Kincaid's chest and used the sensation of his skin to drive away everything else. Tomorrow she would think. Now she'd just delay the inevitable.

Chapter 20

Regan woke with the smell of coffee on her tongue and the heat of a sunbeam on her cheek. In the seconds between sleep and wakefulness, Regan with closed eyes relived the past twenty-four hours. The smell of pine and horses, the moist warmth of Kincaid's mouth, the taste of his skin, the sound of water and harsh breathing. The things he'd done to her body, the intimacy they'd shared.

It had been a long time since she'd touched and been touched in that manner, and as the analytical side of her brain attempted to place concrete terms to last night's events, the other side reveled in the delicate soreness between her thighs. But the words in her mind didn't match the sound in her ears. "You don't have to pretend to be asleep."

The voice almost compelled her to smile, but Regan fought against the temptation as her ears focused on a scratching noise. It took her mind a moment to recognize the characteristics of a pencil's rapid movement over paper.

Without opening her eyes, Regan turned her face toward the location Kincaid's voice had come from and finally allowed a drowsy grin to curl her lips upward. "Who's pretending?" she asked. Her voice had the deep husky tone only achieved after having a good rest.

"Not your stomach, it's on track to protest again in ten minutes."

Regan opened one eye and glared at him. "Not funny, Sinclair."

"I'm only telling the truth."

She stared as his hand remained poised over the large sketching pad, then followed the curve of his muscular arm to linger on his beautiful chest. Her eyes moved farther downward and she swallowed her disappointment at the sight of a pair of green cotton boxers. Yet all the hunger in her stomach disappeared as it gave rise to a different sort of craving.

"Sugar," Regan drawled, letting her appreciation of his physique reflect in her eyes. "I'm not thinking about food right now."

He chuckled, then placed the pad on the nightstand. When he moved to sit on the bed, Regan rose up to sit beside him as she unconsciously responded to the man her body had recognized as her mate.

"I had this dream last night," he said.

"Go on."

"Something about a beautiful woman, fast cars, and bubbles."

"Sounds like a very nice dream."

"You bet it was. But man cannot live on the stuff of love and dreams alone." Kincaid put his arm around her shoulder.

Regan leaned into his side and placed her cheek on his shoulder while her finger skimmed a figure eight over his bare chest. "We could try for a little while."

"You'd rather stay in bed than sample the breakfast I have for you downstairs?"

"Breakfast?" Her hand, which had up until that moment been leisurely making its way down south toward Kincaid's boxers, stopped halfway between his heart and his belly button.

"Pancakes, bacon, eggs, coffee, and . . ."

"And?" Regan prompted.

"Strawberries."

"Strawberries in winter?" Doubt filled her voice even as her stomach let out a vocal indication of its unhappy emptiness. "Are you trying to trick me?"

He leaned in close and placed a soft kiss on the base of her throat as she put her arms around his neck to draw him closer. His kiss tasted of peppermint, and like a child's, her tongue darted inside his mouth and savored the flavor. But minutes later, she let out a small groan of frustration as he pulled back and playfully nipped her bottom lip. "Never."

He gave her a quick kiss on her brow before moving off the bed. "Now how about you throw on one of my shirts and meet me downstairs?"

Regan threatened to move out from under the covers. "I could just come as I am."

"Rebel, you wouldn't make it past the bedroom door before I had you back in the bed."

"Would that be a horrible thing?"

Kincaid paused from putting on his pants and then turned around. The serious expression on his face caused her a moment's regret about teasing him.

"It would."

"Why?"

He took a step closer to the edge of the bed, and Regan felt a momentary sense of panic. They'd made love three times last night, and however unlikely, each time was more pleasurable than the one before. And into that potent mixture of sex, desire, and affection, her heart had entertained the notion of love. The very same emotion she briefly glimpsed while looking into Kincaid's unguarded eyes.

"Regan, can you spend the day with me?" he asked.

She silently let out the breath she hadn't realized she'd been holding. "Can I flip the pancakes?" She pushed the covers back and proudly sat half nude but for the blanket bunched at her waist. Although the temperature in the room bordered on hot from the gas fireplace and the central heating, her nipples stood erect. Kincaid's eyes went from her face to her bare breasts, and Regan's heart caught at the wolfish grin on his face. Kincaid wasn't unaffected by her presence, not by a long shot.

"Maybe if you hurry. But if not. . . ." His voice trailed off.

"I'll be downstairs in two shakes."

"I placed your overnight bag in the master closet. Your toothbrush is right alongside mine, and I'd be more than happy to take you home to pick up more clothes."

She stopped in midreach for Kincaid's shirt and raised one eyebrow. He was taking a lot for granted and they both knew it. As far as he knew, she would leave Georgia within a week or a month. But the fact was that she wouldn't be disappearing within the next few days or hours. No, her orders had already been delivered and the suitcase filled with weapons and money waited for the proper time for her to have it specially delivered to Paris.

"In the South it's customary to ask a lady first."

"You were in my arms last night and you're in my bed this morning. For me, Rebel, that fact is all the permission I need." He nodded and turned around. "I'll see you in the kitchen."

As she glanced briefly at the alarm clock on the nightstand, her arms automatically pulled the shirt over her head. She'd woken up at six in the morning for as long as she could remember. Noon. Her mind mentally calculated the difference from when they entered the bedroom and when they went to sleep. The answer when it came gave her the second shock of the morning. Ten blissfully long hours. Ever since she'd returned from South America, very few nights had been uninterrupted by dreams of Javier Merona or his men.

Thoughts of her last mission led to thoughts of her next task and Kincaid's involuntary role in the masquerade she would have to play. She hated like hell to involve the man who at that moment was downstairs preparing breakfast.

She had four days until Kincaid left for Paris and five days before she made contact with her next target. And then after that, she didn't know. If the military had given up their recruitment drive, she'd be on a plan to a new posting. If General White still insisted upon her joining the Delta Force, she would have little choice but to quit. Regan sighed before turning and put her feet on the floor, and leaving the warmth of the bed.

I will make the most of every second from now until the night of the gallery opening, she vowed.

She chose the front-page section and Kincaid pulled out the comics. As he settled back into the kitchen chair a sensation of supreme satisfaction rose in his chest. There was no doubt in his mind that he and Regan were compatible in all ways. Last night had been a physical confirmation as memories of their fiery lovemaking ignited a fire in his loins, but the sight of her hand curled around the coffee mug as her eyes leisurely scanned over the text cooled the heat of passion into the sweet warmth of tenderness. The Sunday newspaper spread like a bridge between them.

For the past hour, they had spent a leisurely morning feeding themselves, feeding each other, and sharing interesting tidbits about local, national and international events. For a moment, he closed his eyes against a dizzying sort of déjà vu at the scene. Whenever his parents were together on weekends, his father made it a point for the three of them to sit at the table and read the paper after breakfast. He enjoyed the sight of Regan's bare thighs peaking out from underneath his flannel shirt.

"Oh no," Regan said, her tone so soft he almost didn't hear her.

"What is it?" Kincaid asked. "Did something upset you?"

"Just more bad news," she replied, not so soft this time. Kincaid's sharp glance took in the tense set of her shoulders.

"It's been reported that the president of Makihai, a man I met when I first entered the State Department, is dying."

"I'm sorry to hear that."

"He was . . ." She paused, then seemed to correct herself. "Is a good man."

"Help me out here, Regan." Kincaid's brow furrowed as he drew a big circle on the table with his finger. "Which continent?"

"Africa. It's an island about three miles off the southern east coast. It's very rich with natural resources, but has an unstable government."

Suddenly it occurred to Kincaid that there was so much he didn't know about the woman sitting across the table from him. There was more he wanted to know. If it were possible, he wanted to wade through her life like a spring and bathe in every experience she'd ever had. The artist in him wanted to explore her from beginning to end, but the man who'd observed Regan's reluctance to answer questions held back. At the end of the quick war between the two halves of his personality, the artist won. What was life without risk? Kincaid folded the newspaper closed, then sat forward. "Regan, you never told me how it was that you came to work for the State Department."

"That's because you never asked," she said softly.

Kincaid leaned back into his chair and narrowed his eyes on Regan's lowered face as she closed the Sunday newspaper and then aimed an arch look his way. "It was drilled into us from the first day on the job to always get rather than give information."

"Is that an excuse or a way of getting out of answering the question?" Kincaid asked, with a hint of reproach in his voice.

She sighed. "I wanted to see the world and build a career where my family's money and influence wouldn't follow me. So I decided to pursue an international public service versus a corporate career path."

"Are you really happy with your job or is it just that you're reluctant to leave it because of your family?"

Regan winced. "I am content. My work challenges me in ways I've never dreamed of, and at the end of every assignment I can sit back and feel good about what I've done to help others."

"But you're not happy," he said confidently. His eyes compelled her to agree. "Don't get me wrong, I'm not implying that your career should provide constant feelings of joy, but you love your family, Regan. I see it in your eyes and hear it in your voice whenever you mention their names. Yet you deliberately cut yourself off from them."

Her lashes came down and blocked him from seeing the emotions he knew were racing across her eyes. Finally, Kincaid forced himself to hold back the sensation of triumph. Something he'd said had penetrated the walls of calm Regan surrounded herself with.

"It's complicated, Kincaid." She placed her hands flat on the kitchen table and met his eyes.

"How so?"

She looked surprised but continued, "There are rules and codes of behavior."

He sat forward and put his elbows on the table, all the while willing Regan to meet his eyes. *Thank you, Father,* he thought. Alfonse Sinclair's love of debate had taught Kincaid early on the importance of listening to the details. "Rebel, you break rules."

"Not all the time." She shook her head. "Especially when it could get someone—me—into trouble."

"How could staying in touch with your family get you into trouble?"

"To do my job I have to be able to concentrate. Just as you concentrate on your art."

"My family and my work aren't mutually exclusive."

"Really? Well, you could have fooled me," she replied wryly. "How many of your friends have come knocking on your door in the middle of the day? Where are your parents?

How many visitors have you allowed to enter into your studio?"

He blinked twice, then sat back in his chair and watched her through narrowed lids. Although she had a point, he wasn't happy with the way she'd made it. His art was his life, half of his soul. When Kirsten had walked out on all the promises they'd made and left behind all their plans and dreams, he'd turned to his art. It had helped him survive the aftermath of her desertion, but it hadn't helped him to thrive. Only getting out of the studio and back into the rhythm of life had cured that illness.

"No man or woman is an island. It's taken time but I know that. As a matter of fact, I plan to join the Arts Council and a local environmental group."

"You really are planning to stay here, aren't you?"

"I went through my elementary and middle school years traveling from movie set to movie set with a nanny and a personal tutor. High school and college were a combination of dormitories and apartments. After graduating, my home was wherever my tools lie. Now I feel entitled to have a place of my own. I want to put down roots."

"So you're giving up the traveling life for good?"

"No, not necessarily. I have galleries to visit, patrons to meet, and suppliers to discover. But you bring up a good point."

"That being?"

Kincaid shook his head as he realized that he'd just spent the past few minutes talking only about his life when he'd initiated the conversation to learn more about Regan.

Instead of speaking, Kincaid stood up and then took the chair directly next to Regan. He took her hand from the table, then held it against his cheek before placing a gentle kiss on her palm. "This may or may not be the best time to talk about this, but I have to attend a gallery opening in Paris next week."

"Sounds exciting. When do you have to go?"

Kincaid saw the surprise in her eyes. "This Thursday."

"For how long?"

"A week, maybe more."

She dropped her gaze from his to the coffee cup. It was crazy, Kincaid thought. But her response gave him a flare of hope. It seemed that the thrill-seeking Foreign Service officer wasn't so blasé about their parting company, especially when he was the one who would be leaving.

"Oh." Her voice held a twinge of disappointment. "Will this be one of those situations where we'll cheerfully part with an 'I'll call you or you'll call me'?"

"No."

"Are you thinking that maybe we should say our good-byes before you leave?"

Just the thought of saying good-bye or maybe it was the casualness of her mentioning the subject made his muscles tense. So instead of coaxing her into coming on the trip with him, his invitation was rather blunt and to the point. "Actually, Regan, I'd like you to come with me."

"Kincaid—"

He placed a finger against her lips. "I'm not asking for a commitment, just a trip for the both of us. It's important to me to have you with me at the opening."

"Kincaid—" She tried to get through to him for a second time.

"I know you've probably visited the city before." He was absolutely correct, but her travels were never for pleasure, and for the most part, she barely had time to explore the cultural and historical sights of the countries she'd visited.

Frustrated, Regan hurriedly picked up a strawberry, leaned across the table, and plopped it into his mouth. "I'd love to go with you."

"I'll book us two separate rooms."

"You are such the proper gentleman," she teased.

"Regan." His tone injected a note of seriousness into the conversation.

"Kincaid." She sighed softly. "If you want to throw away your money, then by all means do so. But I promise you, there'll be one empty hotel suite if you book two. Paris is the city of love, and I refuse to sleep alone."

"Is that right?"

"Oh yes."

"So your cousin will be okay with you taking off from work?"

"The garage will be fully staffed this week. I would have just gone in to pick up parts for Grandfather's birthday gift."

This was what Morgan had planned for, what she had waited for. But Kincaid's invitation filled her with dread.

Chapter 21

Later on in the evening after sharing dinner with Kincaid, Regan returned to her cottage, changed into jeans and an old sweatshirt, put on her coat, then walked up to the main house. Unlocking the door to the garage, she flipped on the bright overhead lights. To some people, the utter stillness of the car-filled space invited thoughts of old horror movies and paranoid fears. To Regan, the memories of working on cars with her father, uncles, cousins, and brothers warmed her heart.

She needed to be in her cottage in front of the computer monitor connected to the NSA database, and gathering as much information as she could about Paris. Instead, she switched on the heat, took off her coat, and moved toward the old Ford truck. She didn't ignore her work often; in fact, she rarely did anything but concentrate on mission preparation, since her life revolved around her assignments. However, the thought of going back to the life that she associated with her alias Dominique Nichols made her stomach churn. And so she came here seeking a distraction from the memories of the day and the future consequences of her taking Morgan's assignment.

Regan sat down at the metal table and opened the recently delivered FedEx package. With her mind working furiously on other issues, her hands worked to pull out the box's contents. An assortment of gaskets, valves, accelerator pumps, screws, pistons, and springs emerged from the carburetor-rebuilding kit.

One part of her remained bemused by the two days spent alone with a man who made her forget about everything except the moment, except the heady rush of powerful magic Kincaid seemed to wield over her thoughts.

The other part of her remained skeptical of the events that had taken place in the past few weeks in her life. She wasn't the type of woman to be swept off her feet. She hadn't ever asked for a hero, or secretly dreamed of a love that was larger than life. No matter how many ways Regan cut the truth or sidestepped the reality of the situation, she wouldn't succeed without losing.

Yet no matter how hard she told herself that Kincaid would love hard, hold tight, and wouldn't let things remain simple, she couldn't dismiss him from her mind. He was a good man, an honest man whose sudden appearance in her life had made her emotionally reckless.

Hours or minutes, time ceased as she bent her mind to putting the pieces together. With a screwdriver, gauges, clamps, and drill bits, she worked into the last hours of the night. Finally, when things began to blur and her yawns came back to back, Regan stood up and stretched.

"Working late?"

She turned toward the door and smiled as Marius stepped in and closed it behind him.

"Something like that. Were you looking for me?"

"Not this time. I couldn't sleep so I thought I might as well do something useful."

"I'm just about finished with the carburetor. You're more than welcome to start on the water pump."

He took off his heavy jacket and arranged it behind the seat across from her, and sat down. Regan waited patiently while Marius picked up the part, examined it, then placed it back on the table.

"Ever thought about the times we were on the highway?"

"At least once a week."

"The thing I loved the most was being away from everything. We didn't even talk. You just put a cassette tape in the player and let it ride."

Still curious to see where her brother was going with the conversation, Regan nodded to urge him to continue.

"Have you ever done that in a relationship?"

"No."

"Maybe you should try. It's a lot better than being here late at night."

She drew back and narrowed her eyes. "How do you know I'm here because of relationship issues? I could be here because I want this finished by Grandfather's birthday."

"That's always possible, but not likely. You may have gotten away from the environment, but you can't get away from the genes. We always retreat to the things that are easiest to deal with."

"Like carburetors . . ."

Marius tapped a finger against the table. "And water pumps. Tell me the truth. Are you still upset with Grandfather and Father over what went down with Trent?"

Regan sat back in her chair and crossed her arms under her chest. "No."

"Then why the infrequent visits?"

She shrugged. "Honestly, Marius, it's the job."

"But now that there's a man in your life, things are going to change."

"Not necessarily. Maybe this is just a quick fling."

"So it's like that?"

Regan picked up the screwdriver and toyed with it. "I don't know. I'm in the garage at eleven o'clock at night. This is the kind of stuff I'm trying not to think about right now. How about we examine your lack of a personal life instead?"

"I have a personal life," he shot back.

"No." She shook her head. "You have a personal assistant who schedules your life."

"Caroline is an executive assistant."

"Same thing. I bet she knows you're here and you had to pencil this into your schedule like a board meeting."

"I'm working on other things."

"Another takeover bid?"

"Personal things."

"Like finding a wife?"

"More along the lines of finding Great-uncle William."

The screwdriver in her hand clattered as it hit the table. "What?"

"Yeah. I've hired a private detective."

"Grandfather has hired over a dozen detectives over the years and none of them have found a trace of him. The last man he hired said that William Blackfox probably died making the journey."

"That's because all of them didn't know who they were looking for."

"Explain," Regan demanded.

"Remember that special on PBS about light-skinned mulatto people who moved up North and passed for white?"

"Sorry." Regan shook her head. "I don't get to see much American television."

"Well, it got me to thinking that the detectives were looking for a black man. If you were going to start over and put the past behind you, then what better way?"

She thought for a moment. "Maybe you've got something. But if you're right, the truth will hurt Grandpa badly."

"I know, which is why I'm personally working with the P.I. And if there's a lead I'll be on the plane to wherever I need to be."

"Why are you doing this and why now?"

Marius rubbed his brow. "Because I'm tired, Rebel. The party was the last straw."

"You've lost me here, big brother."

"I'm not a violent man, but I had thought of pummeling Jack Archer into the ground that night."

"Oh no." She grimaced.

"Yeah, I'm not the only one either. The sight of him talking to Savannah did it. All the stories of what his great-grandfather did to our great-grandmother just brought out this rage at the injustice."

Regan leaned forward. "But you didn't go anywhere near him."

"That's because I didn't want to ruin the party and attacking one of Pete Archer's sons would be bad for business. Later that night after everyone had gone I sat down on the sofa and thought about it. I've never met Jack Archer and I still don't want to. But he's never done anything to anybody in my family. I just wanted him hurt because he had the bad luck to be born into that family."

"'Let he who is sinless cast the first stone.' Pull back the rock, Marius. You can't paint the whole family because of one man."

She let out a chuckle at the bemused expression on her brother's face. "Unlike the three of you, I paid attention in Bible school."

"I see that. What I don't understand is why you're determined to defend the Archers."

"I'm not defending anyone. Maybe I'm just tired of the cycle of hate we have in this family. Or maybe I don't want the Archers and the Blackfoxes to become the Palestinians and the Israelis of Cartersville."

"It's not that deep," he protested.

"You wanted to beat the man to a pulp, Marius. I think that's pretty serious." Regan looked at her older brother as he stared down at his hands and she prayed hard that some of what she'd said had gotten through to him. Eventually, Savannah would have to tell the family about Jack and the baby, and having Marius on their side would help a great deal in keeping her cousins from doing anything stupid.

"Me too. Our family needs closure, and I can't be the only one that's got a level head about all this stuff."

"You're awesome, you know that?" She stepped forward and gave her brother a huge hug.

"Thanks."

"Now hand me the pliers and let's get some work done."

An hour later, they both got into their cars and drove their separate ways home. It was after two in the morning when Regan returned to the cottage. After showering and putting on her nightgown, she climbed into her own cold queen-sized bed. For over a month, her life in Cartersville had been one stop short of perfect. Now all she had to do was accomplish her pending assignment and move on to the next. So why wasn't she happy?

Chapter 22

Kincaid stood to the side of his work bench and let his eyes follow Regan as his mind wandered. He'd slept at her place and she'd spent the night over at his. They'd looked through each other's photo albums, bathed in the same tub, and eaten off each other's plates. Yet nothing seemed more intimate and self-revealing as inviting Regan into his studio. Even Kirsten had not set foot into his work space, as he had not entered hers. Only his mother, father, and Dana had ever been allowed into his studio until now.

"Thank you," Regan said.

He watched her touch his tools and run her hands over the mixture of stone and wood pieces. She brushed her fingertips over every object in his studio, and his body, which had until that moment been satiated with their morning lovemaking, grew tight with arousal. It was as though she were touching him when she touched the marble statue. And he couldn't deny the pleasant echo of how good it felt to see the admiration in her eyes as she explored his sanctuary.

"For?"

She gave him a sidelong glance while running a fingertip over an unfinished piece of stone. "Allowing me entrance into your studio. I know that it wasn't easy for you."

He blinked in surprise. He couldn't remember feeling so vulnerable, so readable. Maybe he'd spent too much time with his art and not enough with people. But it never crossed his mind that he could be so transparent. "How did you know?"

"Reading people is my fourth language. You are one of the most private people I've ever encountered. If you were a bear, I would say that this is your den."

He took a few steps closer to her. "A bear, huh?"

"Yep." Her eyes sparkled and he watched the lips that had kissed his skin and brought him to the edge of insanity as they touched his sex curve into a smile. "You'd be a big grizzly bear."

"Well, I'll be out in the open for the gallery opening. It'll be wonderful to have you with me. One thing though."

Her teasing eyes met his, and for the space of a few heartbeats, Kincaid was the happiest man on earth. "Yes?"

"My parents will attend."

"That's fine."

"Really?"

"Yes. It's *my parents* that I'm afraid of."

"I'm stunned. Such a brave, globe-trotting woman is afraid of her parents."

"Everyone has to have their fears. One of mine happens to be my father. Every time I've gone up against him, I got what I wanted but it hurt."

"Who else hurt you, Rebel?"

"What do you mean?"

"What was his name? This man who has you so gun-shy?"

"You're wrong."

"I don't think so. At first, I just chalked it up to wanting to be free from your family. But some things wound deeper than family and that usually involve the heart as well."

"My situation is different from yours."

"Yes, Kirsten walked away. Correction, she ran away and didn't have the courage to face me and tell me that she was unhappy. She couldn't make herself tell me the words."

"You loved her, didn't you?"

Kincaid nodded. "So much that had she come to me and told me that she was unhappy, I wouldn't have fought. I would have let her go."

"And you think that she and I are alike?"

"No, you're different. You put up your career as a barrier and warn men off. Don't get too close because I'm going to leave.'"

"I think you should stop this."

"Stop wanting to get around your barriers? Stop wanting to crawl into that warm corner of your heart the same way you have mine? I don't think I can."

"Trent Griffin," she admitted.

Kincaid blinked. "The actor?"

"We dated throughout high school. Everyone in town had us married and living next to my parents' estate. My grandfather had secretly had an architecture firm draw up designs for the house he planned to give us as a wedding present."

"What happened?"

"Over Christmas break I happened to wander near my grandfather's study after our annual Christmas party. What do I behold? I overhear my grandfather and my boyfriend planning my life as his wife and broodmare. They'd planned everything from our wedding date to the house, and even our four children's names."

In the silence, the heating cycle clicked on and the studio began to warm. "I'm not him, Regan. I won't lie and tell you that I'm not going to do my best to change your mind or at the very least make it hard for you to leave, but I won't manipulate you."

"I know. You proved that when you told me about Marius's bribery attempt. That was a risk you didn't have to take. You are one of the most honest men that I've ever met, Kincaid. I see it in your art. I see it in your eyes."

"What else do you see in my eyes?" he asked, moving in closer to her.

His voice got even huskier at the sight of her tongue darting out over her lips. "Come on, Regan, tell me what you see."

"Desire," she whispered.

His hands of their own accord came down gently on her shoulders and moved southward to explore. Front to back, he put his hands under her sweater and ran his fingers along the curve of her spine, her bare back, the slight swell of her belly. "I've wanted to sculpt you since the first day we met."

"Sculpt or touch, Kincaid?" she asked in a breathy voice.

"Both," he replied before leaning down to nip her lower lip. It didn't matter if she were a mirage, nor that their time together would disappear at the first rays of sunlight. And so he moved into her, placed his hands around her waist, and lifted Regan atop the workbench. It was having her in this place, his place, that reached down into the core of everything he was and that inner voice in his head came out with a vengeance. And everything inside him demanded that Kincaid brand Regan, to mark her as his in every way and make her need him as much as he needed her right now.

Kincaid lifted up her sweater and drew it roughly over her head, and before she could think, before she could regain her balance, he moved forward between her legs and moved his head down to run his lips over the curve of her throat. And at the moan from her lips, he locked his mouth over her pulse and sucked. And while his mouth enjoyed the vanilla taste of her skin, his hands reached around and unsnapped her bra.

Then without a shred of delicacy, he ripped down the zipper of her jeans and pulled them down over her legs along with the slip of her panties. He moved his mouth from her neck and sought her lips. Without hesitation, her lips opened and as his tongue slipped into her mouth, his fingers found her entrance. Kincaid entered and, finding her wet, he withdrew.

With his eyes open, Kincaid circled his fingers around her sensitive mound, enjoying the look on Regan's face, the sound of her low whimper. Masculine pride rose in his chest as he watched her eyes darken and her breath catch as her legs wrapped around his waist and pulled him closer to her. He pushed against her, rubbing his jeans against her inner thighs. He felt her tense and relax, heard her breath catch in her throat as he worked his fingers in and out, while his mouth suckled her breast.

"Don't go," she moaned when he pulled away. Regan opened her eyes in time to see his hands ripping apart the condom packet and covering his erection in latex. Regan wrapped her legs around his hips and pulled him closer. Her breath caught and her eyelids drifted closed when his tip touched her entrance.

"Open your eyes," he commanded.

Regan moved her hips forward and growled her frustration as his hands locked onto her hips, keeping her still. There was no doubt in her mind that she would explode from the sexual tension, and when that happened, she wanted him deep inside her. Her eyes opened and Regan stared mesmerized, caught by the intensity of Kincaid's stare.

Between one breath and the next, he surged forward. And his entrance wasn't too fast or too slow, but perfect. Regan buried her face in his shoulder and closed her eyes. She wanted to block out everything, everything but the sensation of him inside her. The feel of her inner walls stretched and full, the sweet pleasure brought by the rhythm of his thrusts and withdrawals. And when Kincaid moved, pulled almost all the way out and returned, each time he hit the spot. That small place sent pleasure rippling through her body as the tension built with each stroke.

"Please . . ." Regan came close to screaming, and it was a plea for him to stop or go faster, she didn't know. The only thing she knew was that nothing had ever felt so good in her life. Every sense heightened, she panted and from one breath to the next, everything stopped and she could feel the cool metal against her bottom; the heat of his hands; his mouth on her throat, nipples. The way his lips sucked while his hand pinched. Her orgasm when it came tore through her body and arched her back with pleasure. Kincaid stilled and wrapped his arms around her, and buried his face in the nape of her neck. Sometime later, after she'd regained control of her limbs and her voice, Regan opened her eyes and stared over Kincaid's back to an object on the floor.

"You were well prepared," Regan commented while eyeing the empty condom packet.

"Hmm?"

"I thought only Boy Scouts carried condoms in their wallets."

Still soft within her body, he grinned. "Let's just say that this was a part of my dream the other night."

"I like your dreams," she murmured into his ear. "Mmm." She snuggled into him as the central air clicked on a draft made goose bumps prickle along her exposed back. "You smell—" She breathed in again. "M&Ms. You smell like chocolate. Vanilla?"

"Yep. Aftershave. I bought it after I discovered your sweet tooth."

Regan drew back and looked into his twinkling eyes. "You're kidding."

"Nope. I might have to go and get more if I can get this kind of reaction."

Regan wet her lips with her tongue and her smile was slow, deliberate, and full of future promise. "You do that, Sinclair."

Chapter 23

France

Paris with its grand boulevards, sleepy waterways, arched cathedrals, and acclaimed architectural buildings had never looked more beautiful, Regan mused as the hired car whisked them toward the Left Bank.

Nor have I ever been more nervous, she thought. Part of her had actually been in denial that she would have to complete a mission. However, all it took was a brief search of the hotel suite to erase that illusion. As promised, Morgan's suitcase of weapons, currency, sedatives, and tracking gear had been tucked under the bed before their plane had touched down at Charles de Gaulle Airport.

"Are you all right, sweetheart?"

She glanced up from toying with the small evening purse in her lap, then smiled at Kincaid. "I'm fine," she automatically replied.

He reached over and took her hands within his own. "Your hands are like ice."

Her lips dipped a little to form a self-conscious pout. "I can't put one over on you, can I?"

"Answering a question with a question may have worked when we first met, but not now. So why don't you tell me why you're jumpy as a water drop on a hot skillet?"

She playfully tapped a manicured fingertip to his chest. "You're overexaggerating, Sinclair."

"Really? Answer me this, what is your favorite Italian food?"

"Besides pizza?" She rubbed her brow in mock concentration. "Eggplant Parmesan."

"And what did you order tonight?"

"Eggplant Parmesan," Regan repeated after aiming a confused look Kincaid's way.

"Rebel, you barely touched your plate at dinner."

For the first time, but she was sure it would not be the last, Regan wished that Kincaid wasn't so observant where she was concerned. "Can't blame a girl for being excited, can you? I'm attending a gallery opening in Paris on the arm of a handsome man. And I'm meeting one of Hollywood's leading power couples. All this on the same night."

"You've met with heads of state and dozens of influential world leaders. This doesn't even compare."

Would there ever be an end to the affection she felt for this man? Regan silently questioned. "You're right." She nodded her head. In the intimacy of the BMW's leather-appointed backseat with the intermittent blinks from the streetlamps, she looked into his eyes and could have lost herself in the warm affection of his stare. "This," she began again after removing her hand from his and placing her fingertips against his clean-shaven jaw. "This means more to me than any official occasion. Tonight, I'm meeting the three most important people in your life. And I can't help but be a little apprehensive."

"They'll adore you, because I do."

It was on the tip of her tongue to ask if the same would be true after she disappeared from his life, but Regan swallowed the response and allowed Kincaid to pull her closer to his side. With her reclined comfortably in his arms, they looked out the window of the chauffeured car. She watched as shop owners closed their stores and the inhabitants of Paris languidly moved along the sidewalk toward their homes or favorite dining haunts.

Guilt, the emotion she'd long thought conquered, sat like a foundation stone on her chest. Regan drew in a deep breath. She'd lied to Kincaid when he'd asked why her hands were cold. Her nervousness also stemmed from the pending assignment. Too many things could go wrong and she hadn't even made contact with her target. Not to mention the very likely possibility that someone who knew her as Dominique Nichols could be in attendance tonight.

Who was he? Why did he need to leave the country? Why was he being watched by the French authorities? Instead of focusing on matters she couldn't control, her mind went over her planned exit strategies. Drive the rental car to Italy, a train to Geneva, then a flight to the United States. Maybe she would use the tour bus tickets and they would have a mock holiday in the south of Spain before flying to America. All those thoughts and more crowded her mind, but everything ended as the car slowed to a stop.

Kincaid turned toward her and gently placed his fingertips underneath her chin. Regan's eyes trailed up from his black-trouser clad thighs, along the inner edge of the charcoal-black suit jacket, and up the perfectly dimpled tie tucked neatly under the soft collar of his dress shirt. Nothing he wore gave hint to the fact that the man was in fact an artist instead of a corporate executive. And try as she might, she couldn't deny the added attraction she felt at the aura of confidence that exuded from him like a fine cologne. "I love you in jeans, Kincaid. But in a suit, you are certainly impressive."

His lips curved upward into a grin and his hand automatically came up to adjust his tie. "I feel like a fake, but Dana would kill me if I didn't show up properly attired. Did I tell you how much I like your dress?"

"No, you didn't." Although her coat covered her dress, Kincaid had gotten a very good look at the luxurious dress when she had requested his assistance in zipping up the back. After visiting four different boutiques, she had finally decided on an antique-white wool crepe sheath dress that clung to her curves while flowing down to her ankles and matching heels to complement her dark hair, which she had pulled back into a chignon with a few tendrils to frame her face. She had topped off the look with her favorite diamond pendant necklace.

"Your beauty makes my hands ache."

Her heart melted at the honest sincerity in his voice. "I'll take that as a compliment, Monsieur Artiste. You don't look so bad yourself."

"Ready to go?" Kincaid squeezed her hand as the driver opened the back door to the cold.

Regan looked past Kincaid's shoulder to the waiting crowd of photographers. "As ready as I'll ever be. I don't like the press."

"Just hold on to me and you'll be fine."

With her heart beating a mile a minute, she gingerly rose from the car and, wrapped in her cashmere coat, the cold no longer mattered. The car lights, camera flashes, streetlamps, and the Louvre, a museum above all others—in whose pathway Kincaid's gallery would sit. Gathering her nerves, Regan turned toward Kincaid's arm and used her hair to shield her face. And with the flashing of more than a dozen lightbulbs, they went in.

Since accepting the mission, she'd had a tiny ball of tension in the back of her throat. Now as she walked through the gallery doors with Kincaid's arm securely around her waist, the knot of anxiety sank to the pit of her stomach. But she had no choice and she smiled and began to pray.

Earth Art Fusion Gallery was painted in a rich swirl of sepia. Geometric shapes of varying colors and sizes hung from the steeped ceiling, inviting the eyes upward only to return to the walls. Six-foot painted canvases hung against monochromatic sections of mobile steel-gray dividers with multiple textures. While other artists' paintings graced the walls, Kincaid's signature creations lay tucked on pedestals displayed on shelves, ropes, and strings. Her eyes caught sight of a birch tree toward the rear section of the main room and underneath sat a wooden sculpture of a child playing. It was so lifelike that for a moment she expected to hear a little girl's laughter.

Black-clad waiters flowed through the crush of people and held aloft crystal flutes of champagne garnished with strawberries. Other servers clad in earth-toned clothing served a variety of ethnic appetizers, from Cajun-style pan-seared catfish with saffron *fume* to Italian Ravioli stuffed with Argentinean shrimp and wild mushrooms foie gras, decadent smoked salmon and avocado balanced atop fresh-baked Greek bread, and countless other treats, not to mention dessert.

Music floated through the air, and the heavy tremble of a cello caught her ear as a muted trumpet set the leather-clad foot of a man she recognized as the head of the International Red Cross to tapping. Kincaid's manager, Dana, had pulled off a spectacularly successful showing.

Old French wealth mingled with their newly arrived European and American cousins. Regan noticed that all of Kincaid's guests were stylishly dressed in the latest Paris and Italian fashions. Everyone seemed to enjoy themselves as they chatted, laughed, murmured, and admired, strolling over gleaming wood floors to view the extraordinarily diverse collection of world art.

Regan sipped on her glass of champagne and nodded again at the celebrity artist as he sought to enlighten her about secret proclivities of some of the European socialites in attendance. As he talked she let her eyes stray to her watch. She groaned quietly; it was still at least four hours before the party would end, four hours she would have to wait for her target. Regan's fingers strayed to the delicate chain around her neck; just the feel of the silver between her fingertips restored her composure. The party had ramped up to full swing, but he had yet to arrive.

Her estimation of her lover rose yet another notch as Regan observed Kincaid unconsciously charm everyone in the room. He did it naturally, just as his famous mother and father who had managed to enter into the gallery without generating undue excitement. And Regan watched it all from her spot by the terrace window, early in the evening after she'd met his family and shared a plate of appetizers with Kincaid's mother and his best friend Dana. His mother was style personified from the top of her elegant pin curls to the tips of her dress-matching Hermés shoes. Regan had met royalty and the wives of various dignitaries, but Mrs. Sinclair was indeed the epitome of a lady.

Much later, after Kincaid's opening speech, countless toasts, and a whirlwind of introductions, Regan stood admiring one of Kincaid's many sculptures. She'd just taken a sip of champagne before catching sight of the man of the hour coming to a stop by her side. She slid an arch glance his way while suppressing the smile that at any moment could curl her lips upward.

He had been magnificent and she couldn't blame the female eyes that continued to watch him as he stood by her side. She reached up and playfully pulled on his double-button-collar black dress shirt as he nervously tugged on one of the sterling silver cuff links she'd placed on his cuff a mere two hours before. "I hadn't realized you spoke French."

"The language of diplomacy isn't for you alone, *ma pétit*."

"*Ma pétit*, Kincaid?"

"*Ma chéri, pétit chou, mon coeur*." He leaned over and placed a gentle kiss on the side of her cheek. "You can have all the pet names you want. Just tell me what you like."

Regan suppressed the large grin from her lips and pretended to be in deep contemplation, then replied with an expression of utter seriousness, "For now you can just call me yours."

"Nothing would make me happier."

"Careful, the sentimental artist in you is showing."

"Can't handle it, Rebel?"

"You must be joking."

"I don't know. You seem to have an aversion to public displays of affection."

"Blame the U.S. State Department. Those kinds of things are frowned upon."

"Sweetheart . . ." He moved closer to her ear and whispered, "I have a secret."

"What?" Regan lowered her voice to mimic Kincaid's as happiness tickled every nerve in her body.

"We're in Paris and you are on vacation."

"The opening is fantastic. And the evening has only just begun," she asserted.

"They love you, by the way."

She watched his eyes go toward his parents and their entourage. "How can you tell?"

"Well, you impressed the heck out of my mother by politely kicking that reporter out of the bathroom."

"She told you about that?"

Kincaid grinned. "Yep. I don't think I've seen my father laugh so hard in years."

"She told your father too?"

"He might put it into his next film."

"How are things?"

"According to Dana, we've got offers on everything except the light fixtures and the champagne flutes."

"That's wonderful."

"Dana's over the moon, but it also means that I'll be tied up most of the day."

"What about your nights?"

"They belong to you."

"Then that's all I need." She patted his muscled arms gently. "I'm a big girl, Sinclair. I think I can manage by myself."

"I don't doubt that. It's just I want to spend every moment I can with you."

"You will. We may not be together during the day, but I plan on having you make it all up to me during the night."

"You are truly something special."

"Because I'm not making you feel guilty for working?"

"That among other things."

"Don't worry. I wanted to get some shopping and a little sightseeing done anyway. And you don't seem to be the lug around shopping bags and calmly sit on a tourist bus type."

"You're right. Damn, Gustav just arrived."

"Go." She pushed him. "You are the host, owner, and the artist. Go work your magic and I'll be here waiting when all this is over."

"Rebel, I can't wait to get you back to the hotel."

She winked, then smiled seductively. "Remember that."

It was an hour until the official end of the gallery opening and her target had yet to appear. With each passing moment, while her expression never changed, Regan's stomach turned a quarter of an inch to form an even tighter knot. As she returned from her second trip to the ladies' room, two tall men wearing identical dark suits, dark shoes, and earpieces entered the gallery.

When the bodyguards spread out to reveal their client, she took one look at the man and cursed. The world was indeed too small. Mosi Amacha, former classmate, first-born son of an African president, international playboy, and academic stood basking with the attention brought by his entrance.

She observed the slight darkening of his eyes as his pupils widened, a tightening of the muscles in his face, a change so slight she wouldn't have caught it if she weren't looking. Her target not only remembered her from graduate school, he also recognized the symbolism of her all-white outfit.

The low light softened Mosi's face to the point of boyishness and played lover's tricks on the hard angles of his face. He was shorter than Kincaid, older, with lazy eyes and lips that had a permanent crook of laughter. Taking a sip of the champagne in her hand, Regan turned to study a nearby painting, confident that her target would come to her. Sure enough, only five minutes passed before a shadow dropped over her shoulder.

"Regan Blackfox," he announced warmly. He laid his hand lightly on her shoulder; it was warm and firm and meant to establish a subtle possessiveness. She moved off a step but kept smiling for the watchers.

"I didn't expect to see you in Paris," Mosi said as Regan examined him. Up close, she could see the dark circles under his eyes; chapped lips and deep tension had etched lines into his features. Fear, she thought.

"I didn't expect to see you in such a hurry to leave." She smiled noncommittally. Neither by tone nor by expression did she reveal her true feelings. She took the lead by walking toward the back French doors, which led out to a walled garden.

"I can't go back home nor can I remain in France."

"So you're ready to give this all up to be a regular American citizen?"

"No, but going back home means certain death and an unstable country. Staying here is living under the constant threat of assassination and under the gaze of French guards. Your country offered me a new life."

"And you jumped at the opportunity to absolve yourself of your father's sins?"

"No. I'm honoring a dead man's last wish. My father's crimes are not mine and he used his power to secure my freedom."

Regan shrugged even as her skin crawled with nervous energy. It was not her place to judge, just to carry out orders even if she disagreed with them. "Are all your affairs in order?"

"Almost."

"Have you transferred your funds into the dummy accounts?"

"Yes."

"You have until the end of the week. Make no changes in schedule, keep your behavior, habits, and financial transactions as far above suspicion as possible, understand?"

His coal-dark eyes narrowed at her tone. "Of course, I'm not a fool."

"Good, then don't act like one. Any hint that the French are on to us and it's over."

"When exactly do I leave?"

She ignored his question. "I'll come for you before Friday. You can take nothing with you and leave nothing that can be traced. Your bodyguards are getting antsy, so try to kiss me and I'll pull away."

He did as she directed and as if on cue, Regan reversed Mosi's grip on her and twisted his wrist in a way that forced him to drop to his knees in pain.

He held up his hands "What the hell? Woman, are you insane?" he asked incredulously as he backed away.

"Keep your voice down." She folded her arms across her chest.

At the movement, two men converged on their position. Regan studied them as they pinned her with their eyes, and with her arms crossed and a furious expression on her face, she became the picture of virtuous outrage.

"Sir, are you all right?"

"No, don't touch her. We had a disagreement, that's all."

Regan took a deep breath and forced an angry tremble into her voice. "Your manners are beneath contempt. I advise you to leave before Kincaid gets here. I won't have you ruining his moment."

Chapter 24

Three days had passed since their arrival in Paris. For Regan, tonight would be the first of many lasts. She curled more tightly into Kincaid's side as they strolled along the lamplit Champs-Elysées. They had shared an early meal with his parents at an exclusive Parisian restaurant, then leaned close sipping cappuccinos over a small round table at a French café.

And all that wonderfully perfect happiness of living in the moment began to dissipate as her mind dwelled on a harsh reality. This could be her last night with Kincaid, her last day in Paris, her last chance to abort her mission, her last day spent with the impenetrable wall between Dominique Nichols and Regan Blackfox. More importantly, tonight would mark the last falsehood she would utter to the man who walked beside her.

Earlier that afternoon, she'd made all the final arrangements to get Mosi out of the country without detection. Behind the wheel of a minicar rented to a fictitious woman from Canada, she had followed his daytime movements for three days. She'd taken notes and gathered intelligence. How many doors and windows did the target's building possess? What kind of weapons did the bodyguards carry, where did the target like to eat, jog, party, shop? When did

he work, when did he sleep? What side of the car he sat
in, what side of the street he walked on. In essence, Mosi
Amacha had become her obsession.

In between waiting for her target, Regan had wandered
into stores and museums to purchase items to show Kincaid and gather stories to tell of her afternoon of shopping
and sightseeing. Then when she was sure that Mosi's
apartment would be empty and safe to enter, she paid him
an unexpected visit.

Upon entering into the luxury apartment building,
which had at one time been the home of an illustrious
French duke and played host to foreign businessmen,
she'd passed unhindered through the gilded doors simply
because she was dressed in haute couture, spoke fluid
French, and looked the part of someone's girlfriend, mis-
tress, or wife. After picking the lock and searching the
abode, she'd found Mosi's daily planner locked in the
upper compartment of his desk.

It was then that she discovered the best time and place
to execute her plans. On Friday morning, he was scheduled
to meet with his attorney for three hours. He didn't know
it yet but it would only be a ten-minute appointment. The
rest of the 170 minutes would be spent putting as much distance between them and Paris as possible. By the end of the
consulting session, she expected to be far away from the city.

Yet nothing could diminish Paris, diminish being with
Kincaid. Replete with the best French cuisine, red wine, and
piano music, they strolled along the boulevard close underneath a wide umbrella. The rain came down gently; the
pitter-patter on the dark red brick brought a smile to her lips.

And after they reached a small bridge. Regan turned and
stared at the Eiffel Tower as if she were a child. "Isn't it
wonderful?" she asked.

"Oh yes," Kincaid replied. Regan raised her eyes to stare
into Kincaid's. *Now*, a small voice in the back of her
mind whispered. *Now is the perfect time to tell him.* His
look held so much devotion and tenderness that she had

to turn away. She looked toward the brightly lit symbol of Paris but allowed Kincaid to pull her close into his chest.

"If we were in a movie, this would be the moment we dedicated our love and eternal devotion," she mused aloud.

"But this isn't a movie, Regan," he stated.

Impulse raged against common sense. The wall she'd built between Dominique Nichols, the NSA agent whose life was a shell, and her real identity gave one last shudder and began to tumble down. Regan turned around in his arms and toyed with the lapel of his long coat. "No, it isn't."

She let the gloved fingertips on her chin raise her head. "I feel like this is a dream and you don't know how much I don't want to wake up, Kincaid."

Right there with passing cars, walking people, he nipped her lips, then warmed them with his own. He kissed her. Long and deep, achingly tender, and blissfully sweet. In the aftermath, her alter ego/secret identity disappeared.

He pulled away, and she slowly opened her eyes to see the tiny tendrils of his breath made visible in the cool night air. "Heaven help me but I love you, Kincaid Sinclair."

"Heaven helped me find you, so I think we're going to be just fine, Rebel. Because I've loved you for a while."

"Since the first day we met?" she asked as he touched her cheek.

"Close. I fell in love with you the evening you introduced me to the country-friend steak and taught me how to throw darts."

"That reminds me, we still need to work on your aim."

"No, I think I'm just fine." His eyes sparkled with mirth. "I got just what I was aiming for, your heart."

Her smile faded slightly as reality intruded. Every hour of every day since she'd stepped on the plane from Atlanta to Paris, she'd wavered over whether or not to tell Kincaid about her mission. And what would happen after their trip ended.

"My loving you hasn't changed the circumstances regarding my work."

"No, but I've changed my target, mademoiselle." He affected a heavy Gallic accent. "And you can't help but to fall under ma spell, for I speak French, am handsome, and rich with zee chocolate in my pockets."

Regan giggled like a schoolgirl and playing along placed her arm through his proffered one. Love had made her weak, but she could only hope that come the morning, training and determination would keep her strong.

Later on that evening, Kincaid paused from unbuttoning his shirt at the knock on the hotel suite door. He spared a glance toward the doorway to the bedroom where Regan was at the moment taking a shower and getting dressed for bed.

He crossed the room with a confident stride and opened the heavy wooden door to the waiting hotel attendant.

"Monsieur Sinclair, you have my apologies for the hour, but I have an urgent delivery for Ms. Regan Blackfox."

"I can take it."

"Could you sign here for me, *s'il vous plait*?"

Kincaid took the pen and scrawled his signature across the bottom of a French document. It was only after he'd closed and locked the door that the return address on the big envelope registered. *United States Department of State, Washington, D.C.* Dread settled in the pit of his gut as anger curled like a vise around his heart. His fingers curled on the object of his displeasure, and for a moment Kincaid entertained the thought of hiding it in his suitcase or opening the big brown manila envelope to see its contents.

With an impatient grunt, he tossed it down on the coffee table and walked over to the bar area, turned over a glass, and pulled the stopper out of a crystal decanter of brandy.

The French liqueur burned a rolling path down his throat and proceeded to blunt the sharp edge of his annoyance.

"I hope you poured one for me."

At the sound of her voice, Kincaid gently placed the glass on the table but didn't turn around. "An envelope came while you were in the shower."

Impatient to know when she would leave him, Kincaid turned around and his eyes flicked between a negligee-and-silk-robe-clad Regan and the envelope in the center of the coffee table. Several moments passed with only the sound of the central air-conditioning, and all the while he stared at her. All gold, the sheer chemise and wrap seemed to reveal every inch of her skin from the lace bodice to the high-cut sides. Looking at him with a sultry come-hither smile in her large brown eyes, Regan, with her warm brown skin and generous lips, appealed to every masculine fiber in his body. "Aren't you going to open it?" he demanded brusquely.

A fleeting look of hurt crossed her features, and he steeled himself against it. Love cut both ways. She was leaving him, he reminded himself. Just like Kirsten, just like his mother.

Regan took two steps toward him, but all the while she held his gaze. "Not now."

"Don't tell me that you're not the slightest bit curious about your next post?"

He followed her gaze downward as she toyed with the straps of her robe. "It isn't a new assignment."

"How do you know?"

Her hands stilled, and the unease in the back of his mind that had begun at the knock on the hotel door grew. "I only get my orders after my mission is complete."

Kincaid stood, took four steps toward Regan, then stopped in front of her so close that the floral scent of her skin wafted up to his nose. He stood so close that he had but to move an inch and their bodies would join. Yet it took the look in her eyes for the full implication of her statement to hit him full-on. There was a flat, resigned expression on her face, as if she had been over this entire subject in her mind and had yet to accept the answer. She met his stare and then looked away biting her bottom lip.

"Mission?" His brows came down into an instant frown as his eyes narrowed.

She took a deep breath, then began in an even tone as though reading a science manual. "I have two jobs and two names. My alias is Dominique Nichols. The truth is that I don't just work for the State Department. I'm also an undercover operative for the National Security Agency. In the beginning, my job was to spy on foreign officials, gain their trust, and report to my superiors. As my role began to evolve, I moved to a specialized team that infiltrated foreign communications installations and procured vital codes to allow NSA analysts to eavesdrop on governmental and military agencies. Now my job is to help identify and if necessary acquire and deliver designated foreign nationals in the political or scientific community to the United States."

Kincaid shut his eyes tight, took a deep breath, and then opened them. "There's more isn't there."

"Yes."

And she did. From the morning her NSA recruiter had showed up at the front door of her Georgetown apartment, her first assignment, to her last official mission in Jordan. The hair on his arms prickled and his gut twisted as she recounted narrow escapes with authorities and near capture. Even as she ended her tale, his own intuition told him that she hadn't told him all of it.

"Why, Regan? Why do you put your life in danger?"

Several moments passed and he watched her face as emotions flickered across her features. Yet they finally settled into a look that he was fast coming to dislike: resolution.

"My unit moves fast, adapts, improvises, and I enjoy the importance of lives depending on me. I like the sense of good, that something I do will make my country a safer place," she responded.

"Not to mention the adrenaline rush," he added bitterly. "This changes everything."

"I know."

"The president's son," he surmised, remembering the closely guarded African man from the gallery opening.

"Yes." She nodded. "My mission is to get him safely to America without anyone knowing."

"How are you going to do it?"

"We're scheduled to travel by either train or car to a neighboring country. After I feel it's safe, we'll fly to Canada, then the United States."

"The envelope?" Kincaid gestured toward the table.

"Mosi's new passport and identification."

"What happens if you're caught?"

"I won't be."

"Can you guarantee that?"

She shook her head. "There are no guarantees. You know that, Kincaid."

"No, I don't. His fingers balled into fists. "I don't know a damn thing. Just when I think I know you, it feels like I've opened my eyes to see a stranger."

"Please don't say that. I'm the same woman."

"The Regan I thought I knew wouldn't lie or be capable of committing the acts you just described."

A heavy silence fell between them, and she could hear her heart beating, thudding painfully against her ribs. Although she tried to keep her voice steady, it still shook. "I took an oath never to reveal my true identity. You are the only person outside of the NSA that knows this information, Kincaid. I've told no one, not even my family. Please let that be proof enough."

"Of what?"

It was on the tip of her tongue to say, "my love." Regan bit the inside of her lip to hold back the words. There was too much in the air, but there was also too much at stake. "My love."

"Love requires trust, Regan." Fingers that had been curled into fists throughout their conversation relaxed. Kincaid stared at the woman who had his heart, and before his eyes pieces of a puzzle began to come together. His mind like a wave poured over every detail of their time together and his gut clenched with anger. "It was all a setup, wasn't it?"

She shook her head. "Not by my choosing. In this situation, we were both manipulated. Somehow the agency found out that you planned on inviting me to the gallery opening. Morgan swore to me that he hadn't tapped your phone."

"Damn," Kincaid cursed underneath his breath. "Whoever this Morgan character is, he didn't need to tap the phone because I told him, or one of his agents. Remember when I went to Charleston to check out a shipment of marble?"

"Yes."

"Well, the woman was interested in both the gallery opening and my personal life."

"What did she look like?"

Kincaid rubbed his brow and thought back. "Tall, shoulder-length hair, brunette, and she had a New England accent."

"I'm sorry." Regan shook her head.

"You recognize the description?"

"Yes."

"I guess I should be flattered that they went through so much trouble to set this up," he bitterly commented.

"Would it make you feel better to know that I didn't want this? That I didn't like not telling you the truth?"

"Yes."

"Then feel better. I was impulsive. I was selfish and I regret having hurt you, but I accepted this mission and I can't turn my back on my duty."

This time when Regan stepped close to him, Kincaid didn't move away. He just stood watching her face. The curve of her brow that had once rested against his bare chest. The bow of her lips that had kissed every inch of his flesh. And as he looked at her, the anger of her betrayal bled away, leaving only hurt in its place. He let out a sigh from deep within his chest. "God, Rebel. How can I trust you after something like this? You're a stranger to me."

"A stranger?" A spark of anger lit her eyes and creased her brow. "Maybe I'm not who you thought I was. Maybe I'm not that innocent or simple. Maybe you don't like the side of me that you've never known, but the woman the outside world sees as Dominique Nichols is me. And I hurt, Kincaid. And right now I'm terrified that you won't forgive me." Regan took his hand and placed it over her heart. "Feel this?"

Kincaid gritted his jaw. "And how do I know that your heart isn't racing out of fear?"

"Because of who you are. Because you see into the essence of people, and if you look at me with the eyes of memory and of perception you'll see that regardless of my career or my past I'm telling you the truth. I'm in love with you, Kincaid Sinclair, and I want to make this right. But I'm not sorry about fighting tooth and nail to keep my double life a secret. My only regret is lying to you."

"That's it?"

Regan's heart sank and her eyes started to fill with unshed tears. "What more do you want from me? What else can I give?"

His dark eyes bored into hers. "Actions speak louder than words, Regan. Show me. Show me that the woman in this room is that same one who ran her fingertips over my sculptures, fed me chocolate kisses at midnight, who stood in front of the Eiffel Tower and declared her love."

Regan's eyes widened in surprise. She began to tremble with hope and desire, each potent alone, but mingled together they poured through her, making her light-headed. She'd confessed everything to him. Her lies, evasions, sins, and transgressions. Yet despite it all Kincaid still could forgive her.

All of the conversations they'd shared ran through her mind like a transcription machine on high speed. He'd been a teenager when his parents had decided to enroll him in boarding school, and he'd gone along with it. Time with family is precious, and Kincaid had had so little. As he'd grown from a boy to a man, he'd closed off that part of him that needed to have people close, and only Dana and Kirsten had gotten close enough to touch the artist's heart. One had left him and the other was on the verge of marriage.

Regan blinked back wetness that had begun to gather behind her eyes. Her confession had not changed the facts, only altered the feelings, but no matter what happened past that night, nothing could dissolve the permanent tie the man had on her heart. When the time came to leave him, she couldn't walk away without wanting to turn back.

But what will happen in the morning? her alter ego taunted. She swallowed hard. She didn't want to think about tomorrow.

She slid her hand slowly from atop his, trailing it across the wine-red sweater covering his chest to his throat. Her fingertips lingered over a pulse that beat just as fast as hers.

Regan gave a soft murmur, went to her tiptoes, and brought her face level with Kincaid's. When their eyes met, Regan pushed down every barrier she had and let every one of her emotions, her needs, her love well up and pour out of her eyes. She paused, her gaze searching his in gentle concern, her mouth hovering above his own.

Her arms wound around his shoulders and her fingertips stroked the nape of his neck. "May I kiss you?" she asked softly. She stared into his dark brown eyes and felt her heart stop at their wariness.

"Please?" One word. One plea filled with need and desire. As if the world would change forever once she touched her lips to his, Regan pressed her mouth to his. She kissed him like a first kiss, an innocent kiss. Like discovering a hidden secret. Her lips touched his and discovered all the ways a mouth could fix on another mouth, and then when he responded, when his lips parted under the pressure of hers, Regan found a new treasure. His hand found the back of her neck and pulled her in closer. His mouth shaping hers, tongue tracing the soft inside. Drowning her in the damp heat, the spicy taste of him.

Her hand slid into his hair, pressing him closer, felt the heat of him against her, his hard arms around her back, holding her close. Her breasts flattened against his chest, emphasizing their swollen ache. Mouths fused, melded. But gently, delicately as though asking permission, and then finally parting. His tongue stroked her lip a last time as he slowly drew away, making her tremble and gasp.

"I love you, Rebel" he said.

A shaky sound left her; like a laugh, but more desperate. She realized that her arms were still locked around his neck. Regan loosened her grasp, stroking gently down his neck as she watched him watch her. Her hand stilled against his chest, over the steady throb of his heart. A deep trembling began inside her, an ache and a heat brought on by his declaration, his kiss, his presence.

Locked in one another's embrace, they stumbled together into the bedroom. Now it was Regan whose fingers slipped underneath his shirt and tugged it off. Regan whose fingernails scratched wicked lines over his skin and pulled off his pants. His sweet Rebel, her sharp little teeth biting his lips, sucking hungrily at his tongue as he felt his fingers slip down her back, over her hips and thighs, and then he had her in his hands and he pushed off the flimsy cloth of her negligee and pushed her onto the bed. Their movements were rushed, the fumbling, breathless gestures of lovers too long apart.

Yet in the midst of their lovemaking and bringing her to climax with his fingers, Regan pulled away. She pushed him back on the bed and pleasured him with her hands and mouth. And when she'd brought him to the brink of climax, Regan covered his maleness with a condom.

She was guiding him between her legs, and he forced himself to slow down, one hand on hers as he buried his face in her neck, smelling her sweet scent, his tongue leaving hot trails up her neck. Her legs wrapped themselves around his waist, and holding him there, tightly, flung back her head and moaned.

He plunged into her slick, tight heat, and she cried out, with his hands on her hips as he thrust into her, harder and harder, relishing the way her breasts moved with his thrusts, the dark nipples just visible in the room's low light.

She moved her hands over her head and clutched at the headboard, her head thrown back, her full, sensuous lips open as she panted and fought to keep the wanton screams at bay. The sense of his touch, the sense of heightened feeling that was going to take her high. Regan held her breath, held that time, held that moment as he thrust into her as deep and as hard as he could, held the roughness of his breathing, held back her impending climax. A few more moments. And as every one of her senses seemed to overload with impending release, Regan gasped, "I love you!"

After he released himself and fell onto her chest, Regan held him close and bore his weight. When Kincaid could find the strength to move, he rolled over, bringing her with him.

As Regan's pulse began to quiet and she buried her face in his shoulder, hot tears crept from underneath her lashes.

Fingers gently touched her face.

"Did I hurt you?" Kincaid asked.

She opened her eyes and in the half shadows of the room looked up into his face. "No, you could never hurt me. It was beautiful. You are beautiful," she whispered.

The confusion in his gaze seemed to touch her all the more, and the tears fell harder. This was all her doing. As she lay in a luxurious bed in the center of Paris with the man she loved, Regan could do nothing but cry. After he'd kissed her tears away and cradled her close, Regan closed her eyes, and as sleep stole over her she wished that everything would stop and tomorrow would never come.

Only after he was assured that Regan slept, Kincaid opened his eyes and looked down on her still face. He let his hand rest on her skin, enjoying the feminine softness of her stomach. Into the night, he lay awake dreading the morning.

I cannot let her go.

Memories of the short time he'd spent with Regan flowed from his heart and sped through his veins. Moreover, the thought of her leaving him like shards of glass cut at his throat, but he kept breathing. Yet the thought of seeing her cold lifeless body, the idea of a phone call telling him she was in a French hospital, or the vision of Regan in jail felt worse. No, when the time came for their relationship to end, he would have it happen at her volition, not circumstance.

If he'd made a mistake by falling for her, it was a mistake he could live with. Quickly and silently so as not to wake her, Kincaid slid out of the bed, left the room, and gently closed the door behind him.

He would make the phone calls tonight, and tomorrow one way or another Regan would make a choice and everything would come to an end.

Chapter 25

Regan moved from sleep to full awareness in the digital chirp of her watch alarm. Sitting up, she blinked owlishly in bemusement as a yawn welled up in her throat and pried her jaws open. This was the first time before a mission that she hadn't spent the night tossing and turning. Last night in Kincaid's arms, she'd slept as though the guardian spirits of her ancestors, which her grandmother had spoken of when she was a child, had stood beside the bed and their unwavering protection kept her from all harm, even her own nightmares.

"Good morning." A familiar deep voice drew her attention.

She twisted around to see Kincaid standing beside the night-darkened window. The sun would not shine upon the city for hours. And by the time the first morning rays sparkled off the Seine, she planned to be halfway out of Paris.

Unconsciously, a soft smile curved her lips upward as she looked into his eyes. Warmth blossomed like honeysuckle and spread sweet nectar through her veins. "Good morning."

"Did you sleep well?"

"Very thank you." She paused as something she couldn't identify in his voice registered in her mind. "And you?"

"I didn't sleep," he answered and abruptly turned and left the room.

Letting go of the sheet, Regan arose naked from the bed, then bent over to pick up her light robe from the floor. A cool draft wafted across her bare legs and a wave of chill bumps skimmed over her body like a strong breeze through chaff.

Regan walked across the bedroom suite and entered into the bathroom. While her feet automatically moved over the cool tile floor toward the shower, her mind continued to process the events of last night. Her right hand turned on the shower, while her left hand untied the robe. And when she stepped into the spray of hot water, fear and unease poured over her skin.

The NSA had taught her that the first step in the process of bringing a target over would always be the hardest. But on-the-job training had taught her the opposite. The last step was the hardest. It was toward the end of the mission when those she brought to the United States looked back toward their homeland, remembered the family they were leaving behind when they looked at Regan to keep them going. These targets, mostly men of high military or government rank, would continue their lives in relative comfort while their relatives might pay the price of their defection. The negative thoughts came one after another until Regan could finally push them to the back of her mind.

She breathed in the steamy water and choked back a sob. Now it was her turn. It was only after she completed her shower and wrapped the towel around her body that she figured out what had her so upset. Regan opened the bathroom door and headed straight into the bedroom.

The sight of Kincaid once again standing close to the window brought her to an abrupt standstill as both the visual and the emotional clues came together in one observation: her lover had clothed himself in all black. Her eyes took in everything about him. From the microfiber to the lightweight turtleneck. His tall, well-built frame caught her attention and sparked a flame in her libido.

Yet it was the new look in his eyes that most concerned her. Not because she had not seen it before, but the opposite. She'd seen it in the faces of some of the most dangerous men to roam the earth. She'd seen it in Ace's face before their last mission. She's once seen it in the mirror as she'd prepared herself to leave the high-class brothel with Merona. The heady mixture of anticipation and resolve could not be mistaken. "What have you done?" she asked slowly.

He nodded his head toward her open suitcase. "Room service should arrive shortly. After you're dressed and we've both eaten, we'll talk."

Regan opened her mouth and then closed it, while every instinct and shred of pride rebelled at being ordered about. But the chirp of her watch, which sat on the nightstand, injected reality into the situation. Her mission came first, and as of that moment, time was of the essence. Their gazes locked and she let some of the emotion churning in her mind show. This would not be an easy good-bye. Clutching the ties of her towel, Regan turned and walked swiftly toward the bathroom.

Less than five minutes later, Regan took out the Glock 26, a.k.a. Baby Glock, and hit the point back near the gun's magazine. The clip fell into her palm; she checked the bullets and slapped it back into place. Even the cool reassurance of the hard grip in her palm didn't help erase the foreboding that had haunted her since seeing Joseph's bodyguards at the art gallery.

For all her training, she wasn't perfect. And now with her identity purposefully compromised, the mission had become even more perilous. Although she didn't plan to use the small gun, Regan tucked it into the ankle holster anyway. Her primary weapon, a modified M9 pistol, lay on the bed. Although to the uninformed eye, the weapon resembled a semiautomatic with a silencer attached, in actuality it came loaded with tranquilizer darts containing a small charge that detonated on impact, injecting a highly concentrated drug into the target's bloodstream.

In twenty minutes, she had completed dressing in monochrome black. Her having packed her suitcase the night before, nothing of her presence remained in the hotel. Gripping the duffel bag filled with all the items she should need until the end of her mission, Regan took a deep breath and left the bedroom and walked into the living room suite and a waiting Kincaid.

Her eyes sought and found him standing in front of the hotel door. "If you could arrange for my suitcase to be shipped home, I would appreciate it," she said into the silence.

"There's no need. You'll be traveling with the luggage."

"Kincaid." She took three purposeful strides in his direction, but stopped after catching a glimpse of the muscle twitching in his jaw. "I don't want to hurt you, but I work alone and I need to go."

"I'm not moving."

Regan bit the inside of her cheek to suppress the urge to let loose a string of curse words. Anger wouldn't do her any good. He knew she'd rather cut out a piece of her own flesh before harming him. "Please don't do this."

Kincaid uncrossed his arms, yet didn't move from the door. "I'm not going to step aside and let you go into a dangerous situation alone."

"You can't be involved."

"I was involved the minute your boss decided to use my gallery opening as a meeting point to smuggle the president's son out of France."

Regan choked back her irritation and tried to stick to the facts. "Kincaid, I have been doing this for years. I'm very well trained. Actually, I'm one of the best."

He crossed his arms over his chest before shrugging.

"Doesn't matter." His eyebrows slanted downward into a frown. "I'm not letting you leave without me."

"Your interference could get me . . ." She paused. "Could get us killed."

Kincaid used a softer tone than the one he'd used earlier. "I'm not a spy or a secret agent. I've never held a gun or illegally entered a country with false identification. But I am a man who cares for you."

"And I you," she confessed. "But—"

Kincaid interrupted, "Look at your watch, Regan. Every second you spend arguing with me decreases your chances of completing the mission."

"Why are you being so stubborn?" A frustrated growl erupted from her throat. For a millisecond, Regan considered pulling out her tranquilizer gun and shooting him. But her stomach heaved at the idea.

This time he moved toward her and Regan kept her eyes locked on his. And in those smoldering brown eyes, she glimpsed something that threatened to bring her to her knees.

"How can you ask me that question, Rebel? I told you that I have few friends, few people who have entrenched themselves into my soul as you have. And I don't want to let you go. But if the time comes, then you will end things by choice, not circumstance."

Not waiting for her response, he moved away from the door and stood alongside the food-filled table. Absentmindedly he picked up a pineapple slice and bit into it before continuing. "I've talked to my father and the pilot of their jet. We're scheduled to fly out to the destination of your choosing at two o'clock this afternoon."

Regan dropped her hands to her side. "What?"

"You're in luck. The Gulfstream should be fueled and can take us anywhere we need to go."

Regan took a deep breath and blew the air out her nose as all of her carefully laid plans crumbled into dust. Turning on her heel, she headed toward the bedroom.

"Where are you going?"

She stopped but didn't turn around. "Since you've just blown my plan to pieces, Mr. Hero, I need to make some phone calls."

After placing the duffel bag that carried all the items she would need for her mission in the back of the nondescript silver Mégane Renault, Regan gently closed the hatch. The cold burned her ungloved hands, but she welcomed the sensation as it helped her to focus. All of her plans were set in motion. She'd chosen the car because the handling and performance would matter in a chase, but if everything went as planned, only the fact that the Renault would be near impossible to trace would matter. Before moving to sit in the front seat, Regan spared one last lingering glance at the hotel.

How she would miss this place, miss the wonderful time she'd spent there.

With fewer than thirty rooms and less than ten suites, La Chateau, originally the Parisian winter town house for a wealthy merchant, stood in the center of the lush French gardens on the Rue du Faubourg St. Honoré. The exclusive town house hotel played host to numerous celebrities, politicians, and wealthy individuals who wanted the wonders of Paris without having to deal with the annoyance of paparazzi. Since the hotel was located within walking distance of an avenue, where glitterati of Paris fashion kept the wealthy clothed in the best of haute couture, a girl would never lack for shopping opportunities.

The hotel's fine furnishings and artwork were old-word elegant and heavy in style, yet the rooms offered every imaginable ultramodern comfort and the staff gave personalized service with attention paid to every detail. They had just spent time indoors wandering from room to room looking at the furnishings or talking Kincaid's parents while sharing a bottle of wine in the upper-level salon. The rear rooms were situated over a Zen-like garden that was perfect for both Kincaid and his parents. The tranquility, not to mention the discretion of it, showed itself when their intent to check out at five o'clock in the morning or Kincaid's request to have their luggage delivered to the airport barely raised a bushy eyebrow. An exceptional collection of French antiques made it feel like an elegant, private residence.

"Ready?" Kincaid paused before slipping his six-foot frame into the two-door hatchback. She looked into his handsome face and examined every inch of his expression. The resolute set of his gaze cleared away most of her doubts. This was the man she'd longed for in her midnight dreams. As surely as she knew she couldn't hurt him, she knew that he would die to protect her. Reagan nodded and gave him what she hoped was a reassuring smile. Time to show and prove. She just hoped that Mosi Amacha was worth it.

Chapter 26

For the thirtieth time in an hour, Kincaid looked down at his watch. Uncaring of his mounting anxiety, the second hand continued to tick. Putting the keys in his pocket, he got out of the car and zipped up his coat. "Sorry, Rebel, but you've been gone too long," he muttered under his breath as he headed down the sidewalk.

Claude Morlet's law office was housed on the fifth floor. Kincaid strolled confidently through the empty lobby and stepped into a waiting elevator. He found the law office easy enough, but he felt his steps falter the closer he came to the entranceway.

"May I help you?" the brown-haired secretary asked in French.

"I'm here to see Monsieur Morlet." He enunciated his words closely, in English. "I just flew in this morning and took a cab from the airport. He is helping me on a large deal."

She responded in flawless British-accented English, "I'm sorry, he is sick. The poor man has a stomach virus."

Kincaid schooled his features into an expression of disappointment and concern. "He won't be in today?"

"Nor tomorrow, I'm afraid. Monsieur Morlet's illness will last for a few days. May I get your name and have him call you to reschedule?"

"Yes, yes."

"Your name, please?"

"Michael Smith." Kincaid gave her the fake name without blinking.

"I shall have him ring you the moment he returns to the office."

Kincaid smiled as his mind furiously raced to come up with a way to get into the attorney's office to tell Regan. And desperation seemed to kick his mind into overdrive. He grabbed his stomach and mimicked a heaving gesture. "Airline food," he barked. Ms. . . . I hate to ask you, but could you point me in the direction of the closest bathroom?"

"Of course. There's a private bathroom in Monsieur Morlet's office. Follow me."

She opened the door, and just at the moment the phone rang. "It's behind that door."

He smiled. "Thank you."

Quickly and efficiently, his eyes scanned the room searching for Regan's possible hiding place. First, he looked out the window and onto the fire escape, and then Kincaid opened the closet door and, finding it empty, gently closed it. Next, he opened the bathroom door and stepped inside. True to its residential beginnings, the bathroom boasted a bathtub, sink, and toilet.

Without saying a word, he pulled back the bath stall door and stopped breathing when his eyes landed on Regan lying faceup in the tub with a gun aimed at his heart. The dark hair of her wig spread like a fan around her face. Even with his life in near jeopardy his pulse quickened with arousal.

"Damn it, Sinclair," she hissed. "You could have said something. I almost shot you."

"Do you know that you call me Sinclair only when you're emotional?" He held out his hand and she grabbed it. After helping her out of the oversized porcelain tub, he stood back and grinned.

"What are you doing here?"

"Thought you would like to know that the attorney came down with some kind of stomach virus. He canceled all of his appointments."

He watched as she tucked her gun away. "And how do you know all this?"

"Morlet's secretary is very helpful."

Regan's eyes narrowed a bit, and Kincaid would have bet his bank account that jealous sparks were shooting out of those brown eyes. "I bet she is."

"Monsieur Sinclair, are you all right?" The woman's voice came from the other side of the door.

Without missing a beat, Kincaid reached around Regan and flushed the toilet, then called out, "I'll be out in two minutes."

"You need to go," Regan hissed, nudging him toward the bathroom door.

"Okay."

"Now," she whispered urgently.

"What about you?"

"I'll be down in a minute," she bit out. Her brow wrinkled and he fought the urge to bend down and kiss her nose. Maybe his thoughts were reflected on his face, but her look of impatience made him want to grin even more. Even with the impending possibility that a French woman old enough to be his grandmother could walk through the door and catch them, Kincaid lowered his head and kissed her. "Be careful."

It took Regan less time to get out of the building than it did to enter, but it took her over ten minutes to make her way back to the rental car. Slamming the door and falling back into the driver's seat, she closed her eyes and tried to formulate a plan B, but Kincaid's voice intruded upon her thoughts. "Do we wait until tomorrow?"

She shook her head, opened her eyes, then turned to face him. "We can't. Everything's scheduled for today. Come hell or high water I have to have Mosi on that plane. The NSA can't turn on a dime, and there have been certain preparations made for his arrival."

"So what now?"

Regan leaned her head back against the headrest and closed her eyes. If she let it, the small ache behind her temple would grow to consume her entire being. Instead, she concentrated on breathing deeply as her mind worked overtime to come up with a new plan.

Several minutes later, when she turned toward Kincaid her gaze stood halfway between resignation and resolve. She gave a Gallic shrug, then reached to collect the keys from his lap, keyed the ignition, and shot out into the narrow Parisian street. "We improvise.

One hour later after a quiet stop at a French bakery, Regan parked the car off a busy side street near Mosi's home.

"I already know what you're going to say," she announced before taking the key out of the ignition.

Kincaid released his seat belt and unlocked the car door. "Good, then let's go."

Catching sight of the navy blue sedan from the corner of her eye, Regan quickly leaned toward Kincaid and pulled him in for a kiss. And what had started as a distraction changed as his hand settled onto the back of her head and pulled her mouth and gave his tongue deeper access. A moan worked its way up from her throat and spilled out. That sound coupled with the laughter of a passing group of teenagers jerked Regan back to the present.

"What was that?" Kincaid asked.

"France's finest government agents," she murmured against his lips. "They're like clockwork and the second shift just arrived."

"How did you know?"

Regan bent over to unfasten her seat belt. "A girl can only shop so many hours. I've spent most of my time watching the watchers."

A moment passed as they both stared out the windshield to the busy intersection. "How will you get him out?"

Regan reached into the backseat and put her hand inside her duffel bag. She retrieved the schematic of Mosi's apartment building, and then spread it over the dashboard. "There are ten exit points from the building and all of them are under camera surveillance. Four have motion detectors, exit alarms, and steel doors. Two are only reachable via the elevators and a resident-assigned key card." She pointed them out as she ran through the list. "That leaves us with four more. This exit is sealed tight and leads to the adjacent building, which houses the Brunei consulate and is therefore not an option. There's the service entrance, but it has a manned guard station. Last but not least, we have the main entrance and the third-floor public terrace."

"You don't plan to jump, do you?"

"I'm not that crazy. I'm going to enter the apartment and immobilize one of the guards. I plan on using the other as a driver."

"What am I going to do besides sit in the car out of my mind with worry while you risk your life?"

Regan reached back into the bag and pulled out a scarf. Flipping down the mirror, she draped the scarf over her hair to create the perfect image of mystery and allure. Assured that she looked the part, Regan pushed the visor up and returned her attention to Kincaid. "I need you to do something far more important. I need to you wait in the car for Mosi to come out."

"Where will you be, Regan?"

"I'll be in the back of the Mercedes."

"No," Kincaid shouted.

Regan closed her eyes and sighed. She wasn't going to lie to herself. His actions, although contrary to her mission, went to justify what it was about Kincaid that made her love him. If their roles were reversed, she would do the same thing. And that fact made it even more difficult to ask him to comply with her next request.

"Sinclair, someone has to distract the French authorities and I need for Mosi to be on that plane this afternoon. The agents will assume Mosi is in the Mercedes and they'll follow. Once I've led them on a wild-goose chase and given the two of you plenty of time to get to the airport, I'll make my way to the plane. If I'm not there by takeoff, then leave."

"I'm not leaving without you."

"Please, Kincaid," she pleaded. "I promise you that I'll be on the first commercial flight to Atlanta."

"And what happens when we land and you're not there?"

"Everything is set up on that end. Someone, most likely CIA, will come to take Mosi off the plane before you get to the terminal. If they ask questions, answer, but don't volunteer, and if they try to recruit you, say no."

"I don't like the sound of this. What happens if you're caught?"

"If I'm caught I can use my credentials as a shield to keep the incident covered up. The worst that can happen is that I'm interrogated and then kicked out of the country. You, on the other hand, can be imprisoned without charges and made to sit in a Paris jail for a long time. Trust me when I say you do not want to be in a French jail for a minute, much less days."

"I still don't like it."

Regan reached into the backseat and collected a bag of hastily bought items from a French bakery. "Neither do I. But it's a solid plan. Now wish me luck."

He leaned in and kissed her full on the mouth. "Good luck."

Regan opened the door to the car and got out. She carefully buttoned the lower half of her coat but made sure that she would have access to the tranquilizer gun resting in a holster against her left side. Her breath came in tendrils as the cool wind whipped through the air. Gripping the handles of the brown bag, she joined a small group of Parisians on their way to work and masked her tension in the form of mimicking coldness.

Even while the flurry of French voices went on around her she kept her eyes glued to her destination, and concentrated so that the sight of the French authorities parked in their normal spot across from the luxury apartment building didn't cause her to lose a beat. The men in the vehicle were overconfident, not untrained.

For the second time, Regan entered the apartment building, but her steps faltered slightly. The concierge behind the desk was young and impeccably groomed, not the older gentlemen she'd met earlier in the week.

"*Bonjour*," he said. "*Puis-je vous aider,* mademoiselle?"

She smiled sweetly and turned her face away so that the camera monitor wouldn't capture her likeness so easily. Her eyes sought the young man's name tag.

"*Oui, Phillipe, je cherche Monsieur Mutabe,*" she replied.

When his hand moved to pick up the phone, she placed hers on top of his and gently pressed it down. Taking a chance that he spoke English as well as French, she pleaded, "Please, I am late for our rendezvous, and he will be irate."

She lowered her eyelashes and delicately shuddered. "He is not so nice when he is angry. That is why I brought him his favorite breakfast. I cannot sing, so I will bribe him with croissants and fruit."

Regan opened the large brown bag filled with a madcap splurge in a neighborhood store.

"Mademoiselle—"

"Henri," she interrupted, with the name of the usual morning doorman. "He understood. Please, I only ask this once." Regan turned the charm on full force and met his eyes with a pleading glance she'd learned as a child. After watching the family dog get away with everything except for mauling her father's leather slippers, she'd picked up a thing or two about how to get what she wanted.

"Well . . . because it's a surprise."

She leaned over and gave him a kiss on the cheek. "*Merci, beaucoup.*"

Then with a smile and a playful swing in her walk because she knew he was looking, Regan stepped into one of the waiting elevators and pressed the button to the tenth floor. For a split second after the doors opened and she stepped onto the carpeted hallway, she felt a momentary feeling of guilt at what might happen to the young man once Mosi's guard woke up from his drug-induced slumber and discovered his boss was missing. Yet she banished it easily. With one hand, she loosened the first button of her coat. With the other, she reached out, pressed the doorbell, and then stared into the surveillance camera above the doorway.

She noticed the darkening of the keyhole and kept a smile on her face as the adrenaline shot through her veins when the door swung open.

"*Bonjour*, Mosi." Regan smiled. The way his round eyes bulged in surprise would normally have sent her into laughter if the situation had been different.

"I'm surprised to see you, Regan." He rubbed his cheek all the while keeping eye contact. "The last time we met you weren't so eager to see me."

"I'm sorry, but I was not without cause. I still owed you one for stealing my Diplomacy 301 study notes."

"So can I conclude that my debt has been repaid?" he questioned after closing and locking the front door.

"Of course. Shall we seal it with a kiss?"

Stepping forward still within plain view of his bodyguards and moving her body so that they looked more intimate than they actually were, Regan kissed him on the cheek and moved her lips toward his ear. "Remember, you can take nothing with you and things are not always as they appear. After I leave, wait exactly seven minutes. Exit the apartment building through the front, make a left, walk two blocks. You will see a silver Renault with Kincaid behind the driver's seat. He will take you to the airport while I distract the French authorities. Do you understand?"

"Yes."

"Now that that is over with, aren't you going to offer me a tour of your place?" She pulled back with a sultry smile on her face.

"Of course. I need to get dressed first. As you can see I'm not properly clothed for company."

On that they both agreed. He wore a long gold-colored robe, and from the feel of the cotton, Regan judged it to be high-end Egyptian. She patted him on the shoulder, then pointed to the bag sitting two feet from them. "I have brought you breakfast. *Pain au chocolate*, fruit, cheese, and some baguettes."

He turned toward his bodyguards, who still eyed Regan with suspicion, and spoke briefly in Arabic. Regan pretended to admire a painting on the wall as she caught snippets of the conversation. Mosi had just introduced her as his future conquest.

As soon as Mosi entered the hallway, Regan turned and strolled over to the smaller of the two bodyguards. The muscles in her lips began to ache, but she turned up the charm another notch. "Could you please put it in the kitchen for me? There is plenty for all of us, so help yourself."

Although her eyes were directed elsewhere, her attention on the position of the second bodyguard never wavered. Anjim. His bulk marked him as the muscle man and not the thinker. In all the days she'd followed the group he had sat in the passenger side of the vehicle and walked one step behind Mosi. Once the other, Tahir, left the room, she unbuttoned the last button on her coat. And before he could offer to put it away, she'd grabbed the tranquilizer gun, aimed, and shot the bodyguard in the heart.

The sedative-tipped dart took less than ten seconds to send him slow and easy down onto the thick rug.

Lowering her weapon, Regan quickly unlocked the front door. Keeping an eye on the hallway leading to the kitchen, she walked over to Anjim's prone body, bent down, and pushed hard. It took a lot of effort to turn the six-foot-five man onto his side. After removing the empty dart and placing it in her coat pocket, she released a small vial of tomato juice near his side, then made her way toward the kitchen with the gun behind her back. Just as she'd hoped, Tahir had taken her invitation and she crept up to his unprotected back and placed the barrel of the gun against his neck and ordered in slow and clear terms, "Chew, then swallow. I need you alive and as long as you do as I say your chances of survival are quite high. Now don't move."

With one hand, she patted him down for weapons. By the time she'd finished, Tahir had shed fifteen pounds. She was sure that the mini arsenal of knives and guns on his person would have raised the bushy eyebrows of the French gendarmes.

"All right, let's go." She gestured toward the kitchen door.

She arrived back in the living room mere seconds before Mosi's arrival.

"About that tour . . ." His voice trailed off as his eyes went from her holding what looked like a real gun, to Anjim's prone body on the floor. "What the hell?"

"Do as I say and neither of you will get hurt." Regan kept her gun steady and pointed toward Tahir.

"Woman, are you mad?" he practically screamed.

Regan raised an eyebrow and kept the gun steady. "No, I'm greedy and have a penchant for the diamonds. My partner is in the study working on your safe. You will join him and give him the combination."

She aimed a sideways look at the second bodyguard. "To ensure your cooperation, Tahir and I are going for a little ride. Once my partner calls me, I'll release him. If you try anything, your bodyguard will be the next to die, and you really don't want to have two deaths on your conscience, now, do you, Mosi?"

Six minutes later, the heavy metal gate securing the building's underground parking garage rolled upward and the tinted-windowed Mercedes sped out into the morning snow flurries. Regan relaxed her finger on the trigger of the gun in her hand. Something of a smile made its way to her lips as she turned her head to look out the back window. Three cars back and on the left, she spotted the French undercover car.

"Excuse me, mademoiselle."

"Yes?" Her attention snapped back to the front.

"Where?"

"What?"

"Where . . . do I go?"

Regan blinked, then couldn't help but grin at the bodyguard's anxious reflection in the rearview mirror. "Centrale Louis," she replied, then relaxed back into the opulent seat with a smile on her face. "This is Paris, and a girl has to do some shopping."

The 120,000-square-meter megamall located between Charles de Gaulle Airport and Paris's city center with its three hundred shops and five-thousand-square-meter parking garage was one of the largest mall shopping centers in Europe. The hotel concierge guaranteed all that a woman desired could be found there. Too bad, all she wanted was a parking space.

For all Kincaid knew, Regan could have been sitting in the back of a French police car. In the hour and a half it had taken him to get from the center of Paris to Terminal One at Charles De Gaulle Airport, she could have been lying in a hospital bed or worse. An infinite number of scenarios played in his mind as he followed the pilot out onto the tarmac toward the waiting G-V.

His father had purchased the well-equipped business jet because it was the only private plane that could fly non-stop from Rome to Los Angeles. Although it could carry up to fourteen passengers, his parents rarely traveled with an entourage, and so they had the rear of the cabin converted from an office area into comfortable sleeping quarters. It had also come equipped with a gallery, an entertainment center, and a restroom fitted with a toilet and shower.

The sounds of airplane engines, refueling tanks, and the wind forced him to raise his voice to be heard. "Captain Lang, after you drop us off in Atlanta will you be returning here to pick up my parents?"

"Yes, sir. My copilot will take over while I get the required sleep. Is there a problem?"

"The person I'm expecting may not make it on time. She may travel back to the States with my parents."

"Of course."

Kincaid ducked down a little and entered the private airplane. Although he'd flown numerous times in his parents' jets, he still felt uncomfortable in the small plane. Breathing deeply, he walked across the carpet and took a seat in one of the leather chairs.

He didn't turn from looking out of one of the airplane's oversized panoramic windows as Mosi perused the cabin. "I didn't know artists made so much money. Maybe I should change my profession," the African man said, finally breaking the silence, which had begun the moment he'd taken a seat in the rental car.

Just then, the stewardess stepped into the room from the full-service gallery. "Good afternoon, would either of you like something to drink?"

"Water, please."

Mosi sat down on the three-seat coach across the aisle from Kincaid. "Whiskey, neat."

"And I thought you were Moslem," Kincaid commented.

"What gave you that idea?"

"It was in your file."

"Regan let you read my file?" Mosi's voice rose with indignation.

Kincaid didn't try to hide the humorless grin that curved his lips upward. He shrugged. "I needed something to do while I was waiting."

"You don't like me, do you?"

"I don't like the fact that Regan could be risking her life for you."

"Funny, I would have thought it was more than that. Regan and I were close during university. I wouldn't be surprised—"

Between one blink and the next, Kincaid leaped up from his chair and crossed the aisle and gripped his fingers tight around the other man's throat and squeezed. All the frustration and anger he'd felt for the past twenty-four hours had found a physical target. "I promised Regan that I would make sure you got on the plane. Don't push me or you might not be able to walk off."

"Sorry," Mosi choked out, ". . . I was lying."

Kincaid gave him a look of disgust and let go. "Don't talk to me, Mosi. And you'd better pray to the Prophet whose rules you don't obey that Regan gets here all right."

"Did someone say my name?"

Kincaid spun around and found Regan stepping through the doorway. "You made it."

"I would have been here sooner if it wasn't for traffic."

Out of the corner of his eye, Kincaid caught Mosi's movement and blocked his path toward Regan.

"You killed Anjim."

"No, I put him to sleep. I used a tranquilizer dart and some red paste, Mosi. He'll wake up in about an hour."

"And Tahir?"

She smiled and took off her coat. "He will wake up in about two hours."

"You should have told me," Mosi complained before picking up his drink.

"And ruin the element of surprise, not a chance."

"Mr. Sinclair, have all of your passengers arrived? We need to get going."

"They're here."

Kincaid took Regan's hand and led her over to the leather seats. Only after they'd buckled their seat belts and the plane began to move did she speak. "You weren't worried about me, were you?"

"Every second."

"I didn't have any problems. You?"

"Besides wanting to deck the president's son? No." He grinned.

Regan blinked, then smiled and laid her head on his shoulder. "You didn't."

"No." He rested his head on top of hers and closed his eyes as the adrenaline rush began to fade. "I choked him."

Regan's soft chuckle followed him into sleep.

Chapter 27

Georgia

The wind cut through the wool coat over his shoulders and the sky remained covered over with stone-gray clouds, but with Regan by his side, as Kincaid exited Hartsfield Airport's main terminal his breathing got a lot easier. Just as Regan had said, NSA agents waiting on the airport tarmac boarded the jet and took custody of the president's son before the plane's engine had cycled down.

As for him and Regan, the swiftness with which they'd passed through immigration and customs amazed him. With the post–September 11, 2001, security environment, vehicles were not allowed to park at the curbside, so the streets in front of the terminal were sparsely populated with people rapidly loading and unloading their luggage and passengers.

Yet in the midst of the managed confusion of police cars, traffic directors, and flashing lights, Kincaid pointed the baggage cart in the direction of the adjacent parking deck while his gaze focused on the unusual sight of two large black Hummers with tinted windows parked directly in their path.

It was only then that he noticed that Regan's footsteps

had slowed, then come to a stop just as the car doors of the vehicles opened.

"Kincaid." Her normally steady voice quivered. He reached out and took the hand that had fallen from his waist. Her wide-eyed expression kicked adrenaline through his system.

Kincaid looked back toward the Hummers as three men stepped down onto the sidewalk. He was by no means a small man, but the individuals who stood watching them could just as easily have been cast from the stone statues of the Greek warriors he'd studied during his travels through the Mediterranean. "What's happening, Rebel?"

She opened her mouth, then closed it. Her eyes flicked nervously from him to the strangers. "I can't tell you."

"Can't or won't?" he challenged.

In the space of a few heartbeats, two airplanes roared overhead, and the sound of their ascent prevented conversation.

"Tell me, Regan. Is this a new assignment?" He took her hand and held it tight, only realizing the strength of his grip at the sight of Regan's tattletale wince. They had come for her. Not in his parents' airplane after smuggling out the president's son, not when they'd entered into the terminal. No, they'd waited until he felt a modicum of safety. Betrayal, hot and heavy, curled up next to rage in the pit of his stomach. "Did you know about this?"

She shook her head. "They're not NSA, Kincaid."

"Then who the hell are they and what do they want?"

"Now isn't the time to argue," she practically shouted. "Just keep walking toward the car."

"Fine," he returned angrily and took her hand to draw her away from the men and into the stream of passengers heading across the passageway toward the parking ramp. Only her resistance stopped him.

"Sinclair," she said as she pulled her hand from his grasp. Regan stood mere inches from him, yet it might have been miles as the icy wind blew. "I have to go with them."

Regan had seen many things in Kincaid's eyes, but the heat of his gaze burned. "You don't have to go anywhere except my truck," he said curtly.

"This isn't the typical nine-to-five job that I can just walk away from."

Kincaid gestured angrily toward the waiting vehicle. "The last time I checked, the government hadn't reinstated the draft. Don't go with them."

"Don't tell me what to do! I get enough of that from my father and brother." Anger sparkled in her eyes for a moment, then faded. Her eyes grew brighter. How the brown of her irises sparkled as though lit by a flame.

It fascinated him that she could control her facial expressions. "Is that what you think I'm doing?"

"Aren't you?"

"I guess you don't know me at all."

She reached out to touch his shoulder but stopped and let her arm fall back to her side. Regan drew a heavy breath, as a weight seemed to press against her chest. "It doesn't work the way you think it does. They'll follow me home. Watch me twenty-four-seven, and no matter how good they are at hidden surveillance, someone in my family is bound to notice and I can't have that happen."

"Maybe it's time you told them."

"No. Not like this. Not by them. If my brothers get a whiff that something is up, both my parents and grandparents will be on the first plane back and Grandfather will call in every favor he has to get me kicked out of the State Department. If the day comes that they have to know, I will choose the time."

"So it's all about what you want?"

"No, it's about what our country needs," she countered.

Kincaid took a step back, and the dull ache in her heart intensified into an acute pain.

"More secrets, Regan? This cloak-and-dagger isn't working for me. I thought this was over."

She rushed on. "I know the man behind this. He'll push and he won't stop pushing until something breaks. Until I break. He's also not averse to using anything and anyone to get his way."

"And how do you plan to fight that?"

Uncaring of the many sets of eyes focused on them, some in curiosity, others in annoyance, Regan walked forward and placed her fingers on the rough warmth of Kincaid cheeks.

She blinked twice as a wetness filled her eyes. She dropped her arms and took his hands within her own. It seemed that for a moment her heart would split in two. She had dreamed of adventure and travel, and that dream had become a reality with the NSA. Until Kincaid she'd only had to choose between her career and family. Now she would have to choose between her sworn oath of secrecy and love.

With great care, she raised Kincaid's hands to her mouth and kissed their backs. "Trust me this one last time."

"I'll trust you if you tell me what's happening or take me with you."

She stared into his angry brown eyes and kept silent.

"Regan, this bond that we share is once in a lifetime. I can understand that you love your job, and I can be man enough to acknowledge that it burns in my gut that you risk your life. But you can't expect me to stand here and let you leave me without a fight."

"You can't keep me," she replied without thinking.

Kincaid's head moved back as though her words had been a physical slap. "It's like that, then." He steeled himself against emotion. In his heart, which had in the past been a gateway through which his deepest emotions and artist's muse flowed, slammed shut. Regardless of what Regan asked, she'd made her choice, and it wasn't him.

"No." She reached out for a second time, but like the first, something kept her from touching him.

"If you need to travel, to move around, fine. But, damn

it, no more secrets. No putting yourself in harm's way. Leave the NSA and I'll follow you wherever the State Department sends you."

Regan didn't know who was more surprised, Kincaid or herself. The possibility of a compromise had just entered his vocabulary, all for the sake of love. But she still couldn't reveal that the men waiting for her were members of America's elite Delta Force. "I'm sorry, but I can't tell you."

When a flicker of emotion crossed Regan's face, a fist slammed into Kincaid's stomach. He'd seen that look. For a moment, his mother stood in front of him, then Kirsten, and Dana. They'd had the same look of regret before saying good-bye. Kincaid blinked and Regan stood facing him. She'd made her choice, so he would make his.

He raised his hand to cut off her words. "You demand too high of a price, Regan. I can't watch you leave and hope that you come back." He stepped back and pulled his suitcase from the luggage trolley. A sense of utter calm washed over him. This time he would leave.

The sun shown through a crack in the clouds. Shards of salmon pink spread over the cars and the wind blew her hair and stung her cheeks. Regan didn't notice. Her face, just like her emotions, had frozen. She didn't feel a thing as he walked away and Ace drew to a stop by her side.

"New look, new name, huh?" He picked up her suitcase. "I like the short hair."

Still Regan didn't look at him.

"Come on, Nichols, it'll be okay."

Like a sleepwalker, she turned her gaze from Kincaid's back as he disappeared into the parking deck.

Numbly she allowed Ace to escort her into the back of one of the waiting Hummers. After fastening her seat belt, Regan laid her head back and closed her eyes as an overwhelming weariness settled into her bones. One of the DELTA operatives turned up the volume on the radio. She opened her eyes again and watched the passing cars.

Chapter 28

Later that next night, as Ace and his Delta teammate drew the Hummer to a halt outside the front door of her cottage, Regan was exhausted to the point that she could hardly speak.

"Do you want me to check out the house?"

She smiled. "No, thanks, I'll be fine."

With nothing in her hands except for her thoroughly searched purse, she stepped down from the vehicle. Without looking back, she walked toward the door of her house and pulled out the key from her purse. She'd just spent over five hours with a bullheaded, argumentative old general and two hours with two very persistent Special Forces officers who deliberately tried to goad, trick, and coax her into joining Delta Team Three. Although she loved Kincaid with all of her heart, she didn't want to see another male for at least twenty-four hours.

After unlocking the door and disengaging the security alarm, Regan dropped her purse on the side table. Reaching out to turn on the light, she went completely still at the sound of rustling. Silently and quickly, she pulled up the leg of her trousers and removed the Baby Glock from around her ankle. Keeping the gun aimed low, she moved down the hallway toward the living room. Regan put her back against the wall and felt along it for the light switch and then flicked it on and pointed her weapon. "Don't move!"

"Go ahead, shoot. Put me out of my misery."

"Damn it, Savannah!" Regan cursed and lowered her gun. "What are you doing here?" She managed to squeeze the question past the lump of fear in her throat.

Savannah stared at the weapon in Regan's hand as though watching a coiled snake. "What are you doing with a gun?"

"It's a part of the job."

"You carry a gun! No . . . no. You need to quit this instant. I swear I'll tell your mother if you don't transfer or something. Do you know how dangerous those things are?"

With her hand slightly trembling, Regan ejected the gun clip, checked the cylinder, then placed the gun on an end table. "Can we get back to the subject at hand?"

"You mean why am I sitting in the dark on your couch with my car in your garage?"

"Yes."

"Because you lied to me. Telling the truth made a bad situation worse. Now not only is Jack furious with me, Clint and T.J. started following me to school, home, the grocery store. They practically camped out in front of my house, and when they had business at one of the dealerships, they hired a private investigator to watch me."

"You can't be serious." Regan looked up through her hair. Her cousins, T.J. and Clint were the sanest members of her generation of Blackfox kids.

Savannah laughed, and the bitter sound echoed through the room. "It gets better. Dad's not speaking to anyone. Mom's having a nursery built, getting out baby books, giving me notes about single-parent support groups, and she's hired a pregnancy counselor."

"Oh, sweetheart," Regan moaned as she walked over to sit on the couch next to Savannah.

"Wait, here's the icing on this cake. Jack's parents and

my parents are fighting. Each blames the other for this mess, and Dad has vowed that he won't let them anywhere near the baby."

She sniffed and Regan got a good look at her red-rimmed eyes. "Everybody's telling me how to feel, how to behave," she stammered. "I don't know what to do."

"First, you should get some sleep."

A sparkle of anger shot through her eyes. "What, so you can disappear again?"

"Savannah, don't start," Regan warned.

Her cousin didn't listen. "You're not the stronger one."

"What?" Regan's brow wrinkled at the statement.

"I always thought that of all the women in our family besides Grandmother, you were the strongest. But you're not."

"Where is this coming from?"

"When the pressure gets to be too much, you run and hide behind your work instead of staying here and dealing with it."

Regan looked at Savannah with different eyes even as denial sat on the tip of her tongue. The truth, no matter how painful it was to hear, kicked off a tidal wave of revelations. She had run. From the pressure of a young marriage, from a family that loved her too well, and she'd almost run from the man she loved.

Savannah continued, "You didn't tell me you were leaving for Paris."

"It was a last-minute trip."

"You gave me that bad advice, then left me when I needed you the most."

"You're right and I owe you an apology, but you can't place the blame on me for your situation."

"Did Kincaid at least propose?"

"What gave you that idea?"

"Marius and Caleb started taking bets on whether or not you'd come back with a ring on your finger."

"No, we are nowhere near that point. But let's stay focused on resolving your problems before we delve into mine."

Savannah sighed and buried her face in her hands. "I've tried so hard to be strong and independent, just like you. But it never works out. One word from my parents and I give in."

"Did Uncle William tell you to stop seeing Jack?"

"He took the engagement ring and personally delivered it to Jack's father."

Regan sat back on the sofa. "Savannah, do you remember when we'd play goldfish for candy?"

"Yes. You'd always win."

"No," Regan corrected. "I wouldn't give up. If I was losing, I'd push you to play another game. If I was winning, I'd quit while I was ahead."

Savannah pushed herself off the couch and stood in the middle of the room wringing her hands. "Why are you telling me this?"

Regan stood as well. "This time the stakes are higher, Savannah, and you can't quit because you're behind." Regan carefully picked each word and spread them out as though laying out a deck of cards. She knew what she was saying, because she had the experience to back up her advice. Once before she'd gone toe-to-toe with their grandfather, the patriarch of their family, and their battle had rippled through the family like a firestorm. "Do you truly love the man?"

"Lord, yes."

"Can you fight for him?"

Savannah's chestnut eyebrows pulled together a little. "Alone?"

"Yes. If you can't stand on your own two feet and make this decision to have a baby and a husband, then your relationship will be doomed. Even if you and Jack get married, the men in this family will chip at your relationship until there's nothing left but a pile of rubble."

"If I go against Dad, if I go against Grandfather and

marry the son of the family who cost him his brother, how could he ever forgive me?"

Slipping back into the role of older sister that she'd played her entire life, Regan pulled Savannah into her arms and gently rocked the crying woman. "Remember the time you put liquid dishwashing liquid into Grandma's new dishwasher and flooded the kitchen with soap suds?"

"How can I forget?"

"You didn't think she'd forgive you then."

"What a mess I made. It took us two days to get it all cleaned up."

"No kidding. The point is that we're family . . . .blood. Nothing can change that but you can change their minds."

"How?"

"By being happy."

"Being with Jack Archer makes me happy. The thought of having our child gives me a feeling that I can't put into words."

"Now that is something." Regan chuckled. "When a librarian and walking thesaurus can't put something into words."

"I know I need to do this on my own, but. . . .

"Go ahead."

"I don't want you to help me, but your just being here means a lot, Regan. Will you stay for a little longer?"

She breathed deeply as the question hung in the air. All the signs pointed in the same direction. *Home*. Her heart was there, her family, her thoughts. In the brief time since she'd returned home, everything had changed.

And to be brutally honest with herself, Regan knew deep down that although she could leave, she couldn't walk away without looking back, couldn't stay away from home for weeks, months, or years at a time. The words she spoke next came from the place in her heart she'd long ago hidden away in order to continue her life as Dominique Nichols. "I'll stay."

* * *

Later that night after settling Savannah into the guest bedroom with a glass of warm milk and cookies, Regan went downstairs and into the kitchen. After rinsing her hands, she caught sight of the red blinking light on the security alarm. Someone or something had tripped a sensor in the garage. Regan took a deep breath, then dried her hands. Without turning around, she spoke. "You can come out now, Morgan."

"How long have you known?"

"Just now."

He pulled back the kitchen chair and sat down. "So what did you tell General White?"

"Same thing that I'm going to tell you. No more."

"No more what?"

She turned around and leaned against the kitchen countertop. "No more Dominique Nichols."

"Regan—"

"Don't try to sweet-talk me, Morgan. You knew when you asked me to take on that assignment that there was no going back. I have spent the past three years risking my life to serve my country. Every person I've helped had two things in common. One, they possessed information vital to the security of the U.S. Two, they feared for their lives. Mosi Amacha could have spent the rest of his pampered existence in Paris."

"All that aside, are you really leaving the group?"

"Yes."

"The NSA?"

She remembered the advice she'd given to Savannah. "Not unless I have to. I need to find a new role. One that Regan Blackfox can fit in. Either you help me to secure a transfer into a more stable position or I leave. It's that simple."

"You'd leave when you're at the top of your career? The military wants you, the directors in the NSA are bandying around your name for promotion, and I'd have a hell of a time trying to replace you."

"Without a backward glance," she replied.

"You want out. Well, I'm not going to make it that easy. First come back to the home office for debriefing, and then you can talk to the appropriate people."

Regan thought about Savannah, her family, and Kincaid. "When?"

"Tomorrow. I want you on the first flight to Baltimore."

"Is this some kind of power trip?"

"No, I heard about what happened between you and the artist."

Regan moved toward the table and sat down. "Kincaid saved the mission."

"Be that as it may, he didn't leave you on friendly terms. You need to get your head together if you're going to have a moderately successful career. Plus, he needs time."

"So tell me more, O Wise One, fix my life," she replied sarcastically.

"I don't have any answers. I'll just meet you at the airport."

With that, he stood and left the house via the door that led into the garage. Regan sat still for a few moments, then turned out the lights and headed upstairs to her bedroom. And after she'd changed into her pajamas, she thought of what she would tell Savannah in the morning, what she could do with her life after leaving. She thought about everything but Kincaid.

Chapter 29

Regan pulled her corvette to a stop in front of her brother's house. Regan knew it wasn't a good idea, knew for a fact that the results of her getting out of the car and walking up to the large brick house would be an "I told you so," but after spending most of the day digging into a half gallon of ice cream, she didn't know what else to do. It seemed like yesterday that she and Kincaid had boarded the plane to Paris, but three weeks to that day they'd gone their separate ways at the Atlanta Airport. Shaking her head, she reached out and rang the bell.

The look of surprise on Marius's face made her want to laugh and run into his arms. But close on the heels of that thought came the vision of the man's arms that she truly wanted to run into.

"Rebel, what wrong?" he asked while pulling her inside.

"I've messed up, Marius," Regan started and stopped as her voice came out hoarse and weak. "And I don't know how to fix it."

"Kincaid?"

She sniffed, then nodded before walking through the entry foyer and heading straight through the house toward the den. Regan threw herself down onto the overstuffed butternut leather sofa.

Marius sat down beside her, crossed his legs in front, and his arms behind his head. "This is one for the record book. I can't believe that you're coming to me about relationship problems." He shook his head. "Snowballs must be dropping in Hades, little sis."

The small dig sparked enough anger to nudge back the mess of self-pity she'd wallowed in for the past three days. Firefights, negotiations, geopolitical meetings, and family reunions she could handle. But confidence to face up to the emotional responsibilities of her own life eluded Regan.

"Look, I came to you for some advice, not to provide you with personal amusement."

The smug grin disappeared from his face. "What happened? Last I heard, you and the artist were strolling the sidewalks of Paris."

She curled her legs underneath her body and muttered, "I can't tell you."

"What did you do?"

"Can't tell you that either."

He sighed, then pulled her in for a hug. "Well, what can you tell me? I'm a CEO, not a psychic."

Regan closed her eyes, then breathed deeply to ward off the fresh burst of tears that threatened to rain from her eyes. "He thinks I chose my career over our relationship."

"I'm not surprised. You've already put it before family."

"Marius," Regan said, exasperation plain in her voice, "now is not the time."

"I'm not trying to point fingers, Rebel. But it's the truth. When you joined the State Department, you put the needs of the country before your family. I'm proud of you for making that sacrifice, but I'd do anything short of murder to have you back home."

"I guess bribery is short of murder," Regan commented.

"He told you?"

"Yes."

"And you're not mad?"

She sighed, then laid her head back against her brother's

arm. "I'm not mad. I had a feeling you would try something."

"Nice to know I'm off the hook."

"Not yet, you aren't. Not until you help me solve this problem."

"The same problem where you can't tell me what happened or why?"

"That would be it."

"First, did you do it?"

Regan's brow drew tight and she refocused her gaze on Marius. "Did I do what?"

His mouth quirked. "Did you put your career before your relationship?"

"No, I put in for a stateside desk job."

During her trip to Maryland, Regan had sat through conversation after conversation, meeting after meeting. Over and over again she'd been asked to change her mind about leaving the team, and each time she'd hesitated. But each time something would remind her of why she had to quit. Wherever she was, no matter what she was doing, Regan found herself caught in the memory of him: tasting the touch of his lips while on the plane, feeling the heat of his tongue in the shower, smelling the scent of his skin while eating a bagel.

Before that moment, Regan could count on one hand the number of times she'd seen her eldest brother speechless. From that day forward, however, she would have to use two. When he'd recovered, Marius asked, "Does Kincaid know that?"

"No."

"Because you haven't told him," he stated. Marius rubbed his chin, then grinned.

For a moment, Regan was overwhelmed by the sense of déjà vu. There had been one Saturday morning when her brother was cruising down I-75 at ninety miles an hour, there hadn't been traffic, but there had been a Georgia state trooper sitting around a wooded curve. Her older brother hadn't panicked, he'd assumed command. And instead of being put in the back of the patrol car and hauled off to the county jail, they'd driven home. Of course, she'd never shown up for her emergency visit to the dialysis clinic.

"I haven't talked to him since we got back from Paris," Regan confirmed.

"And you think he's mad at you?"

"I don't have a clue as to how he's feeling right now. I just remember the look on his face when I said I had to leave." Regan sniffed and closed her eyes again as the memory made fresh hot tears crowd into her eyes. She opened them quickly when Marius grabbed a hold of her shoulder.

"No tears. You know I can't take the sight of a woman crying."

"What else am I going to do?"

Marius gave her a hug and patted her on the back. "Here's what you do . . . ."

Chapter 30

"It took you long enough to answer the door," Regan said as she brushed past him and walked into his house.

Stunned, Kincaid automatically shut the door and watched as she dropped two heavy plastic shopping bags on the floor and began taking off her coat, scarf, and gloves. Automatically, Kincaid reached for her coat, but he caught himself and stopped. As he drew in a deep breath, the scent of her perfume blanketed his senses. For four weeks, he'd battled her memory and pushed through his misery. Four weeks of not knowing where she'd gone or if she'd come back. Half of him wanted to pull her close and kiss her until the air ran out of his lungs, but instead Kincaid held on to the kernel of anger in his gut and stayed where he was.

"Why are you here, Regan?" he asked briskly.

For a moment, their gazes locked and he caught a flash of pain in her eyes before they narrowed. "We need to talk," Regan stated before turning around, opening the foyer closet, and hanging up her coat. Despite his best intentions, his eyes strayed. Regan wore a tight-fitting candy-apple-red sweater and jeans that accentuated her curves. Her hair was tucked behind her ears, but a stray tendril framed her brow.

"I think we've talked enough."

"Maybe you have, but I haven't." She placed her hands on her hips. "What's happened to you, Sinclair? You look like hell."

Kincaid opened his mouth to say none of her damn business. He ate when his stomach growled, slept when doing otherwise might cause him to collapse, and used every other moment of his time taking care of the horses or working in the studio. The only time he left the sanctuary of his property was to get supplies. He frowned. "I've been busy."

A skeptical look tilted her eyebrow at his response. "Well, I'm hungry, and from the looks of things you haven't had a decent meal in weeks. So why don't you clean up while I get this food together?"

He stood there staring as she picked up the bags and made her way toward the kitchen. Kincaid blinked and looked around the entry foyer as the sound of humming trickled back into the room. Not sure how he felt or what he wanted, he shrugged, then went upstairs to his bedroom. He took off his work clothes and let them drop on the carpet and headed toward the bathroom. He'd planned to shower anyway before going into town to pick up Chinese takeout.

After the shower, he stood in front of the mirror and glimpsed the four-day results of going without a shave. He opened the bathroom door and anger told him to tell Regan to leave and he never wanted to see her face again. When he opened the bedroom door, the smell of roasting meat and corn bread hit him square in the empty stomach, and weakened his resolve. He could at least hear what she had to say.

First, knock him off his guard.

Regan busied herself setting the dining room table and lighting the candles as her brother's advice drifted through her mind for the tenth time. In her line of work, failure wasn't a choice. But as she'd made the drive from her cottage to Kincaid's house, doubt had stuck to the back of her fender like a fierce competitor.

Her parents and grandparents would return in a few days to find her cousin sleeping with the enemy, her request for a transfer would go before the bureau chief, and as she had slowed to make a left turn, Regan had no idea what would happen when she knocked on the door of the man she loved. Yes, love, was in love with, wanted to spend the rest of her life sleeping beside. And that knowledge, far from making her feel more confident, gnawed at her. Ate at her composure like a stray dog on a turkey bone. So, for the past week, instead of making a left turn on the street that went to Kincaid's home, she'd made a right and returned home.

She'd gone over it a hundred times. As though she were on a mission, she pictured herself knocking on his door, waiting for him to answer. She heard the words she would say and the expected polite response when he let her in. And that was as far as she got. The rest of her images shed like their clothing on the stairs and then it would all end with daybreak where she would wake wrapped in his arms.

As soon as she heard the sound of Kincaid's footfalls coming toward the dining room, Regan straightened up and stepped from behind the damask covered dining table. She ran her hands nervously over her pant legs, and then said a short prayer. She watched him walk into the room, and her heart stopped. Regardless of the fresh shave and the clean clothes, he looked tired. The smile that she'd grown so used to seeing had disappeared. Regan summoned up a sad smile. "Dinner's ready."

"Smells good."

"Take a seat, I'll get everything out of the oven." Regan swallowed hard and was about to retreat to the kitchen when Kincaid spoke.

"Wait. Why are you doing this to me?"

Regan froze and met his eyes. Kincaid's anguished

gaze sent the air out of her lungs. Then summoning her composure, she chuckled softly, not with amusement, but at herself. She'd prided herself on being able to stick to a plan, and this time she couldn't. All the pep talks and promises she'd made to her brother flew out the window. "This"—she gestured toward the dining room table and the kitchen—"this was Marius's idea. First, knock you off guard, hence the surprise visit. Second, overpower your senses with a good home-cooked meal. Third, apologize. Fourth, if all else fails, cry."

He took two steps forward and stopped. Regan placed her hands behind her back to keep from throwing herself into his arms.

"So those are Marius's ideas. What are yours?"

She shook her head sadly. "I love you and I'm sorry that I hurt you. I can apologize until the cows come home, but I can't change the past. And I can't change the fact that I had to leave. I just hope that I can help you understand."

"I lied at the airport, Regan. I can't live the life I once did with my parents. Traveling around the world only seeing home for a few weeks at a time. I want what you had all of your life, roots. And I want to grow them here with you, and our children can't live the life I once did when I was a kid. Yeah, everybody dreams of traveling the world, but I just want a family and a home. I love you enough to let you go, but I can't follow."

She took the final step forward, closing the gap between them. In the past few weeks, she'd spent hours looking back at her life, reliving in detail the times she'd placed her life on the line, made midnight phone calls to her family before a mission and told them she loved them because there was always the possibility it might be her last chance. And after all that soul-searching, she'd uncovered some long-denied truths. Savannah was right; Regan had run from her family instead of dealing with her grandfather's manipulation. But none of that mattered at that moment. "I know. I'm home, Kincaid."

"For how long?"

She reached out and took his hands within her own and looked into his eyes. "Until you stop loving me. Officially, my job with the State Department has been terminated, unofficially I've requested a stateside position with the NSA. I can't promise to be here to have dinner on the table every night, but I will always come home to you."

Hope flickered in his eyes, then died. "No, Rebel. I know what you're trying to do, and believe me it won't work."

"What exactly am I trying to do, Kincaid?"

"Ignore the truth and believe that you can come back here and pick up where we left off."

"No, I'm trying to start something new here."

"And how do I know that weeks from now or months from now you won't wake up and resent me for making you give up your dream?"

She shook her head. "I can't give up a dream when it includes you, Kincaid. There's no hard and fast rule that says that I can only have one dream and that it can't change."

"Are you sure, Rebel? What if it comes down to your having to choose between our relationship and work?"

Regan let go of Kincaid's hands and placed hers on his chest. She felt his heart beating underneath her palms, and that sensation warmed her hotter than any fire. Her eyes searched his. "One day I may have to trade in my Corvette for a minivan, but if it ever came down to choosing between my job and my husband, I'll leave the NSA without a second thought."

His arms wrapped around her in the signature way that made her feel loved and protected. "Regan, are you saying what I think you're saying?"

"Maybe . . ." Her lips turned into the first hint of a smile she'd had in the last few weeks. "I don't believe in long engagements and I won't live in sin, especially with the man I'm in love with."

She drew back to look into his eyes and was rewarded

with the sight of the easy grin she'd missed. "You're proposing?" he asked.

Regan's brow wrinkled. "You were taking too long."

"I thought you'd left the country."

"I saw you at the grocery store the other day and you didn't say a word."

"I didn't see you." He laughed and shook his head. "Regan, why are we arguing?"

"Because I'm halfway frozen with fear," she confessed.

He lowered his head and covered her lips with his own. Regan opened her mouth, and his tongue darted inside, teasing her own. And they didn't stop until an electronic ping from one direction broke the silence. Kincaid gave her a quizzical look.

"It's the corn bread."

"You made corn bread?"

He grinned broadly while following her into the kitchen. "From scratch," she said.

"After we eat, how about you help me in the barn?"

Her brows rose in surprise. "You haven't fed the horses?"

He shook his head. "I did that this morning."

"Cleaned the stalls?"

"All done."

"What else do you need to do?"

He leaned over and whispered in her ear. Despite all her travels and worldly experience Regan blushed even as her body heated at the image Kincaid painted with his words.

She reached over to the counter and picked up the oven mitt. "Sinclair."

"Yep."

She pulled open the oven door, then aimed a sidelong glance in his direction before licking her lips. "Eat fast."

ABOUT THE AUTHOR

A Southern girl by way of Tennessee, Angela Weaver penned her first novel on a dare and hasn't stopped since. In addition to writing romances, she scuba dives, travels, and grooms horses. The author of four BET Arabesque novels, she lives in Atlanta where she gets most of her inspiration.

An avid reader and occasional romantic optimist, when Angela isn't at work on her next novel, she can be found on the web at www.angelaweaver.com

SIZZLING ROMANCE BY
Rochelle Alers